I've travelled the world twice over,
Met the famous: saints and sinners,
Poets and artists, kings and queens,
Old stars and hopeful beginners,
I've been where no-one's been before,
Learned secrets from writers and cooks
All with one library ticket
To the wonderful world of books.

© Janice James.

McLEAN TO THE
DARK TOWER CAME

A young man is offered the loan of a country cottage in Dorset to write his first novel, but his peace is most rudely interrupted when his aged benefactor is found murdered. Inspector McLean, who takes over the case from the local Constabulary, is deeply puzzled. What is the meaning of the cryptic anonymous message left at the house? Why is the murdered man's daughter ready to commit perjury rather than tell the truth about her past? Who, in fact, poisoned the old man in the middle of the night?

Books by George Goodchild
Published by The House of Ulverscroft:

GEORGE GOODCHILD

◆

McLEAN TO THE DARK TOWER CAME

Complete and Unabridged

ULVERSCROFT
Leicester

First published in Great Britain

First Large Print Edition
published 1998

British Library CIP Data

Goodchild, George
    McLean to the dark tower came.
    —Large print ed.—
    Ulverscroft large print series: mystery
    1. Detective and mystery stories
    2. Large type books
    I. Title
    823.9′4 [F]

    ISBN 0–7089–3989–9

Published by
F. A. Thorpe (Publishing) Ltd.
Anstey, Leicestershire
Set by Words & Graphics Ltd.
Anstey, Leicestershire
Printed and bound in Great Britain by
T. J. International Ltd., Padstow, Cornwall

This book is printed on acid-free paper

1

The weather was incomparable when Philip Barrington started out on the journey which was destined to change the whole course of his life. Never had the English countryside looked so entrancing, nor the sunlit villages and hamlets, through which he passed, more peaceful and inviting. The old patched-up car which he had inherited from his father made an awful fuss of the slightest gradients, and boiled furiously on the steeper hills, but it possessed the one blessed virtue of never completely breaking down, and since he had good reason to believe it would be many years before he stood the slightest chance of getting a new one he treated it with the greatest affection and consideration.

His objective was Strafford Park in the county of Dorset. It was marked clearly on his road map, and it pleased him to notice that its southern boundary was not far from the sea. Arriving at Dorchester he left the main road and very soon was in the wildest country imaginable. He checked the turnings against the very detailed instructions contained in a recent letter from the owner

1

of the estate, and was satisfied that he was on the right track. Finally the narrow undulating lane led him to a pair of handsome wrought-iron gates, on the right of which was a lodge built in stone. Through the gates he could see a Palladian mansion set on a hill, and backed by a dense forest of trees. But this was not for him. His instructions were to take the lane alongside the stone wall for half a mile, and to enter the park at the secondary drive. A hundred yards up that drive was the cottage which had been placed at his disposal for as long as he wished. It was named Deepwater Cottage.

Barrington checked the distance on his speedometer and found the secondary drive exactly where it was reputed to be. It was narrower than the main drive, and fringed by gigantic elms. Away to his right he could hear the murmur of water. Then suddenly an old half-timbered cottage swam into view, with a long expanse of water behind it. He made a turn and brought the little car close to the front door, which was wide open. For a few moments he remained sitting in the car, gazing with appreciation at the beautiful place, in its still more beautiful setting. He had not expected anything quite so idyllic, and he found it difficult to believe his good fortune. How different from that horrible third-floor flat at Battersea, with a huge gasometor as his main *pièce de résistance!*

'Good evening!'

The sound of a human voice startled him, and he turned his head to see a middle-aged man in breeches and gaiters approaching from the rear.

'Oh, good evening!' he replied. 'I suppose this is Deepwater Cottage.'

'Yes. You, of course, are Mr. Barrington? Sir John told me you would be arriving this evening. My name is Weston, and I am bailiff to the estate. I presume you know that Sir John is away from home for a few days?'

'Yes. He told me that in his letter.'

'Then I had better show you over the place, and give you a hand with your baggage.'

'Thank you.'

'The cottage has no garage, but there's an old boat house along the lakeside. I'll show you presently.'

The interior of the cottage was as attractive as its exterior. Two downstairs rooms had been knocked into one, and a bay window thrown out. This window was quite a feature of the place, for it framed the most pleasant view imaginable — a green lawn running down to the water's edge, and then the whole length of the beautiful lake.

'This is marvellous!' said Barrington. 'Is there really deep water out there, or is the name merely euphonious?'

'There's deep water all right at this end. Twenty-five feet at least. Plenty of trout, too, although we haven't been able to restock it for some years. Where will you have this typewriter?'

'Anywhere. I'll find a place for it later.'

Weston took him into the kitchen, and explained the mysteries of the hot and cold water systems.

'It's an efficient contraption,' he said. 'My wife and I lived here for a while. There's electric light, you'll notice, but no power. We've had a cable brought here from the house plant. You're lucky to have the telephone. It was installed only a month ago, after waiting about five years. The nearest village is Instone — three miles away. The tradespeople deliver daily. My wife has stocked you up for a few days with bare necessities. You'll find a bill somewhere. Oh, there it is — on the mantelpiece. With regard to domestic help I've arranged with the cowman's wife to come here every morning for an hour or so. She'll start tomorrow morning round about eight o'clock. Two shillings an hour.'

4

Upstairs there were two bedrooms, a box-room, and a bath. The largest bedroom had the same view as the sitting-room below, and was tastefully furnished. Weston put his hand on a protuberance in the bed.

'Hot-water bottle,' he said. 'Glad she remembered that. Well, I hope you'll be comfortable.'

'I'm sure I shall. I am very much obliged to you for all you have done.'

'Not at all. If I can be of any service you'll find me at the 'Gables'. That's the villa farther up the lane. Shall we go to the boat house now?'

Barrington did not take the car at once, but walked with Weston up the drive, where the evening sunlight filtered through the immense trees. Very soon Weston turned down a narrow track, and pointed out the boat house which was but a few yards ahead. It was a commodious timber erection, with a thatched roof and wide doors. Inside were a couple of canoes, a rowing boat, and a lot of old fishing gear.

'Plenty of room for your car here,' he said. 'And ample room to turn outside. I'll have one of the canoes put into the water. It should be usable in a day or two.'

To Barrington it was all novel and delightful, and he wished his host were there that he might express his gratitude for his generosity. But that could wait. At the moment he was hungry and dirty, and in need of a night's sleep. Tomorrow would start a new day, and what a day it would be!

Back at the cottage and alone he investigated the larder, and found a good array of edibles. The bailiff's wife certainly knew how to shop, for there was a pound of butter, a dozen obviously fresh eggs, and a great mass of bacon, four or five different kinds of vegetables, and sundry tins. When he tried the bath water it came out hot, and a few minutes later he was removing the stains of travel from his person.

By the time he had cooked his evening meal on the excellent stove the light was going. He ate in the sitting-room facing the lake over whose still waters the sunset was working a miracle. What a change after that almost endless roar of the London traffic, to which he had never become used. In this silence, broken only by the music of running water, and the evensong of birds, his mind seemed strangely awakened, and the need which had brought him here completely satisfied.

On the following morning the new life commenced. Having no swim-suit he hesitated to yield to the invitation of the clear water in the lake lest he should be caught in an embarrassing predicament, so he made a note to buy a swim-suit that day. The sitting-room contained no table stout enough to take his typewriter, so he removed a heavy table from the kitchen, and soon had the few tools of his profession where he wanted them. From the brief-case he took a bundle of notes which were to be the basis of his first long novel, and after sitting before the machine for a few minutes, silent and inactive, he began to type.

An hour later he was interrupted by a ring of the doorbell. It was the cowman's wife come to do the chores. She said her name was Sawyer, and apologized for being a little late, but she had to get the children off to school first. She seemed amazingly young to have children old enough to attend school.

'That's all right.' replied Barrington. 'I was just about to get my breakfast.'

'Oh, I'll do that, sir. What would you like to eat?'

'Nothing substantial. Just tea and plenty of toast — and marmalade.'

Mrs. Sawyer stared at Barrington's six feet two inches and marvelled at his simple requirements, but she went about her business and was soon spreading a cloth over a table in the sitting-room, casting a wondering eye at the busy typewriter. Barrington, completely unaware of her presence, went on until the tea and toast arrived.

'Oh, thank you, Mrs. Sawyer,' he said. 'What about you? Have you had your breakfast?'

'At six o'clock,' she replied with a smile.

'Six o'clock! Don't you ever sleep?'

'We go to bed early. You have to if you've cows to look after. They're worse than children.'

After the meal Barrington worked steadily for two hours, during which time Mrs. Sawyer did all there was to do in the small place, which included preparing vegetables for his lunch.

'Will you cook your own dinner?' she asked.

'That's the idea. If I make a hash of it I can always run into the village. But I won't. I've done it too often.'

Upon her departure Barrington went for a walk round the lake. He had no notion as to what was expected of him in regard to perambulations, but obviously some limit had to be set upon his wanderings, or he might find himself barging into a private party from the house, which would be a poor return for the hospitality afforded him

8

by his old wartime comrade. So he kept rigidly to the pleasant path round the big stretch of water, from which no part of the house was visible.

As he walked his mind went back to the day when he had first met young John Medding — in the stewing heat of a Burma jungle. The boy had just got his commission, and was subordinate to him. He had been a nervous, sensitive creature, and for a time his brother officers believed he would crack under the strain of that arduous campaign, but Barrington, who himself had gone through that same phase of fear and horror, never lost faith in his young lieutenant, and this faith was later justified when Medding was awarded the Military Cross, and promoted to a captaincy, giving him equal rank with Barrington. He had not known in those days that Medding was heir to a baronetcy, and four years were to pass before they met again, following the death of Medding's father. He had read the announcement in a newspaper, and had written expressing his sympathy with his old comrade, whereupon John himself called at the flat and found the late Captain Barrington engaged in the hard job of producing literary works in the worst possible circumstances, and just managing to keep his head above water. It was then that the invitation to Deepwater Cottage had been mooted, and instantly accepted, for it was the answer to Barrington's dreams. London was getting him down, and too many of his shorter writings were coming back, with the usual regrets that lack of space et cetera. But in the book publishing business there was at least ample printing paper. The sensible thing to do was to turn over to novels, and let the bread-and-butter stuff go. He knew it required a different technique, but he believed he could do it, and he had in his mind an idea which had intrigued him for years. Now, here he was, in this enchanting spot, with nothing to disturb his thoughts, no rent to pay, and his flat let for four guineas a week for three months.

The prospect was delightful and he found himself more clear-minded than ever before. Country born, he was recapturing some of the thrills of his early youth, long forgotten in the blood and noise of the war years. Here were peace and beauty unalloyed, and a sense of fellowship with Nature. The thick woods at the head of the lake were a veritable bird sanctuary. He halted here and listened for a while, identifying the flute-like notes of the blackbird, the thrush's theme sung twice over, the unmistakable chiff-chaff, and the voices of several warblers. A little bridge which crossed the stream which fed the lake brought him to a region of dense rushes, passage through which was afforded by a stone causeway. He was turning from this into the open when suddenly he came face to face with a girl who was carrying a basket full of wild anemones.

'Oh!' she ejaculated. 'I didn't know — '

'I beg your pardon,' said Barrington. 'I hope I'm not trespassing.'

The steady brown eyes regarded him for a moment, while he noticed the exquisite lines of her form, and the smile which banished her temporary confusion.

'Can you be Captain Barrington?' she asked.

'Mister Barrington — for a long time now. I'm staying at the cottage yonder.'

'Oh yes, of course. John told me you were coming, but I had forgotten. I'm Felicity — John's sister.'

'Glad to meet you. What a delightful name.'

'A little difficult to live up to. I have to apologize for John's absence. He really meant to welcome you in person, but was suddenly called away. This morning he telephoned and said he would be back this afternoon. I hope you're comfortable at Deepwater.'

'Very comfortable indeed. This is one of

the most beautiful places I have ever seen.'

'Yes, it's lovely, but somewhat isolated. You've known John a long time, haven't you?'

'Quite a while. We helped to kick the Japs out of Burma.'

'I can't imagine John kicking anyone out of anywhere. He's so gentle and peace-loving. My mother told me that when he was a boy he used to faint at the sight of blood. Even now you can't get him to shoot a partridge or pheasant. It's as much as I can do to get him to catch a few fish. Oh, dear, I'm talking too much. I'm the chattermag of the family, to quote mother.'

Barrington smiled at her delightful ingenuousness, and now for the first time he saw a fleeting resemblance to her brother in her facial expression, and in the slight graceful gestures of her shapely, free hand.

'So you fish?' he asked.

'Oh yes. My father taught me how to cast a fly almost as soon as I could walk. He was mad on fishing. Are you an angler?'

'I'm no Izaak Walton, if that is what you mean. My catches have been mostly of the size one throws back, and I don't know one fly from another.'

'I think you're just being modest. John told me you were the most versatile man he had ever met, and John, I happen to know, always tells the truth.'

'There are such things as little white lies.'

'Not with John. Oh, tell me something.'

'Well?'

'Are you writing a novel?'

'I'm trying to.'

'What fun! What's it all about?'

'Men and women — saints and sinners.'

'Any murders?'

'Certainly not, unless any of the characters get out of hand. I shall try to keep them well in hand.'

She looked at him searchingly.

'You don't look much like an author,' she said.

'How should an author look? I should like to know, because I'm only a beginner, and I should hate to be considered a blackleg by the more experienced members of my fraternity. Should I wear my hair long, and sport a flowing tie and a sandy beard?'

She broke into a rippling laugh that was as musical as the song of a bird.

'I asked for that,' she said. 'Now I must go back to the house. It's my job to do the flowers for the tables, and to read *The Times* to my grandfather, who is nearly blind. You must come up soon and see our menagerie. Nice to meet you.'

She went off through the trees at a walk that was nearly a run, and Barrington stood looking after her for quite a while. When she had vanished he gave a little sigh of amazement. Was she real or a figment of his imagination? Then he laughed. Of course she was real, but how different from any other girl he had met. John had never even mentioned that he had a sister, but that was not remarkable for John had never been in the habit of discussing his family, although at their recent meeting he had mentioned his wife. Since Felicity had talked of her mother and grandfather it looked very much as if the big house held three generations of Meddings. He continued his walk back to the cottage.

2

A trip to the village resulted in the acquisition of a swimsuit, some beer and a bottle of sherry, and a few angling oddments. Later in the day he did another spell of work, at which he was interrupted by a ring at the bell. When he opened the door he came face to face with the young baronet, dressed in a pair of very old corduroy trousers, and a dazzling blue shirt, open at the neck.

'John!' he said.

Medding's pale, lean face broke into a smile of pleasure as he gripped Barrington's hand.

'Hard at it already?' he asked.

'Yes. Can I offer you some tea?'

'No thanks. I promised to have tea with the family. Sorry I couldn't be here when you arrived.'

'That's all right. Your bailiff was here, and put me wise about most things, and Mrs. Sawyer comes and does the chores. I also had the good fortune to meet your sister.'

'Felicity? She didn't tell me.'

'We met quite by accident. She took my breath away.'

'Why?'

'I had no idea you had such a beauty in the family.'

'Is she beautiful, or just unusual? I can never quite make up my mind. Until a year ago she was in Switzerland, being finished off, as they call it. She's just a little difficult.'

'In what way?'

'Wants to go on the stage, but my mother has rooted objections. The trouble is that my grandfather sides with Felicity, so mother is in a minority of one against two.'

'What about you? Don't you have a vote?'

'I'm neutral. It makes for less friction. Actually my opinion doesn't count for much. You see, Phil, the estate doesn't belong to me. After the First World War my mother's people — the Graylings — paid off the various mortgages and saved it from being broken up. It is the old man who has the real power here. From my father I inherited the Baronetcy, and nothing more. My mother has private means, inherited from her mother who died only two years ago, shortly before my father. When the old man dies she will be quite indecently rich, but he hangs on to life like a limpet. This little cottage is mine. My father, despite his penary, managed to keep it unencumbered. That's how I was able to

16

let you use it without consulting anyone else. One of these days Lucy and I may retire here, for I'm getting tired of the mausoleum.'

'Lucy, I presume, is your wife?'

'Yes. I want you to meet her, Phil.'

'I should very much like to.'

'Then come up to dinner tomorrow — say seven o'clock. Mother will be delighted, especially when I tell her you play a good game of bridge. But I'm sorry to confess she cheats.'

'What!'

'Oh, I don't mean she keeps spare aces up her sleeve, but she makes it quite clear to her partner what suit he is to lead by staring at the wanted suit in 'dummy'.'

Barrington laughed at his friend's frankness.

'I'll watch out for that — if I'm her partner,' he said. 'There's one snag. I've nothing in the shape of dress clothes.'

'Splendid! That let's me out. So you'll come?'

'Of course.'

'Good! The quickest way by car is across the park. Follow the road outside until you come to the farm, then branch right and it will bring you round to the back part of the Hall. You may have to open a gate or two on the farm, but the road isn't bad. If you prefer to walk you go up by the right-hand side of the lake, and over the bridge. Then the footpath past the gazebo, and up over the terrace.'

'I'll walk, if it doesn't rain.'

'It won't. Seven o'clock, then.'

'I'll be there.'

'Good. I had a look at the canoe which Weston has put afloat. It seems to be making no water at all, so please use it when you feel like it.'

'Thanks. What about that old fishing-rod in the boat house?'

'Use that, too. The lake hasn't been fished for years. There used to be plenty of trout in it, but I expect most of them have died from boredom.'

Barrington used the canoe that evening, between periods of work. It was a beautiful little craft, and had a turn of speed which surprised him. It did not take long for him to be assured that the trout had not died of boredom. On the contrary they were very busy rising to flies that were executing wild dances over the surface of the water. After a spell of hard paddling he lay back and let the canoe drift where it would.

On the morrow he promised himself a bit of fishing after a modest amount of work on the book, but it never materialized for he found himself caught up in an attractive situation which would allow him no respite until the typewritten sheets had grown into a considerable pile, and he realized that it was evening, and that he had missed both lunch and tea, and completely forgotten his appointment with the trout. There was barely time left to have a bath, change his clothes and walk over to the Hall.

At the stroke of seven he reached the huge portico and rang the bell. An apple-cheeked girl with the reddest hair he had ever seen answered the summons, and he was shown into a vast and over-furnished lounge. The room was empty except for Medding, who was reclining in an easy chair, smoking. He rose as Barrington entered.

'Dead on time,' he said. 'Your punctuality puts me to shame. I'm the first one down. The ladies are powdering their noses, and grandpa is probably having a quiet drink in his bedroom. How's the great work going?'

'Fairly well. John, there's one thing I must know. How do I address your mother?'

'Just Lady Gertrude. My wife, of course, is Lady Medding, but for heaven's sake don't call her that.'

'What else can I call her?'

'Lucy, of course.'

'Isn't that a little familiar?'

19

'Not a bit. No frills about Lucy. She's the most sensible woman I've ever met. That's why I married her.'

The door opened and into the room came Felicity, clad in a very simple but most becoming frock.

'Oh, Felicity — this is . . . but of course you two have met before.'

'We have,' said Felicity. 'And far from the Medding crowd.'

'I should have warned you, Phil, that my sister cracks that kind of ghastly pun when she is in the mood,' said Medding. 'Her taste in humour is deplorable.'

'All the best humorists were punsters,' said Felicity. 'I am in the tradition of Tom Hood, Charles Lamb, et cetera. Am I right, Mr. Barrington?'

Barrington was excused from answering by the entrance of a most attractive woman of about his own age. There was a quiet dignity about her that was most impressive. She did not wait to be introduced but came to Barrington and offered her hand.

'You must be Philip Barrington,' she said. 'I have been looking forward to meeting you. You are exactly as John described you.'

'And you, too,' replied Barrington.

Sir John pushed up a chair and his wife

thanked him with a smile. Both men followed her example, but Felicity was like a cat on hot bricks.

'Isn't it time Susan brought the drinks?' she complained.

'Susan has her instructions,' replied her brother.

'I know,' she said, striking an attitude. 'Susan, you will serve the drinks immediately upon my arrival. No sooner and no later.'

Lucy contrived to cover up a smile, but the gratuitous piece of excellent mimicry seemed to annoy Sir John, although he let it pass without a word, and a moment or two later Lady Gertrude put in an appearance. For a woman of over fifty she carried her age extremely well, and it seemed to Barrington impossible that she could be the mother of Sir John, although he suspected that her marvellous figure was to some extent due to excellent corsetry, and her hair to certain unnatural additions. She looked very much the Grande Dame, and Barrington felt convinced that her word was law in the big house.

'Mother, this is Philip Barrington, of whom I have often spoken,' said John.

'Delighted,' said Lady Gertrude in a rich, fruity voice, and Barrington, who, feeling instinctively that shaking hands was not the correct response in this case, made a neat little bow.

While John was making his mother comfortable in the beautiful old needle-worked armchair, Susan arrived with a large tray on which were glasses and sundry short drinks. This she deposited on a side table, and then silently vanished. John now took charge of this and was soon serving drinks, much to Felicity's obvious delight.

'Grandpa is a long time,' commented John.

'I'm sorry to have to make his excuses,' said Lady Gertrude. 'He has a headache, and will eat in his room. Felicity, do you think you should drink that old sherry?'

'I'm sure I should,' replied Felicity. 'It gives me a nice warm, comfortable feeling inside.'

'When I was your age I wasn't permitted to drink sherry.'

'That was before the great liberation,' retorted Felicity.

'Liberation of what — bad habits?'

'No — women.'

Lady Gertrude shook her head and then turned her gaze on the guest.

'How are you getting on at Deepwater?' she asked.

'Splendidly,' replied Barrington. 'I think

it's the nicest little cottage I've ever seen.'

'It's certainly little. I feel suffocated whenever I go there. I hear you are writing a book.'

'Yes, but only a novel.'

'Don't be so modest,' said Lucy. 'All the best classics are novels. Is it your first?'

'Yes. Since I left the army I have published a fair number of short stories, but have never had the courage to tackle a full-length novel. It's more than possible I may make a complete mess of it.'

'Most interesting,' said Lady Gertrude. 'My dear husband was a great novel reader, but I must confess I prefer history. Yes, John, I will have another sherry. Not you, Felicity, I absolutely forbid it. You gulped down that one as if it were lemonade. I don't want a dipsomaniac daughter.'

'Dipsomaniac!' gasped Felicity. 'Why, at Lausanne we threw a sherry party every week, and no one can ever accuse me of ever being tight.'

'Tight! What a vulgar expression. And I imagined that was a respectable school. Mr. Barrington, if you ever rear a family make sure they are all boys. Girls are most disappointing — most disappointing.'

'I'll try to remember that,' replied Barrington. 'But at the moment my plans for the future include neither sons nor daughters.'

'Just a crusty old bachelor,' said Felicity. 'But mother's right, you know. Women are a poor lot. No wonder Joan of Arc insisted on wearing trousers. Don't laugh like that, Lucy. I really mean it.'

Sir John wagged a finger at his irrepressible young sister, and helped Barrington to another glass of the excellent sherry.

'You should put Felicity in your book,' he said. 'In many ways she's unique.'

'Don't you dare,' said Felicity, 'unless you draw me as a really bad character, then I can sue you for libel. And it's no use your trying to get out of it by printing some lie on the fly-leaf about all persons in the book being purely imaginary. Mother, can I have another sherry? Everyone else has had two drinks.'

Barrington found the conversation quite amusing, but he got the impression that Felicity was far from being the impulsive scatter-brained creature she purported to be. That her mother was determined to keep her in check was obvious enough, and that the girl resented it deeply was equally obvious. Of the three women Lucy was by far the most transparent. No one, watching her, could doubt that she was supremely happy, with no complexes or inhibitions. Unlike Felicity she was incapable of putting on an act, and her devotion to her handsome husband was in evidence all the time — a fact which her mother-in-law appeared, for some reason or other, to find distasteful.

A little later Susan entered to announce that dinner was served, and the party moved through a communicating door into the dining-room, where a flower-decked table was laid for six. Lady Gertrude took the seat at the head of the table, John and his wife on her right, and Barrington and Felicity on her left. Lady Gertrude stared at the place that was laid at the farther end.

'There are only five of us, Susan,' she said. 'I told you to lay for five.'

'I did, my lady,' replied Susan, blushing. 'But Mr. Edward rang for me and told me he was coming down.'

'Nonsense! He is much too indisposed. Take the plate and cutlery away.'

'Yes, my lady.'

'Thereby hangs a tale,' whispered Felicity to Barrington.

Barrington had no notion what that remark signified, until Susan was about to remove the unwanted articles, when the door opened and into the room staggered a very old man, whose scanty, grey hair looked like a birch broom. He wore a velvet coat and very baggy trousers, and a pair of old carpet slippers.

'Father!' gasped Lady Gertrude. 'I told you — '

'Yesh — yesh — I know. Susan, my gal, put those things back.'

The nervous girl did as she was told, and now Barrington got Felicity's meaning. Her mother had tried to keep the old man in his room, not because he was unwell, but because already he had had ample access to the bottle, and was in his cups. That good lady was now regarding him with the strongest reprobation, until she remembered her obvious duty.

'Mr. Barrington, this is my father, Mr. Grayling. Father — Mr. Barrington.'

Barrington stood up for a moment, and nodded.

'Pleased to meet you, Mr. Barrington,' hiccoughed the old man. 'But damned if I can see you. Left my spectacles upstairs. Susan, run and get my glasses.'

'I'll get them,' said Felicity. 'Susan is very busy.'

Felicity was quickly back with the spectacles, which her grandfather placed over his thin nose, while he peered at Barrington in a way that was somewhat embarrassing.

'The fat's in the fire,' whispered Felicity, with quite ventriloquial immobility of features.

26

'The family skeleton has jumped out of the cupboard. Mother did her best to keep it locked up, but failed.'

'Were you saying something, Felicity?' asked her mother.

'No, Mother — just breathing hard.'

During the meal Lucy introduced a controversial topic, with quite satisfactory results, and to which the old man appeared to be completely aloof. He was quite content to eat heartily, and to drink wine between the courses. The only contribution he made to the conversation was to say 'rubbish!' a couple of times, when Lady Gertrude ventured her opinion.

To one who was trying to be a writer the whole set-up was interesting. Even the presence of a guest did not prevent the frequent eruption of the unseen family volcano, and the precise cause of the trouble was not easy to locate. It might be that Lady Gertrude regarded herself as head of the family, and resented the slightest word or deed which questioned her claim. But Barrington felt certain that the quiet and gentle Lucy would never raise her voice in protest, and yet there was no sign that Lady Gertrude had any great affection for her daughter-in-law. If she loved anyone at all it was John, and John on his part seemed quite content to let her throw her weight about.

Dinner over they all adjourned to the lounge where coffee was served, the old man being helped on his unsure path by Felicity, to whom he displayed the best part of his nature. He insisted in sitting near Barrington, and soon made clear the reason for this.

'D'you happen to play chess, young man?' he asked.

'A little,' replied Barrington, unthinkingly.

'Fine! I haven't played a game of chess in years. The Rector used to come here and play. Then he retired and some young jackanapes took his place, whose only game is tiddly-winks. Felicity, my gal, get out the chessmen — '

'Father,' interrupted Lady Gertrude, 'you can't monopolize our guest in that manner. I was about to ask Mr. Barrington if he would make up a bridge four. I know that John and Lucy would enjoy it.'

'You too,' snorted the old man.

'Naturally. What do you say, Mr. Barrington?'

Barrington, caught between two fires, knew what was expected of him.

'I should like it very much, Lady Gertrude,' he said. 'Perhaps, Mr. Grayling, we could play chess some other time.'

'Jam tomorrow, never jam today,' muttered the old man. 'But who knows where I may be tomorrow? Never grow old, Barrington. The world is for the young — always has been. There's no consolation in old age, but dreams of the past, and some of them none too pleasant. I'll go to bed. That's the place for old fogies. The bed or the grave. Don't stare at me, Gertrude. I hate being stared at — like that.'

'Help him, Felicity,' said Lady Gertrude.

The old man shambled out, with Felicity holding his arm. When the door had closed behind them Lady Gertrude sighed.

'He can be very trying,' she said. 'Lucy darling, find the bridge cards while John brings the table. Oh, and we shall need some pencils.'

The bridge party was well into the first rubber when Felicity returned, and Lady Gertrude, with Barrington as her partner, was holding all the cards, and enjoying herself for the first time that evening.

'I'm so glad you play Blackwood, Mr. Barrington,' she said. 'It's the only way of knowing when there's a slam. Oh, Felicity, is anything wrong? You've been such a long time.'

'Grandpa wanted me to write a letter for him, and to post it so that it would catch

29

the early morning collection.'

'What an extraordinary thing to do at this hour. You shouldn't have encouraged him.'

'I didn't. But he was insistent.'

This information seemed to trouble Lady Gertrude so much that she made a misdeal.

'Sorry,' she said. 'You really mustn't talk to me while I'm dealing, Felicity.'

'Well, I like that,' retorted Felicity. 'You asked me a question and I — '

'Yes — yes. Run away, now.'

Thereafter came dead silence, except for the bidding. Again Lady Gertrude held all the cards, but she played them abominably, leaving three tricks in dummy to which there was no re-entry.

'I'm dreadfully sorry,' she said to Barrington. 'I don't know what I was thinking of.'

But Barrington was in no such quandary. He had noticed Lady Gertrude's instant reaction when Felicity had explained her long absence. It was one of huge surprise, mingled, he thought, with grave anxiety. After that Lady Gertrude went to pieces, and at a comparatively early hour she begged to be excused as she had one of her headaches coming on. Since Felicity did not play the game it killed the bridge party stone dead.

'I'm sorry, Phil,' said Sir John. 'Mother has these attacks of migraine periodically.

I think she lives too much on her nerves. Felicity, would you like to play the piano to us?'

'Nothing I should hate more,' replied Felicity. 'I'm out of practice, and I'm pretty sure that Mr. Barrington is a critic.'

'I assure you I'm not,' replied Barrington. 'But I happen to have a passion for music.'

'Do play, Felicity,' begged Lucy. 'If I could play a quarter as well, I should be proud to perform.'

Felicity switched her gaze to Barrington.

'Do you really want me to play?' she asked. 'There's no need to be polite.'

'Felicity!' remonstrated her brother.

'I really mean it,' said Barrington quietly. 'Just now I saw a volume of Chopin on the piano. He happens to be my musical god.'

'Very well. But remember, you asked for it.'

She went to the piano, switched on the light of the standard lamp, turned over some pages of the volume, and then commenced to play one of the 'Studies'. Barrington sat quite still, enraptured by the excellent interpretation. It was a short piece and soon over, but she went on, with a second and a third piece, no longer bothering to turn the pages of the volume, and Barrington, who knew the 'Studies' intimately, could not find a single fault. Finally she stopped and closed the volume.

'Oh, please don't,' begged Barrington.

Felicity shook her head and came over to the couch and sat next to him. The music seemed to have affected her as much as it had him. She was breathing heavily, and her eyes held an expression difficult to understand.

'Thank you,' said Barrington. 'That was splendid.'

'No, it was third-rate. I've come to a kind of corner which I can't get round, and never shall. There was a time, when I was younger, when I believed I should make a name in music. It was all a pleasant dream while it lasted. Now I know the truth about myself. Music has no place for me.'

'You underrate yourself,' said Barrington.

'Oh no. I've no modesty at all. I don't want to talk about it. Mr. Barrington, I should like to show you the conservatory. Just now we have some blooms at their very best. John and Lucy will excuse us, won't you?'

'Of course,' replied Lucy.

The conservatory was clearly a later addition to the house, standing out at right angles to the dining-room, through which it was approached. Barrington was amazed when, having passed through a short corridor, Felicity opened a door and pressed a switch, to reveal an immense glass dome full of most unusual plants, and pungent with strange odours. He knew very little about floriculture, and could name scarcely any of the things there.

'Mostly orchids,' said Felicity. 'It was my grand-mother's hobby. She spent thousands of pounds adding this place to the house, and employed an expert to keep it going. Since her death it has been going to seed. The expert left, and the general gardener does what he can, but mother now finds it necessary to economize, and I rather think that soon this place will be empty, or completely demolished. There, look at those.'

She stopped before a magnificent orchid, which had thrown out half a dozen incredible trumpet-shaped flowers, striped like the skin of a zebra, and dazzling to the eye. Each bloom was as long as a human hand, and exuded a scent that was almost overpowering.

'Marvellous,' said Barrington. 'But it's like a drug.'

'Yes. Mother told me it was the first time it has bloomed in ten years.'

'What's its name?'

'I don't know. Grandma knew them all by name, but nobody else seems to.'

'You remember her?'

'Oh yes. She died only two years ago. All very tragic.'

'In what way?'

'Her body was found in the lake — not far from Deepwater. I was home at the time. It was awful.'

'You mean she fell in the lake?'

'That was the verdict at the coroner's inquest, but I don't think mother believes it. You see, there had been a great quarrel between grandma and grandpa that evening, and grandma had gone out of the house in a huff. She had a very violent temper, and was most impulsive when in a rage. I believe all the family knows she committed suicide, but naturally wish to cover it up. Perhaps I shouldn't tell you this, but I don't believe in keeping secrets, when they can serve no good purpose. Poor grandpa has never really got over his wife's death. That's why he drinks to excess. I think that he holds himself partly responsible for what happened. Mother, of course, handles him quite wrongly. He wanted particularly to meet you this evening, but just because he had had a few drinks he was forbidden to come down to dinner. So he had some more drinks to back up his courage, and then defied her. It's very hard on John and Lucy, who are compelled to live here until John can find a place of his own. He's hoping to get a post in the Foreign Office, but it seems to be taking a long time. It's all very difficult.'

'It must be. Until yesterday I was under the impression that the estate belonged to John.'

'No such luck. It was grandma who had all the money. She inherited several hundred thousand pounds from her father, who was a shipbuilder. When mother married father the estate was bankrupt, and about to be broken up and sold at auction. But grandma had some business acumen, and bought the thing as a whole. When she died she left mother an income in her own right, and grandpa took the rest. How grandpa is going to leave his money is anybody's guess. I hope he'll remember John, because John is a grand person — like father, who was crippled in the First World War, and scarcely had a penny to his name.'

Barrington appreciated this burst of confidence. It was, he thought, due to pent-up emotion which had to find an outlet somewhere. How different too was her whole demeanour now. The nymph he had met only yesterday by the lake was no longer in evidence. She looked, and spoke, like a fully matured woman, with vexing problems which went very deep, and she was regarding him as if she expected him to utter words of divine wisdom.

'You're not very happy?' he asked.

'No. I try to persuade myself I am, but there's too much friction here. Too much possessiveness. I don't want to be possessed. I don't want to have to wait for someone to die so that I can live a useless life. I want to be free.'

'So does everyone. But perfect freedom is an illusion. There is always a point at which we are no longer free. We all have obligations to the other person whether we like it or not. The great thing is to recognize the obligation, and to like it.'

'Now you're talking like a parson,' she said, with a sudden return to her old facetiousness. 'How very like John you are in some ways. But, then, all men have much in common, while all women are completely different. Why wasn't I born a man?'

'You don't really mean that.'

'But I do.'

'What is it you want — power?'

'Yes. Power to make the world a better place.'

'Or a worse. Be careful of power, Felicity. It creates more misery than it cures.'

They had come to the end of the circular

walk and passed again into the house. John and Lucy were sitting close together on the couch, and the whole place was very quiet.

'Well, what did you think of Grandma's Folly?' asked John.

'The conservatory? Quite wonderful. Is that what you all call it?'

'Grandpa started it. He objected to the enormous sums of money which grandma spent on it. She had only to read of some uncommon orchid, and she had to have it, if it cost the earth. Still, it was her money, so no one had a right to complain. Like a nightcap, Phil?'

'No, thanks. I think I had better be going.'

'But the night is young.'

'I have promised myself an early bathe, then some fishing, and then a full day's work. Also I have to walk back, as I didn't bring the car.'

'But I'll drive you back with pleasure,' said John.

'Thanks, but there's a full moon, and I shall enjoy the walk. It was very kind of you to ask me here.'

'Not at all. We have to thank you for tolerating us.'

Finally Barrington shook hands with John and Lucy, but Felicity insisted on seeing him off the premises. At the door she gripped his hand warmly.

'Don't take any notice of what I said,' she begged. 'As John will corroborate, I talk the most awful drivel at times.'

3

On the morrow Barrington rose at the crack of dawn, and proceeded to carry out his programme. It was a pearly morning with dew on the grass, and the promise of a warm, calm day. As he got into his swim-suit he saw through the wide open window a great bird sweep down at the far end of the lake, and rubbed his eyes in amazement as he soon realized it was a heron. Judging from its actions it had found a nice school of innocent young fish, and was having a breakfast off the estate. It was still outlined against the distant rushes when he left the cottage, clad in a dressing-gown and a pair of tennis shoes, but before he took his plunge it rose and went soaring away over the treetops.

Kicking off the unlaced shoes he dived into the still, clear water, and gasped for breath as he came to the surface. The water was ice cold, and for some minutes he swam at full pelt, until slowly he felt a warm glow surging through his limbs. After that every moment was a joy. As a change from swimming he lay on his back and kicked the water into the air where every drop gleamed and scintillated like a faceted diamond. Testing the depth by sinking feet first he was satisfied that that end of the lake earned its title of Deepwater, for he was unable to touch bottom.

Finally refreshed and invigorated by the exercise he sat down on the grassy bank in the warming sun, lit a cigarette, and browsed for a few minutes. It was good to be here. Good to feel a hundred per cent fit. Good to have a very definite job of work to do, with no interruptions, and good to have met John again.

It was good too to feel assured that John and his lovely young wife were happy, despite their impecunious state and their dependance on Lady Gertrude. He wished he could feel the same about the other members of the family. Felicity had admitted her unhappiness, and the old man wore his misery on his lined face. Certainly Lady Gertrude put up a show, but no one but an idiot would have been deceived by so shallow an exhibition.

He went back to the cottage, dressed in leisurely fashion and then got his borrowed rod ready for action. He had been assured that the flies which he had bought were just right for trout at that time of the year, but he had to take that assurance on trust. Anyway, it would be fun, even if the trout merely came up, looked at the fly, and went away in disgust. Choosing a likely spot he commenced to cast, making rather a mess of it the first few times, for it was many years since he had done that kind of fishing. But before long he was operating with some degree of skill, and suddenly there was a swirl in the water and he raised a big rainbow-coloured fish. His heart bounded, but alas, the fish got back to its natural habitat, and only the widening circle in the lake was left as consolation. The second rise was no more successful, so he moved along the bank for a short distance and tried again. Another half-hour must have passed when suddenly the water was broken and up came one of the biggest trout he had ever seen. In a split second the fish took the fly, and the hidden hook. There was tension on the rod as the line reeled out. Certain now that the trout was firmly hooked he began to play it, until the furious resistance began to slacken. Then foot by foot, yard by yard he brought it inshore, until he could see its marvellous coloration a foot or two beneath the surface. Then the landing-net was put into use, and the fight was over.

He found some little difficulty in getting the barbed hook out, but finally the two-pound trout was safely, and literally, in the bag. His feeling of triumph was now complete. The trout had gasped its last gasp and he sat for a few moments admiring the thing, and feeling a little sorry for it. So intent had he been in his pastime that he had quite failed to notice a figure half-walking, half-running towards him. It was Felicity, and he saw her only when she was but a few yards in his rear.

'Oh, Mr. Barrington!' she gasped.

There was something in her expression which puzzled him, and commanded his whole attention.

'Is anything wrong?' he asked.

'Yes. Grandpa is dead. Mother found him dead in his bed half an hour ago.'

'I'm terribly sorry. He seemed well enough last night. Is there anything I can do?'

'I — I don't know. But I haven't told you all. We telephoned the doctor and he came at once. He was most strange about it, and asked all sorts of queer questions. Then finally he said he couldn't give a certificate at once, and — and rang up the police.'

'The police!'

'Yes. Mother is terribly upset, and John told me to come and tell you, and to ask you not to go out in case the police should want to question you.'

'But why . . . ?' commenced Barrington,

and then stopped. That question was quite unnecessary. Clearly there must be medical evidence to indicate that the old man had not died a natural death.

'It's ghastly,' said Felicity. 'All this questioning. And now the police.'

'What sort of questioning?'

'The doctor wanted to know what food and drink grandpa had taken last night. Mother told him about the dinner-party, and that we all ate the same things.'

'So he suspects poison?'

'Yes.'

'Did he attend your grandfather regularly?'

'On and off. But for an old man grandpa was very healthy, except for his failing sight. The doctor used to say he would live to be a hundred. He asked me if grandpa appeared to be in good spirits when I last saw him, and I said that he was grumpy because he had more or less been sent to bed. Then he asked me if I had seen any drink in the bedroom, and I remembered grandpa's early morning drink.'

'What was that?'

'Susan always left him a glass of lemon and water on his bedside table. He used to drink it early in the morning. I told the doctor that I had seen the glass on the table, with a saucer over the top of it. He wanted the empty glass, but Susan had already washed it up.'

'That disposes of one useful bit of evidence,' mused Barrington. 'But, of course, there will be a post-mortem. Felicity, I think I had better come with you up to the house. The police are bound to ask for you, if not for me. I'm dreadfully sorry about all this. Quite spoilt my fishing.'

'Have you caught anything?'

'Have a look in that bag.'

Felicity investigated the rush bag, and gave a whistle of surprise as she saw the splendid trout inside, but her interest in angling, like Barrington's, was for the time being very diminished. They hurried back to the cottage, where Barrington handed over the fish to the cowman's wife, who had just arrived, and who was yet ignorant of the tragedy at the Hall. Then Barrington changed into less weather-beaten garb and drove Felicity back in the car.

On arriving they found John pacing up and down the terrace, and Felicity noticed that another car was parked close to the doctor's. John hurried to meet them, his face very set and grim.

' 'Morning, Phil,' he said. 'The police are here. It didn't take them long to get moving. Nasty business this.'

'It is indeed. Any fresh facts?'

'None that I know. Mother is now being questioned by the inspector about last night. But one thing is quite clear. Grandpa never died a natural death. Oh, Felicity, there's one thing I meant to ask you. To whom was the letter addressed which you wrote for grandpa last night, and posted.'

'To Mr. Brayton.'

'Grandpa's solicitor?'

'Yes.'

'I suppose I ought not to ask you what was in it, but grandpa is dead — '

'It was simply to ask Mr. Brayton to call as soon as he possibly could, as grandpa wanted to discuss a certain matter. Nothing more.'

'A certain matter of business,' mused John. 'That's rather extraordinary, isn't it?'

'Why?' asked Felicity.

But Barrington was not so innocent. A man who might be contemplating suicide would not be likely to dictate a letter making an appointment with his solicitor. He gave John a long look and John winced.

'Oh!' ejaculated Felicity. 'I see what you mean. But that's a terrible thought. I — I suppose the doctor could be wrong?'

'He's a very experienced doctor,' replied John. 'I can't imagine him taking the action he has taken without good grounds. But it might have been an accident of some kind.'

This suggestion did not soothe Felicity, and she gazed at Barrington as if to read his thoughts, but Barrington did not feel like advancing impulsive and gratuitous theories in so grave a situation, and he was remembering the old man's parting remark: 'That's the place for old fogies. The bed or the grave.'

Lucy then came from the house to greet Barrington with a forced smile, and to impart the information that breakfast was ready, having been greatly delayed by what had taken place. Barrington accepted an invitation to join the party and they all entered the dining-room through the casement window.

'Is mother still with the inspector?' asked John.

'Yes,' replied Lucy. 'They're all in the study. But Dr. Bragg has just left.'

'Have they questioned you yet?' asked John.

'No. I'm expecting to be called at any moment. Felicity, aren't you going to eat anything?'

'No thanks. Only coffee.'

'But, my dear, we must eat, despite this shocking business, which I don't understand at all. Mr. Barrington, poached eggs or cold ham?'

Barrington accepted the poached eggs gratefully, for he had put a particularly keen edge on his appetite. A few minutes passed and then Susan entered and said that Inspector Young would like to see Miss Felicity, at which Felicity almost jumped in her chair.

'T-hank you, Susan,' she stammered. 'Tell him I'll be there in a few moments.'

Susan vanished and Felicity stood up and hesitated.

'What am I to say?' she asked.

'Just answer their questions truthfully,' replied John. 'There's no need to be nervous. We've nothing to hide.'

As Felicity left the room Lady Gertrude returned to it, and her powdered nose and eyes suggested that she had been weeping. John immediately stood up and placed her chair into position. As she sat down she realized that Barrington was present, and nodded to him.

'It's all so bewildering,' she complained. 'All those questions as if to try and trap me into some inconsistent remark. All I know is what we all know. Oh, nothing to eat, Lucy dear. All I want is something to revive me. Just coffee, without milk. They asked me about father's will, but I don't know that he ever made a will. If he did I've no idea where it is, or what it contains.'

'There's something which you must know,' said John. 'That letter which Felicity posted last night was to Mr. Brayton, asking him to see grandpa as soon as convenient.'

Lady Gertrude stared at her son.

'Did Felicity tell you that?' she asked.

'Yes.'

'She never told me. Why didn't she tell me?'

'You never asked her.'

'No, that's true. But it's of no importance.'

'I can't help thinking it is important,' replied John. 'And I feel sure the inspector will consider it so. Have you any idea why grandpa should want to see Brayton?'

'None at all. You know how secretive he was about his personal affairs.'

'Mightn't it have been about his will, presuming he has made one, or about a will which he wished to make?'

'It might, but there are other things he might wish to see Brayton about. I know that Dickenson is keen to buy the freehold of 'Riverhead'. Brayton might be able to tell us something. Why not telephone him?'

'Not now. I think the police would take a poor view of that. The matter is completely in their hands. I saw the sergeant at the telephone a little while ago, and it's possible he may already have spoken to Brayton. There's nothing we can do but be patient, and hope that the doctor is wrong.'

Lady Gertrude stared at her son.

'You don't think he is wrong?' she asked.

'No, Mother. We have to be realistic about this. There are certain post-mortem symptoms of poisoning which no good doctor can mistake, and Bragg is a man of long experience. How grandpa got the poison is, of course, another matter.'

'Didn't Bragg say what he thought the poison was?' asked Lucy.

John shook his head, and for a few minutes there was silence, which was broken by a ring at the doorbell. A few moments later Susan knocked and entered, with half a dozen letters on a tray.

'The post, my Lady,' she said.

'Thank you, Susan.'

'The one with no stamp on I found in the letter-box, my Lady,' said Susan. 'The others the postman handed me.'

Lady Gertrude nodded, and then handed a letter to John, and a postcard to Lucy.

'Will you excuse us, Mr. Barrington?' she asked.

'Certainly.'

49

She recognized the handwriting on the several stamped letters and laid them aside, unopened. The unstamped one she looked at for a moment, and then slit it open. From inside she took a strip of paper measuring about eight inches by two. It bore handwriting in large capitals, and her brow became furrowed as she read it, apparently again and again.

'Curious,' she muttered. 'John, what do you make of that?'

She passed the slip to her son, who read what was written in a voice just loud enough for the rest of the party to hear.

'CHILDE ROLAND TO THE DARK TOWER CAME.'

'What does it mean?' asked Lucy.

'It's Shakespeare,' said John. '*Macbeth*, I think.'

'No,' said Barrington. 'It's Edgar's song from *King Lear*

Childe Roland to the dark tower came;
His word was still — Fie, foh, and fum,
I smell the blood of a British man.

No one has ever made any sense out of it.'

'And no one does now,' muttered John.

'Was it addressed to you, Mother?'

'Yes.'

'And you've no idea what it signifies?'

'No idea at all. The envelope is also written in capital letters. It must have been left since yesterday afternoon's postal delivery, because that was left in the box, and I cleared the box myself.'

Barrington found himself deeply intrigued by this strange business. Unless it was the work of a lunatic it must have significance, and since it was addressed to Lady Gertrude it was natural to assume that she had been chosen by the writer to interpret it. But Lady Gertrude still shook her head, and looked as pale as death.

Time passed and Felicity did not return. Lady Gertrude, looking like a pricked balloon, begged to be excused. The events of that day were proving too much for her. She needed rest. Perhaps Lucy would call her if the inspector wanted to see her.

'Of course,' said Lucy.

'You'd better leave that mysterious note and the envelope, Mother,' said John. 'The police should see them.'

When she had gone John gave a little sigh, and rang the bell for Susan.

'You can clear the table, Susan,' he said. 'Miss Felicity has had all she needs. I

51

suppose she is still with the inspector?'

'Yes, Sir John.'

'If she should be wanting me I shall be in the library.'

'I must go and dress,' said Lucy.

Barrington and Sir John walked through the large hall and along a corridor to the library. It was a commodious panelled room with splendid views across the park, and the excellent book-shelving was carried up to about six feet from the floor. All the shelves were packed with books, stoutly and splendidly bound, and Barrington was fascinated by this goodly array. But John seemed not to notice his friend's interest in them, for his mind was elsewhere.

'What do you make of it, Phil? The message, I mean.'

'I think it has a definite connection with your grandfather's death.'

'In which case one must rule out both suicide and accident.'

'We had already ruled out suicide, hadn't we?'

'Yes. It means we have to face the ugliest possibility of all. That's what I find difficult — well-nigh impossible. I feel almost like packing up and going away.'

'That wouldn't be any good.'

'No. But there's Lucy, not to mention

52

Felicity. Consider the effect of all this upon them. Felicity is pretty hard-boiled, but Lucy isn't. I brought her into this family and I feel responsible. At least I could send her away.'

'Would she go?'

'I don't know. Come in!' he called as there came a knock on the door.

It was Felicity, a little short of breath from hurrying.

'Susan told me you were here,' she said. 'Oh, it was awful. They asked me so many questions I became bewildered. They must have already spoken to the solicitor on the telephone, because they knew about the letter which I wrote at grandpa's dictation. The inspector tried to be nice, but some of his questions were almost insulting.'

'In what way?' asked John.

'He wanted to know if I had ever heard mother and grandpa quarrelling. I said there were differences of opinion but no quarrel. Then he asked me if — oh, I really can't repeat it.'

'You needn't,' said John, with a wan smile.

'But I will. He asked me if I had told mother about the letter which I had written and posted to Mr. Brayton. I — I didn't know what to say.'

'Why not?' asked John, almost angrily.

Felicity winced as if she had been struck, for it was not often that her gentle and beloved brother spoke with such marked reproval. Immediately he was contrite, and touched her hand.

'Sorry, Felicity,' he murmured. 'I think we are all a little upset. Forgive me.'

'You see, John, it wasn't one of those questions you can answer in a word. I told him that I had mentioned a letter to mother, to explain my absence, but I had not told her to whom it was written, nor what it contained. The sergeant wrote it all down, and the third officer kept glancing at the inspector as if they had a kind of deaf and dumb code. They were acting as if — as if it were murder.'

'Felicity!'

'You said I must tell the truth. You have always told me that the truth is all that matters. Well, then, the truth is that grandpa was poisoned, and not by his own hand, and that the police suspect someone — someone in this house.'

John took her arms and drew her close to him.

'You really mustn't race ahead like that,' he said quietly. 'This is an enquiry, and the police are bound to ask awkward and embarrassing questions. At the moment nobody knows with certainty the cause of grandpa's death. Only the post-mortem will reveal that. The best thing for us all is to keep our nerve and try to remain calm. Now, I want to use the telephone.'

Barrington guessed that this was a white lie, and that John's immediate intention was to hand over the anonymous letter to the inspector. It was natural that for the time being he would wish to keep that strange development from his young sister, since it seemed to indicate the existence of a deadly enemy.

'Are the police calling other witnesses?' asked Barrington.

'I don't think so. They've already seen Susan, and cook, and when I left they seemed about to hold a conference. Perhaps they've gone as far as they can without hearing the result of the post-mortem. What — what do you think of it all?'

'My opinion isn't worth anything, and it would be presumptuous of me to offer it. As a matter of fact I feel a little uncomfortable here, at a time when you are in such trouble.'

'Oh, don't think of leaving,' she said hastily. 'John needs you. Yes, really he does. He's always needed you — you know that.'

'Nonsense!'

'It's true. By nature he is gentle and timid, but cruelty and violence shock him, and he's not capable of standing up to this alone. Please don't go.'

'I won't — if that is how John wants it.'

John came back a few minutes later.

'They're leaving in a short while,' he said. 'The ambulance is on the way, and after that they will seal the room, and await the further medical evidence. They are not going to call you, Phil, not for the time being.'

'Good!' said Barrington. 'I think a spot of work won't do me any harm. If I can be of any service do let me know.'

'I will,' promised John.

Back at Deepwater Cottage Mrs. Sawyer had heard the news, but knew nothing of the details.

'Went off in his sleep,' she said. 'Well, that's the way it ought to happen. Strange gentleman he was too. Quite rude he was to me when I was working in the big house, but you couldn't help liking him.'

Barrington, to his dismay, found that work went very badly. Try as he might he could not give it the intense concentration it called for. Time and again he would sit still and stare into space and that intriguing mystery message would float before his eye, in letters of fire:

'CHILDE ROLAND TO THE DARK TOWER CAME'.

4

Twenty-four hours later Inspector McLean, at Scotland Yard, returned to his office from a conference, with a sheaf of typewritten documents which had arrived from Dorset overnight, relative to the Grayling case. Sergeant Brook, who knew his chief like a book, could tell from the set of McLean's features that something was undoubtedly cooking. A conference, which was suddenly called and went on for two hours, invariably spelt immediate action.

'A case in your own beloved part of the country, Brook,' said McLean. 'A few miles out of Dorchester. Finish what you're doing and then shut down. I shall be ready in an hour, and we'll go by road.'

Brook's eyes gleamed, for despite his twenty-odd years in London he could never shake off the lure of the country especially that part of the country which was west of Southampton.

'Must be lovely down there just now,' he commented, staring through the window at the spring sunshine. 'Serious case, sir?'

'Serious and interesting, I should say. An

58

old man with a large fortune is found dead in his bed. Doctor suspects poisoning, and calls for a post-mortem. The result is what he expects. The poison is believed to have been introduced into a glass of lemonade which the old man was accustomed to drink in the early morning. But unfortunately the empty glass is washed up before the tragedy is discovered, which is very convenient for the poisoner, and very inconvenient for us. No sign of any poison in the house, and no evidence that anyone has ever acquired any such stuff. A motive as large as a house, but by no means convincing.'

'You mean his money?'

'Yes. It's a big estate — some two thousand acres in all, incorporating a number of leasehold farms, large house and parklands. The dead man, Grayling, inherited the estate from his wife, who died in somewhat peculiar circumstances two years ago. She apparently rescued it from bankruptcy, prior to her daughter's marriage to the late Sir Robert Medding, baronet. Her daughter, Lady Gertrude, is in residence, along with her son, the new baronet, and his wife. Lady Gertrude has money in her own right, but her son and daughter-in-law have no means and live at the Hall on sufferance. But it was the dead

59

man who held the moneybags, and he appears to have left no will. Lady Gertrude, being next of kin, stands to inherit quite a lot of money, so it's natural that there should be a lot of speculation as to how the poison got into the old man's system.'

'You mean this Lady who-is-it is suspected of poisoning her own father?'

'It's been done before, for far less gain than is now involved, and no one else stands to benefit directly by the old man's death. One thing seems certain — it wasn't suicide, for on the night when he died the old man sent a message to his solicitor, asking to see him as soon as possible. That would be an extraordinary thing to do, if he had any idea of taking his own life. The solicitor has stated that he knows of no reason why his client should want to see him, unless it was for the purpose of making a will, which he had always refused to do.'

'Looks pretty murky to me,' said Brook.

'Yes, and it's murkier still when this little slip of paper is taken into account.'

McLean passed the anonymous message across to the sergeant, and smiled as he saw the deep wrinkles appear in Brook's broad forehead.

'What's it mean?' asked Brook.

'If we knew that our case would present

less difficulty. It was left at the Hall on the night of Grayling's death. It may of course be a red herring.'

'To make it look like the work of someone outside the house?'

McLean nodded as he slipped all the documents into a brief-case, and began to tidy up his desk. Already the new case was taking hold of his imagination, for his colleagues in the west country had drawn attention to the strange death of old Mrs. Grayling, which had never been satisfactorily cleared up. How the lady could have slipped into the lake was a mystery, and a verdict to that effect was given chiefly because no one who knew her would believe for a moment that she had drowned herself, since she was notoriously in love with life, and hale and hearty despite her advanced age. In the document covering this matter the date was given as two years previously, but McLean, who liked his facts to be concise and tidy, had already put a telephone call through to Dorchester, and was now waiting for a reply.

They were almost ready to take the road when the office telephone rang and Brook picked up the receiver. It was a personal trunk call for McLean, and Brook handed over the receiver. He spoke a few words, thanked his informant, made a pencil note on a memorandum pad, and then extracted a document from the brief-case.

'Yes, here it is,' he muttered. 'May the twenty-ninth. That seems to get us off to a good start.'

'Did you speak, sir?' asked Brook.

'Did I? Perhaps I did. I was cogitating on the interesting fact that old Mrs. Grayling met her end on the same date as her surviving husband. The odds against that I believe are three hundred and sixty-four to one. Makes one think, doesn't it?'

'By Jove, it does,' said Brook. 'But life is full of coincidences. Take the pools, for example — '

'I should very much like to.'

'I mean a three million to one chance comes off every week. Why, I nearly got one home myself a few months back. Think of me with fifty or sixty thousand quid.'

'I can think of nothing more deplorable; but may I remind you the car is waiting, and we seem to have got a little off the track.'

Brook grinned and shut down his desk. A few minutes later they were threading their way through the incredible traffic in one of the new swift police cars which Brook loved to drive, and before very long they were slipping noiselessly through the suburbs, to where the Great West Road went rolling into the sunlit countryside.

'Straight for Dorchester,' said McLean. 'I have an appointment there with the chief constable.'

The subsequent appointment yielded nothing new in the way of evidence, but from the chief constable, whom McLean knew very well, a lot of useful information was got regarding the various members of the Medding family, including the dead man and his wife who had predeceased him.

'There's a lot of friction there,' concluded the chief constable. 'Some of it is undoubtedly due to the fact that until recently there were three generations all living together, and that old Grayling hated parting with money. The place is understaffed, and what servants there are had difficulty in getting their wages paid when they were due. Lady Gertrude actually has a long bill against her father for monies which she has dispersed from her own private fund.'

'What are her private means?' asked McLean.

'Not great, I believe. She inherited ten thousand pounds from her mother two years ago, but she must have got through a lot of that since she dresses rather extravagantly, and is fond of jewellery.'

'You knew the family intimately?'

'Yes — fairly intimately.'

'What is your private opinion about this death?'

The chief constable shook his head.

'I really don't know,' he said slowly. 'Gertrude is a curious type of woman. She is proud and domineering, and for years she and her father have lived at loggerheads. There's no doubt at all that she resented the terms of her mother's will. She expected very much more than she actually got, and made no bones about saying so in public. All the same, I find it very difficult to believe that she could coldly and deliberately plan and accomplish her father's death. I'm very glad you have got this case, Mac.'

'I had an idea you were,' replied McLean. 'When does the coroner's inquest take place?'

'Tomorrow afternoon at three o'clock, unless you want it adjourned. I've booked you a couple of rooms at the Bull, and told Tyson — the coroner. His telephone number is 12136. If you can find time for a round of golf on Sunday I am at your disposal. On the last occasion you gave me an appalling thrashing. I've been saving myself up for revenge.'

'I'll let you know,' said McLean. 'Now I

think I'll get along to the Bull and leave my baggage. I presume the Medding family know you've handed the case over.'

'Yes. I told Sir John this morning. You'll find him a perfectly charming person. He has an old war comrade staying at one of the cottages — a writing chap named Barrington. An intelligent sort of man, but so far he hasn't been troubled. Well, the best of luck to you. Don't forget about Sunday.'

McLean said he wouldn't, but his mind was far from golf or any other innocent form of relaxation. After leaving their baggage at the very attractive old-world inn, he and Brook had lunch, and then set off for Strafford Park. On sighting the big house from the long drive McLean was deeply impressed by its noble lines. It was all on two stories, with some fine mullion windows on the nearer end, and some other evidence of Tudor origin. Remembering the cryptic message he looked for anything resembling a tower but saw nothing. As they approached it the lovely gardens came to view, backed by the fine trees in the park. Farther away, on undulating land, were fields under crops and here and there a whitewashed cottage, with cattle browsing on lush meadows.

'Gorgeous!' said Brook, now in his element. 'Takes me back thirty years and more, when my father was head-gardener to an earl and . . . Well, here we are.'

Susan answered the summons, and on being given McLean's card she showed them into the hall, and was absent for a few minutes. Finally she returned and led them into the lounge where Sir John was sitting alone. He rose as they entered.

'Good afternoon, gentlemen,' he said. 'I was told to expect you. Inspector McLean, I presume?' he asked, looking at McLean.

'Yes. This is Sergeant Brook, my assistant. You are Sir John Medding?'

'Yes. Do sit down.'

McLean looked around the big room, with its many family portraits, and fine display of antiques. He found it a very pleasant place, with wonderful views, and a most restful atmosphere, which sorted strangely with the grim business at hand.

'You realize that the case is now largely out of the hands of the county constabulary?' asked McLean.

'Yes.'

'I shall do my best to cause you as little inconvenience as possible. The evidence already taken is of a preliminary nature, and I shall have to take supplementary depositions, and possibly recall some of the previous witnesses. If I could have the use of a room for that purpose I should be grateful.'

'Certainly. There is the morning-room, which we seldom use. It has direct entry to the terrace, and will save you the trouble of coming through the house. There is also a telephone extension. Will you see it now?'

'Please.'

He led them to the small room in question, and McLean found it much to his liking. A stout table was drawn up close to the window, and some chairs suitably placed. The telephone cord was long enough to permit the instrument to be placed on the table.

'This will do splendidly,' said McLean. 'Is that the key to the casement window?'

Sir John nodded and McLean took the key from the mantelpiece and opened the windows wide, letting in a breath of perfumed air from the flower beds outside.

'I shall need to spend some time in the sealed room,' he said. 'But I have obtained the key to that. I think that is all for the moment, Sir John. Thank you very much.'

When Sir John had left McLean opened up his briefcase, and perused the various documents for a while. Brook took a new note-book from his personal case, and sharpened a couple of pencils, gazing round the interesting panelled room as he did so.

'I think we'll start with Susan Benson,' said McLean. 'She's probably the girl who answered the door. Find her and bring her in.'

Brook came back in a very short time with Susan, who displayed a natural amount of nervousness.

'Do sit down and make yourself comfortable, Miss Benson,' said McLean. 'I want to ask you a few questions.'

Susan sat facing him, with her hands clenched together in her lap. She looked a very healthy type of honest girl, and McLean had little doubt that he would quickly detect an untruth.

'How long have you been employed here?' he asked.

'Five years, sir.'

'What is your position here?'

'Parlourmaid, sir.'

'Unmarried?'

'Yes, sir.'

'I want you to take your mind back to Tuesday evening — the night when Mr. Grayling died. Did you take a glass of lemonade to his bedroom?'

'Yes, sir.'

'At what time?'

'It was about half-past eight.'

'Where was Mr. Grayling then?'

'He was in the lounge with the rest of the family, and Mr. Barrington, who came to dinner.'

'Did you see Mr. Grayling again that evening?'

'No, sir.'

'When did you see him again?'

'At eight o'clock the next morning.'

'You mean — in his bedroom?'

'Yes, sir.'

'Why did you go there?'

'To draw the curtains. He liked me to do that, because the daylight woke him up. He didn't like to be wakened any other way.'

'Did you take away the empty glass which had contained the lemonade?'

'Yes, sir.'

'You actually saw Mr. Grayling, then?'

The girl trembled.

'Only — the top of his head. I — I thought he was asleep and didn't disturb him.'

'You didn't know that he was no longer alive?'

'Oh no, sir — no.'

'What did you do with the empty glass?'

'I placed it and the saucer on the draining-board in the kitchen. Ethel, the housemaid, was there washing up some of the things that were left over.'

'Had you prepared that lemonade yourself?'

69

'Yes, sir. Just half a lemon squeezed into a glass of water. I always did it at the same time.'

'Did you take it to the bedroom at once, or was it left about for any time?'

'I took it up at once, and made the bed ready.'

'When did you know that Mr. Grayling was dead?'

'About half an hour after I brought the glass down. Lady Gertrude came downstairs, and met Sir John in the hall. I heard her tell him to get on the telephone to the doctor, as she thought that Mr. Grayling had passed away in his sleep.'

'Were you later asked about the glass of lemonade?'

'Yes, sir. The doctor came into the kitchen and questioned me and cook about what food or drink Mr. Grayling had had the previous evening. Then I told him about the lemonade. He enquired about the glass, and Ethel told him she had washed it up.'

'Did you put any sugar into the lemonade?'

'No, sir. It was always plain lemon and water.'

'Have you any idea at what time Mr. Grayling was accustomed to drink the lemonade?'

'He told me once that it was in the early

hours, when he woke up with a very dry throat.'

'Did he ever fail to drink it?'

'Once or twice perhaps, but not very often.'

'And you are sure that when you left that glass on the last occasion it contained nothing but lemon and water?'

'Quite sure, sir. It never left my sight for a moment.'

McLean was quite satisfied that the girl was telling the truth, but he detained her a little longer, in order to secure evidence of quite a different nature.

'What were Mr. Grayling's relations with the various members of the family?' he asked.

'He — he got on with them very well.'

'All of them?'

Susan hesitated for a moment.

'Some more than others,' she said. 'Miss Felicity was his favourite. His sight was very poor and Miss Felicity used to read the newspaper to him every morning. He was very fond of Miss Felicity.'

'What about his grandson?'

'They used to argue a little.'

'What about?'

'I'm not supposed to know.'

'But you have an idea?'

71

'I think it was chiefly about the tenants. Sir John was always trying to get Mr. Grayling to improve some of the cottages, and he wasn't very successful.'

'And his daughter, Lady Gertrude, did he argue with her?'

Here Susan was most reticent. The old man wasn't about very much, but spent a great deal of his time in his large bed-sitting-room. At times he would have his meals served there, especially when Lady Gertrude had guests. Pressed about this Susan admitted that the old man had a weakness for strong drink, and confessed that she had on several occasions taken him a bottle of whisky secretly, which he secreted behind the books in the small bookcase by his bed. Lady Gertrude kept the key of the wine cellar, and so Susan had to buy the whisky in the village.

Finally McLean thanked the girl and let her go. Brook read back the verbatim shorthand version, and McLean nodded his head reflectively.

'A little bit inconsistent, sir, isn't it?' asked Brook.

'Just a bit, but no more than I expected. The girl was doing her best to tell the truth without drawing too dark a picture of the family relationships. One thing seems clear — if the poison was in that drinking glass it can only have been introduced after Susan left the drink in Grayling's bedroom. The medical evidence is that the poison was taken somewhere between two and five o'clock in the morning and that death supervened round about seven o'clock. It is in evidence that the grand-daughter, Felicity, took her grandfather to bed at nine o'clock the previous evening. She has stated that she saw the drink on the side table, but of the various persons in the house she is the least suspect, because there is little doubt that she was fond of the old man. Moreover, as far as I can see, she stood to gain nothing from his death. We have to look for someone who could have entered that bedroom while the old man was absent, or while he slept. Someone who had a very good motive. That brings us to Lady Gertrude, who has already testified that she was not in the room between the old man's retirement and her discovery of his dead body the next morning. I think I shall have to see her.'

'I should think so, sir.'

It was half an hour before this could be accomplished, for Lady Gertrude, overwhelmed by the tragedy and its consequences, was trying to make up the sleep she had lost. When at last she came McLean saw the signs of acute mental suffering on her handsome face.

'I am sorry, my lady, to have to bother you with further questions,' he said. 'But you will appreciate that since the result of the post-mortem has been made known this case takes on a more serious aspect.'

'I understand perfectly,' replied Lady Gertrude, in a firm voice. 'I understand too, that I am under suspicion.'

'That is an over-statement. There is no doubt at all that Mr. Grayling met his death by poisoning. This enquiry is an attempt to discover how he got that poison, whether by his own hand, by accident or by design. I shall be glad of any help you can give me.'

'I wish I could help, but I can't. To imagine that anyone in this house would commit such a crime is senseless. I won't say we all loved him, because at times he proved very difficult, but none of us were lacking respect and affection. I can't help believing that for some reason or other he decided to end his life.'

'A few hours after he had dictated a letter to his solicitor asking to see him?'

'That I don't understand.'

'It is a very important fact in the case. You have stated that you entered his bedroom on the morning following his death. Had you any special reason for going there?'

'I always did that — after I had dressed, to find out whether he would come down to breakfast or have it served in his room.'

'When you saw him did you think he was dead?'

'Yes. I could see no sign of breathing, and when I touched his hand it was stone cold.'

'Can you think of any person who for any reason whatsoever might wish to accomplish your father's death?'

'No, I can't.'

McLean then took from his brief-case the slip of paper bearing the quotation, and showed it to Lady Gertrude.

'I presume you have seen this before?' he asked.

'Yes. It was addressed to me and put into the letter-box at the front door.'

'Does it convey anything to you?'

'No. I think it must be a practical joke.'

'Do you know anyone who might play such a joke, at such a moment?'

'I'm glad to say I do not.'

'And you do not know of the existence of any will which might have been made by your father?'

'No.'

'Did he never express his intentions

regarding his property, in the event of his death?'

'Never to me.'

'Did you never suggest to him that it was time he thought about the ultimate disposal of the estate?'

'I did so on many occasions but always he refused to discuss the matter.'

There was a pause while McLean turned over some documents, and when he spoke again his question seemed to cause Lady Gertrude some embarrassment.

'After the death of your mother, did your father suffer extreme remorse?'

'Naturally. They had been together for a very long time.'

'Was there not some doubt about the manner of her death?'

'Not with us,' retorted Lady Gertrude. 'It was quite clear that she slipped into the lake and was drowned. I know there was a lot of vulgar gossip, but it arose out of complete ignorance of the facts. I can't see what this has to do with my father's death.'

'Do you remember the exact date of your mother's death?'

'It was about the end of May two years ago.'

'Yes, the twenty-ninth of May, the same date as that on which your father died.'

Lady Gertrude gave an involuntary start.

'I see now,' she said. 'Yes, it is rather a grim coincidence. Is it possible that my father might have remembered that day, and . . . No, it makes no sense. I wish it did.'

'I wish it did, too,' said McLean. 'I don't think I need detain you any longer.'

Lady Gertrude rose and Brook escorted her to the door, and closed it after her.

'A very self-possessed lady,' mused McLean. 'But I think her grief is just a little overdone. Why grieve so much about the death of a very old man, with whom she was at loggerheads most of the time, and who was foolish enough to die intestate, leaving his upstart daughter the income from nearly a quarter of a million pounds?'

'As much as that?'

'So I am informed.'

'One would have thought the old man would have made some provision for the young baronet and his wife, not to mention the grand-daughter, of whom he was fond.'

'Perhaps that is the reason why he wanted to see his solicitor. If it was he was a day too late.'

'Looks bad, doesn't it — for Lady Gertrude, I mean?'

'It certainly brings her well into the picture. But we mustn't forget the person who quoted that phrase from Shakespeare.'

'So it was Shakespeare?'

'Yes. A great many people have cogitated over its meaning. You should read Shakespeare when you can spare a moment from your football pools.'

'To find phrases which nobody understands?'

'You score one mark there, Brook. What I want you to do, Brook, is to keep your eyes open for any writing paper resembling this strip, also envelopes like the one in which it was enclosed. Take a good look at them.'

Brook did so, holding them both to the light in search of watermarks. The envelope was void of them, but the notepaper had part of a watermark.

'Looks like a bird's wing,' he said.

'Yes. Pity there is no lettering.'

'You think it may originate from inside the house?'

'There's a bare possibility. Now I think we'll go upstairs and investigate the bedroom.'

5

Barrington, wrestling with his novel, found the task more than ever difficult. His active and inventive mind, upon which he had been accustomed to rely most confidently when in any literary quandary, now seemed to have deserted him, and his concentration was ruined by an irresistible desire to know exactly what was going on at the Hall. Out of consideration for the Medding family he had remained within the immediate precincts of his cottage, and had seen no one who knew anything about the matter, except Mrs. Sawyer who by this time had some inkling of the family drama, which was made clear to Barrington by the fact that she spent two hours bustling about the place without a single mention of it. It was when she was about to leave for the day that her unusual oyster-like silence broke down.

'People are saying such queer things about poor Mr. Grayling,' she said.

'What kind of things?' asked Barrington.

'I'm not a woman who repeats a lot of silly gossip,' she replied. 'But I've heard that the police are making enquiries because — because Mr. Grayling didn't die a natural death.'

'It's not wise to believe all one hears.'

'That's what I told my husband, but he said that several people on the estate have been questioned by the police, and some people in the house. He said that only happens when the doctor has doubts.'

'He may be right, but whatever may be the truth it is nobody else's business but the family's. If I were you I wouldn't repeat anything you have been told.'

Mrs. Sawyer sniffed at the mild rebuff, and Barrington went back to his forsaken typewriter. For two solid hours he wrote steadily and pugnaciously, and then ate the cold luncheon which Mrs. Sawyer had left. He read what he had written, shook his head despondently and tore it up. Half an hour later John Medding called to find his guest sitting in the garden, under the shade of a giant walnut tree, smoking reflectively.

'I rang the bell, but couldn't make you hear,' he said.

'Sorry,' said Barrington. 'I'm having a rest. Can't resist this enchanting view. Do take a pew.'

'I'd better not. I'm on my way to the 'Gables' to see the bailiff. Thought I'd tell you of the new development.'

'Is there one?'

'Yes. The county police have handed the case over to Scotland Yard. One of their best men is already here — Chief Inspector McLean of the C.I.D.'

'Did you expect that?'

'Not quite so quickly. Phil, I won't disguise the fact that I'm worried out of my life. This man, McLean, impresses me immensely. He'll move heaven and earth to get to the truth of this matter, and in getting there every scrap of family pride will be trampled in the mud.'

'But surely this kind of enquiry is restricted to relevant matters, even if you do keep a skeleton in the cupboard.'

'Everything is relevant in a murder enquiry.'

'Aren't you going a little too far?' asked Barrington.

'I don't think so. I've lain awake all night pondering the matter. Accident, suicide, murder. Those are the three alternatives. There is not a shred of evidence to support the first two possibilities. It leaves only murder. When Inspector McLean is certain of that, which he may be even at this moment, he will put us on the rack. Of course we are all innocent, but in the process we shall be stripped naked.'

This vehement outburst astonished

Barrington, who had hitherto regarded John as a man of few, if any, deep emotions.

'I don't quite understand,' he said.

'Of course you don't. You have only seen us when on our best behaviour. You saw the old man only once, and grandmother not at all. My father was a grand person — an easy-going, charming personality who knew nothing about business, and cared little about money. When he inherited the estate he had no notion that it was hopelessly bankrupt. Shattered in the First World War, he was incapable of taking any post, and when at last the balloon went up and somebody foreclosed on him, Mrs. Grayling, bulging with wealth, came to the rescue, almost on her own terms. What more natural that she should save her prospective son-in-law from the publicity of the bankruptcy court? My father was left with Deepwater Cottage, one small private spot among all these hundreds of acres. He willed that to me before he died. The Graylings took the rest. They were a strange pair, ruthless in business matters, and outside the pale socially. Grandpa was a penniless actor until he met the woman he married. She was attracted by his good looks, and he no doubt by her wealth, for Grandma was never a good-looker.

'From the day of the marriage grandpa

never did a day's work, but drank himself into a dipsomaniac. He got so bad that he was sent away to some sort of clinic for a year. Finally he came home, partially cured, but cynical and hateful. He and grandma used to engage in fearful quarrels, but grandma always held the whip hand — her money. It was in that atmosphere that my mother was brought up, but my father was unaware of it until after his marriage. It was a painful revelation, and it caused friction between him and my mother, who from a mistaken sense of loyalty invariably sided with her parents. Now the Graylings are no more, but that breath of healthy fresh air which should be blowing through Strafford Hall is poisoned by this mystery of the old man's death. I don't mind so much for myself, but there's Lucy, and she is to have a baby. I don't want that child to be born here. I want its surroundings to be peaceful and happy. All this beauty which you see everywhere is a mockery. Behind it there is horror and everlasting unrest.'

Barrington knew not what to say in the circumstances, but he could not help feeling that John, despite his candid admissions, was still keeping something back. The one reference to his mother was, in the circumstances, remarkably brief, and

Barrington was left with the feeling that in the tirade against the Graylings, Lady Gertrude was not entirely excluded.

'Is it possible that your grandfather had an implacable enemy?' he asked.

'He had many. But forgive me for boring you with these details.'

'I'm very far from being bored. How is Felicity taking it?'

'Very badly. I had expected something better of her, because she has always been so remarkably self-controlled. Now she seems to have gone to pieces. If you see her, Phil, try to take her mind off this tragedy.'

Barrington nodded and John went on his way. It was late in the afternoon when Barrington was walking in the lower garden of the Hall that he came upon Felicity, sitting on a seat above the lily-pond. She seemed to be in a brown study and was not aware of his approach until he was within a yard or two of her.

'Good afternoon, Felicity!'

'Oh!' she gasped, coming to her senses. 'I — I didn't hear you. Been working?'

'Yes,' he replied as he sat beside her. 'Am I trespassing?'

'Of course not. It's nice to see someone in the garden. It's so lonely here when the gardener has gone; and the house is lonelier still. I suppose you've heard about the Scotland Yard invasion?'

'Yes. John told me. He looked in at the cottage.'

'Do you think they'll solve the mystery?'

'I hope so, for everyone's sake. But if I were you I wouldn't worry too much. Nothing is gained by worrying over matters outside one's control. Leave it to the police. It's their job, and they're used to it.'

She looked at him with her very impressive eyes.

'You wouldn't say that if it were someone you liked very much who had been murdered.'

'That hasn't been proved, Felicity.'

'It will be. I have just come from that new inspector. He can't be fooled. He'll find out everything.'

'Isn't that what you want — what we all want?'

'Yes — I suppose so.'

'Well, let's try to forget it for a while. What about coming out in the car, and you can show me all the local beauty spots.'

For a moment she looked as if she would accept the invitation, then she shook her head.

'I want to see John. He's gone to look at some of the labourers' cottages with the bailiff, and may be back at any moment.'

'Won't it wait?'

'No. It's very important. I must see him the moment he comes back.' There was silence for a few moments, while she stared into the pond. 'You see,' she resumed, 'I'm going away.'

'You mean — for a holiday?'

'For good.'

'Felicity!'

'Why do you look so shocked?'

'Because I think that would be an unwise — even cruel — thing to do.'

'Cruel to whom?'

'To your mother — and John. You would merely add to the troubles they are now bearing, and for you to leave in the middle of this enquiry would start all kinds of horrible suspicions. The police might even take steps to prevent your leaving, since you are a witness in this case.'

'Let them try,' she muttered.

'Listen, Felicity. I'm convinced that now is the time for the family to stick together. If you leave — '

Felicity stood up and put her hands to her ears dramatically. Then she turned and, without a word, hurried away. Barrington stared after her until she had disappeared from his view, then he walked back to the cottage, deep in thought. The question now was whether he should warn John of the intention of his headstrong sister. He disliked the idea, but found it equally repugnant to sit and do nothing while Felicity committed an act which he was certain would cause heartbreak on both sides.

How confused things were. Felicity repining the death of her reprobate grandparent. John in fear and dread of something emerging from the investigation which would drag his name into the mire, and both of them talking wildly of taking flight. The police apparently believing in the existence of a calculating murderer. The workpeople whispering among themselves, and most probably advancing theories which they dared not put forward openly. And all the time the blessed sun shone from a clear sky, and the birds in the gardens and woods praised creation in their own spontaneous and inimitable way.

Back at the cottage he rang up the Hall and asked for Sir John. Susan's unmistakable voice informed him that Sir John wasn't at home. Would he leave any message.

'No,' he replied. 'I'll ring again — later.'

Within a quarter of an hour the telephone rang, and he heard John's voice on the line.

'I was told you telephoned me, Phil,' he said. 'But I've only just got back. Anything I can do?'

'Is Felicity there?'

'I really don't know. I haven't seen her since I came in.'

'John, I must tell you something. I met Felicity and had a very brief chat with her. She's thinking of doing something silly.'

'What do you mean?'

'She's thinking of leaving.'

'You mean — running away?'

'Yes. I tried to reason with her, but it was no use. Whatever you do please don't tell her I told you, or she'll hate me for it. But watch her, because I believe she is in earnest.'

John's voice came back, low and tremulous. 'Thanks, old chap. I understand. I must do something about this. Excuse me now.'

Barrington breathed a sigh of relief as he hung up the receiver.

★ ★ ★

John, shaken to his foundations by what he had learnt, rang the bell for Susan, and asked her casually if she had seen his sister. Susan replied that she had seen her half an hour ago, but believed she had gone out for a walk. Not satisfied with this John went upstairs and rapped on Felicity's bedroom door.

'Who's there?'

'It's me — John.'

'Oh, don't — '

But John had already opened the door. He saw Felicity standing by the bed, with a suitcase behind her. A drawer in the dressing-chest was wide open, and some under-clothing was lying on a chair.

'What are you doing?' he asked.

Felicity met his gaze fearlessly.

'I'm going away,' she replied.

'I don't understand. Where are you going?'

'To the home of a girl I know — in London. I telephoned her a short while ago.'

'But you haven't said a word about it.'

'No. I was going to leave a note.'

'Felicity, what is all this? Why are you running away?'

'I — I can't bear this any longer. Don't try to stop me, John. My mind is made up.'

'But, Felicity, you must listen to me. We are in great trouble, but we shall overcome it. I feel like running away too, and taking Lucy with me, but just now it would be rank cowardice. Mother needs all of us just now and — '

Felicity cut him short with a toss of her lovely head.

'Mother can fight her own battles,' she said acidly.

'Aren't they also our battles?'

'Are they?'

John winced at his sister's staring, challenging eyes. Never in his life had he seen her like this.

'What is it that is troubling you?' he asked.

'Lies. I can't stand lies. Don't ask me any more. Please get out of my room.'

'Not until you are a little more explicit. You are making accusations which you should justify. Who is telling lies?'

Felicity shut her mouth grimly, and placed some of the underwear in the suitcase.

'Felicity, you must answer me,' said John, raising his voice in anger.

'I'll answer no more questions. Why don't you leave me alone?'

'Because you are behaving badly. If you went away how could we explain your absence in the circumstances? It would look as if you knew more about this shocking business than you do. I should have to tell the police where you could be found. Now tell me the truth. What exactly is driving you away from here — ?'

The door opened suddenly and Lady Gertrude entered the room, very scantily clad, with her hair untidy, as if she had just been roused from sleep.

'What is going on here?' she demanded.

John hesitated a moment, and in that moment Lady Gertrude was able to size up the situation.

'Why are you packing?' she asked Felicity. 'And John was saying something about going away. Answer me, Felicity. What is the meaning of this?'

Felicity gave a curious little sigh, and then faced her mother courageously.

'I'm going because I can't face any more questioning. I've lied already and I won't lie again.'

John screwed up his face as if he had been hit, and Lady Gertrude regarded her daughter incredulously.

'You mean you lied to the inspector?' she asked.

'Yes.'

'Well!'

'But why?' asked John.

'Because — someone else had lied first. You, Mother.'

Lady Gertrude pushed back her untidy hair, gave a little gasp and sank into a chair. For a moment she was quite incapable of speech.

'Felicity!' cried John. 'How dare you?'

'Ask her,' retorted Felicity. 'She told the police she did not see grandpa between the

91

time when I took him up to bed, and the next morning when she entered the bedroom and found him dead. Ask her if that was true.'

'Of course it was true,' snapped John.

'Ask her.'

But there was no need to put the question, for Lady Gertrude was half gasping in the easy chair, her eyes downcast and her features twitching. John turned away from her.

'Wait!' wailed Lady Gertrude. 'It's true I did visit grandpa — just before I went to sleep. Felicity, how did you know?'

'I saw you. I was going to the bathroom. It was nearly eleven o'clock.'

John turned on his mother, trembling with emotion.

'Why didn't you tell the police that?' he asked.

'How could I? It would have looked as if I . . . John, dear, don't you understand?'

'No, I don't. Why did you have to visit grandpa at that time of night?'

'I wanted to ask him something.'

'But you knew he would probably be asleep. Did you intend waking him up to ask him something?'

'If necessary — yes.'

'And was he asleep?'

'No. He was wide awake.'

'Did you put your question?'

'Yes.'

'What was the question?'

Lady Gertrude made a very unsuccessful attempt to regain her lost dignity.

'It was an entirely personal question,' she said, stiffly.

'But, Mother, this is ridiculous,' protested John. 'If you tell the police you were the last person known to have seen grandpa alive they are bound to ask you precisely what I am asking you now.'

'I have no intention of telling the police. Things must go on as they are.'

'Indeed they will not,' said John. 'I refuse absolutely to be a party to deception, or to commit perjury, no matter what the consequences may be. What business did you discuss with grandpa — was it money?'

'What makes you ask that?'

'Because I happen to know you have overspent the income from your investments, and are overdrawn at the bank. I saw the letter which the bank wrote. I couldn't help seeing it, for you left it inside a copy of *Vogue*, and I put it on your dressing-table lest one of the servants should see it.'

'So it was you! Well, if you must know, I asked grandpa to lend me a few hundred pounds to put my account right. He refused, and told me to sell some of my shares. I was disgusted by his meanness and went back to my room. That's the whole explanation, and I hope you are satisfied.'

'I believe you,' said John. 'But I'm not satisfied. You must see the inspector and tell him — '

'No — no. I can't humiliate myself in that way.'

'You will do that or I will refuse to stay in this house, and that goes for Lucy, too.'

Lady Gertrude sniffed and then suddenly dissolved in tears, her shoulders shaking from her heavy sobbing. Felicity passed her a handkerchief, and looked at her brother, but John was too distressed to say or do anything but walk up and down the room.

'I'll do as you say, John,' sobbed Lady Gertrude. 'Perhaps I acted foolishly, but I thought it would look bad if I told them the truth. Felicity, you won't leave now?'

Felicity shook her head and began to take the things from the suitcase. In a few moments Lady Gertrude had mopped up her tears, and looked more like her habitual self, minus a little of her normal composure.

6

Inspector McLean and Sergeant Brook were still in the house. The dead man's room had been thoroughly searched for any letters or documents which might shed light on the tragedy, and further evidence had been taken. Brook, prowling around, had secured specimens of paper from sundry writing blocks, and a number of envelopes.

'None of them anything like the paper used in the anonymous letter,' he said.

'Well, we must persevere. I've just discovered this.'

He held up a small sheet of blotting paper, which he had removed from a blotting pad in the dead man's bedroom, and held it before a mirror. It was nearly a new sheet, and the writing which it recorded in reverse was fairly clear.

'The letter which the girl wrote at her grandfather's dictation,' said Brook, as he read the short message. 'Does it help?'

'In a sense. Felicity has stated that no one but herself and her grandfather knew that she had written that letter.'

'Didn't she tell her mother — ?'

'She told her that she had written a letter, but did not disclose the contents, or the name of the person to whom it was addressed. But anyone, coming to this room secretly, and finding this impression on the blotting pad, would know all about it.'

'Someone who might wish the old man to die intestate?'

'Exactly.'

'There's only one person who stands to gain by those circumstances.'

'Only one that we know of. But it would be unwise to make too much of this discovery, or to exaggerate what appears to be the obvious motive. The old man was certainly a strange character. There is no knowing what enemies he may have made in the past, or what sins he may have committed. From those old letters which have come to light it is clear that he got to hate his wife, and she him. She had him put away for a period to a clinic for chronic inebriates, and that couldn't have pleased him, but there seems to have been a rehabilitation later, for she certainly made a will in his favour, not long before she fell into the lake and was drowned. A turn in the tide of his fortune. It may be that someone, who had good reason to believe Mrs. Grayling didn't slip at all, considered it an act of delayed justice to put the old man quietly to sleep. We simply don't know — yet.'

'It could still be Lady Gertrude?'

'It could — or anyone else.'

'But Lady Gertrude might have the double motive.'

'We're getting away from facts, and must get back to them. The poison used was Atropin — one of the scheduled poisons, and very difficult to obtain. That tends to rule out any theory of accident. People don't keep Atropin in their pantries or bathrooms. It's quite clearly a case of murder, well planned and executed.'

'Then it must be the work of someone in the house.'

'Not necessarily, but certainly the work of someone who knew the victim's habits. There are four different means of entry to the house, and for a period of over two hours all the family were gathered together in either the dining-room or the lounge. An intruder, who knew the lay-out of the house, would only require a minute or two to get to the bedroom and introduce his poison into that glass of lemon-water.'

'If it was so introduced.'

'Don't take me up on that, Brook. We have to make some assumptions or we'll get nowhere. What puzzles me as much as

97

anything is the Childe Roland letter. Is it a fake to lead us on some wild-goose chase, or is it genuine? If it is genuine it would appear to exonerate everyone in the house, but it must have a meaning. I have an idea we shan't get very far until we drag that meaning from it. Now I propose to pay a visit to the young man who is staying at the cottage, as the guest of Sir John.'

'Mr. Barrington?'

'Yes. So far he has not been questioned at all. Pack up everything and we'll lock up here.'

Before this could be done there was a rap on the door, and on going to it Brook came face to face with Lady Gertrude, who was now completely dressed.

'I should like to see the inspector,' she said.

She passed Brook without waiting to learn whether her visit was convenient, and McLean instantly detected a change in her manner since he had last seen her.

'What can I do for you?' he asked.

Lady Gertrude cast a glance at Brook who was politely waiting for her to be seated before he himself sat down.

'It is rather private and confidential,' she said.

'Everything is private and confidential if it

98

has reference to the death of Mr. Grayling. Sergeant Brook is rather necessary for the purpose of taking notes. If it is another matter — '

'No, no.'

'Then I should prefer that my assistant remain.'

Lady Gertrude sighed and sat down, whereupon Brook did likewise and opened his note-book.

'It concerns the evidence I gave,' said Lady Gertrude, in a low and somewhat unsteady voice. 'At the time I was overwhelmed by the circumstances attending my father's death, and scared out of my wits. I want to retract something I said.'

'Indeed! What was it?'

'I told you I had last seen my father alive in the lounge, before he retired. That wasn't strictly true.'

'Then what is the truth?'

'I went to his bedroom, at about eleven o'clock that night.'

McLean continued to look her squarely in the face, in a manner which caused her obvious distress.

'What was your reason for overlooking that rather important fact?' he asked.

'I was afraid — afraid you might think . . . I know it's silly, but I've never been through this experience before. But I swear he was alive when I left him.'

'We know that,' said McLean suavely. 'But why did you find it necessary to visit him at that time of night?'

'I was in need of a sum of money to put my account in credit at the bank. There had been no opportunity previously, as we had a guest.'

'Wouldn't the next morning have done?'

'No. I had received a letter from the bank, and was worried about it. I found I couldn't get to sleep, and I wanted to get the matter settled.'

'Was it settled?'

'No. He refused to let me have the money.'

'Was it a large sum of money?'

'No. Only a matter of a few hundred pounds.'

'While you were with him did you notice the glass of lemon-water on the bedside table?'

'Yes, I saw that. It had a saucer over it.'

'Anything else?'

'No. I went back to my bedroom. That's the whole truth about the matter. I know nothing more — nothing.'

'Thank you,' said McLean. 'This new

100

statement will be on record. It was, of course, a very serious indiscretion on your part, but it is best forgotten.'

Lady Gertrude was shown out, and Brook came back, rumpling his thick hair as he always did when something was agitating him.

'We were talking about the possibility of someone coming here and finding the impression of that letter in the blotter,' he said. 'If you ask me there's a slight shortening of the odds. Gosh, didn't she look sick with herself.'

'So would you if you had to come here and brand yourself a liar.'

'But she didn't have to.'

'I think she did. I very much doubt if her conscience works that way, without a jolt from someone else. Well, let's get moving. We'll call on Barrington on our way to the hotel.'

* * *

When, a little later, Barrington answered the ring of the doorbell, he was not greatly surprised to see the two officers standing in the porch, for he knew that sooner or later this must happen.

'Scotland Yard?' he asked.

101

'Yes,' replied McLean. 'You are Mr. Barrington?'

'I am. Please come in.'

McLean and Brook followed him into the lounge, which was all orange and gold in the slanting rays of the declining sun. McLean's quick eyes took in the typewriter, the mass of loose sheets of paper and the ash-tray overflowing with cigarette-ends.

'Lovely little place,' he said.

'Yes — particularly at this hour, and in the early morning.'

'So you're a writer?'

'Learning to be. I expect you know all about me — I mean the fact that I am only a guest here, owing to the kindness of my friend Sir John Medding?'

'Yes. When did you arrive?'

'The day before Mr. Grayling died.'

'I think you saw him the following evening?'

'Yes. I was introduced during dinner — he arrived late.'

'Was it the first time you had met any of the family, with the exception of Sir John?'

'Yes. Oh no, I had already met his sister.'

'How did Grayling behave on that evening?'

'Rather badly. Lady Gertrude had tried to prevent his appearance at dinner, but he gate-crashed the party, and had clearly been drinking more than was good for him. Later he tried to collar me for a game of chess, but Lady Gertrude had set her heart on a bridge four, and so he was sent to bed.'

'How did he take that?'

'Not very well. But he went.'

'Mr. Barrington, although you had not previously met any members of the family, with the exception of Sir John and his sister, I presume you knew a good deal about them?'

'Practically nothing. I think he only mentioned his father, who was incapacitated in the First World War. Even then I didn't know that his father was a baronet, and that John was heir to a baronetcy. He was remarkably reticent about his family.'

'Have you any ideas about the death of Grayling?'

'None at all. I wish I had.'

The telephone bell rang outside.

'Excuse me,' said Barrington. 'I'd better answer that.'

'Certainly.'

The moment the door closed behind him McLean went to a stationery rack and pulled out an envelope. He examined it for a moment or two and then handed it to Brook.

'Rather like the one which contained that

queer message,' he whispered.

'By Jove, it is!'

'Keep it. We'll compare them later.'

He then went to the table where Barrington's manuscript was piling up. From the left-hand side of the typewriter he took a sheet of manuscript paper and held it up to the light. Towards the top of it was a watermark — a bird with wings outstretched, and under it the words *Eagle Bond*. A little gasp came from Brook, as he peered over McLean's shoulder.

'Quite a discovery,' said McLean, and folding the sheet he slipped it into his pocket. Within a few seconds Barrington was back again.

'Sorry,' he said.

'Not at all,' said McLean pleasantly. 'Mr. Barrington, did you see the message which was received by Lady Gertrude on the morning after her father was found dead?'

'The quotation? Yes.'

'You knew the source?'

'Oh yes. It was from *King Lear*.'

'Did it convey anything to you?'

'Not in these circumstances.'

'Would it in any circumstances?'

'You mean in its original context?'

'Yes.'

Barrington laughed.

'That's an old bone of contention,' he said. 'Shakespeare put it into Edgar's mouth, and Edgar wasn't very responsible. I think Shakespeare was influenced by the Charlemagne legends. Roland, of course, was Charlemagne's nephew and one of the twelve peers — or paladins — of Charlemagne's court. Oliver was another. They outvied themselves in deeds of valour, and were the original knights errant — slaughtering giants and rescuing damsels in distress, if you can believe them, which nobody can. There are also Roland and Oliver in *As You Like It,* and another reference in *Henry the Fifth*. But I expect you know this?'

'I do,' said McLean.

'Then your guess is as good as mine. Also I should remind you that Browning wrote a magnificent poem on the same theme. That you probably know, too.'

'As a matter of fact, I don't.'

'Then you must read it, for Shakespeare has nothing on Browning when it comes to deep psychological insight. But where is all this getting us?'

'To the person who wrote that message. I presume you have no notion whom he might be?'

'I? Good heavens — no.'

'Despite the fact that he has been in this

room — quite recently.'

'Are you serious?'

'Quite serious. That message was written on part of a sheet of your manuscript paper.'

Barrington was still looking incredulous.

'Are you sure?' he asked.

'Reasonably certain. It bore part of the watermark, and from the start I thought the paper was too thin to be an ordinary letter heading. Of course, it could be a coincidence, but I may be able to settle that remote possibility. Has that waste-paper basket been emptied since you came?'

'No. I told Mrs. Sawyer not to disturb any papers at all, and I think she took that to include the paper basket.'

McLean told Brook to go to the car and bring in the briefcase. He was back in a few moments, and from the briefcase McLean extracted the message and the envelope which had contained it. First he compared the envelope with the one he had taken from the rack. They were absolutely identical in size and pattern. Then he turned out the wastepaper basket, and after unscrambling many bits of spoiled manuscript he found what he hoped to find. It was the lower part of a plain sheet, which had been rolled into a ball. When it was smoothed out and the smaller strip added to it it made a perfect sheet — the unevenly cut edges fitting like a jig-saw puzzle.

'Cut with that paper-knife,' said McLean. 'Could anything be more convincing?'

Barrington was dumbfounded for a few moments, for here was a situation he had never dreamed of.

'I hope you don't imagine I wrote that message?' he asked.

'It hasn't quite come to that,' replied McLean with a laugh. 'But tell me — when you go out do you lock the door?'

'No. I never thought it was necessary.'

'Did you lock up on the evening when you went over to the Hall for dinner?'

'No, I'm sure I didn't.'

'What persons have been in here since your arrival?'

'Only Sir John, and the daily woman. Oh yes, the bailiff was here when I arrived, but he hasn't been since, to my knowledge.'

'You mean Mr. Weston?'

'Yes.'

McLean put his two exhibits back into the briefcase.

'I had rather you didn't mention this matter to anyone,' he said.

'I understand.'

'And in future, if I were you, I should

107

lock up when you propose taking a walk, or a drive.'

'I certainly shall.'

'Well, that's all for the moment.'

Barrington saw them both to the door, and then came back to his chair, and stared into space. Whether he was under suspicion or not he had no means of knowing, for McLean was not the man to reveal the true nature of his thoughts.

7

On the following morning McLean had a meeting with the coroner and the chief constable, at which all the available evidence was produced and sorted out. The coroner was expecting that McLean would ask for a postponement of the inquest, but McLean had no such intention.

'An open verdict would, I think, meet the situation,' he said. 'I cannot see that anything is to be gained by a postponement, for nothing that would materially alter the out-look is likely to emerge during the next few days.'

'I agree entirely,' replied the coroner.

The chief constable also agreed. Suicide, misadventure, anything but murder, and since the evidence was such as not to uphold the first two, an open verdict was a very desirable piece of face-saving. When he and McLean were alone, he put a question which he had wanted to ask.

'What do you think of Lady Gertrude, Mac?'

'I haven't quite made up my mind. If she lied about one thing she is quite liable to lie about others. I don't trust her explanation of her bedroom visit.'

'Going there to borrow a few hundred pounds?'

'Yes. She could have raised such a sum by selling a single piece of jewellery. Moreover, she had previously sent the old man to bed like a naughty child. Was that the moment to beg a favour?'

'Yes. That looks bad.'

'And then there's the anonymous message. It was addressed to her and intended for her, yet she swears it has no significance. If it has some reference to the past, where is the Dark Tower, and who, in this case, is Roland?'

'Who was he, anyway?' asked the chief constable.

'Ask Mr. Barrington. He is quite an expert.'

'Barrington! You don't think that he had anything — ?'

'No. I rather wish it was as simple as that. He just happens to have been kicked into this case. I've put an enquiry afoot, but I feel sure we shall find that he has an excellent character. I suppose there was nothing suspicious about the death of the late baronet?'

'Nothing at all. He was very badly knocked about in the First World War — chest wounds and gassing. He lingered for months before he died. I knew him very well — a perfectly charming man, who never complained about his bad luck.'

'Was he happy with his wife?'

'Yes, and she with him. I'll say that for her. She nursed him during the last months of his final illness with the utmost devotion. One could not but admire her. All the same, she is a very strange woman.'

McLean had to admit the truth of the last part of this statement when, the next day, Lady Gertrude gave her evidence at the coroner's inquest. She looked magnificent, and her voice was as steady as a rock. How different from that self-confessed prevaricator who so recently had faced him, almost in fear and trembling!

It was all over in a very short time, and it went the way the police intended it to go. The witnesses and the jury dispersed, and Lady Gertrude went back in her car, driven by John. Barrington, who had been present, but was not called, induced Felicity to take a seat in his old boneshaker.

'You won't like it much after your mother's limousine,' he said. 'I may even lose you on the road.'

Felicity laughed, but it was laughter without mirth. Barrington could see that

111

she was still very disturbed in her mind, and not in the mood for banter.

'It was all a put-up job,' she said, after a long silence.

'The inquest?'

'Yes. Why didn't they say it was murder?'

'Because there isn't sufficient proof — yet.'

'You mean that the proof may come later?'

'Let's hope so. But murder is the last thing any coroner wants to pronounce, unless the facts are incontrovertible. Anyway, it doesn't make any difference. The investigation will go on.'

'And we shall have no peace.'

'Peace lies largely with ourselves. I am in this almost as much as you, for it was my manuscript paper which was used for that cryptic message. I couldn't tell you that before, but it came out at the inquest.'

'But no one suspects you.'

'I'm not so sure. I heard this morning over the telephone that there had been a curious enquiry made as to my credentials. It goes to show that Inspector McLean isn't overlooking any possibilities — foolish as they may seem. But I'm not running away.'

Felicity gave him a sharp look, and immediately he regretted making that quite

112

ingenuous remark, which she obviously misinterpreted.

'I'm sorry, Felicity,' he said. 'That was not intended to have the slightest reference to you.'

'Even if it had I have no right to complain. I did intend to leave, but John persuaded me not to.'

'I'm glad about that. This will all pass, Felicity, and it may even be the harbinger of better times. I know you loved your grandfather, but in any case his days were numbered, and he passed away without suffering.'

'That's true. Tell me, how is the book going?'

'Not very well. There have been too many distractions.'

'It was unfortunate that you came to Strafford Park. You must be very sorry.'

'Sorry! I'm delighted in spite of everything. It has been good to see John again, and to meet the rest of the family, especially you.'

'Me! I'm nothing to write home about. I'm just a bag of inconsistencies, preconceptions, prejudices and illusions. I don't think I quite know what I want, nor have I the application to get it if I wanted it. I live in a kind of nebula.'

'You live in the real world, which is full

of opportunity, of joy and delight, even if it harbours a few wolves and a lot of old bogies. In spite of all that is said it is a better world than it was, and it gets better every day.'

'Do you really believe that?'

'Absolutely. It is ours to shape as we will, and when we complain the complaint should be addressed to ourselves.'

Felicity suddenly laughed.

'You're better than doctor's medicine,' she said. 'Of course it isn't true, but you make it sound true. Can I come and read your book this afternoon?'

'Certainly not. My book is as yet just a slim incoherent embryo, which may catch cold and die on me at any moment.'

'Just a little bit. I've never seen a novel in embryo. I promise not to make any rude comments.'

'No.'

'H'm. I believe it's indecent.'

'It's you who are indecent for believing that.'

'No use arguing with you. You know too many words. So you don't want me to come?'

'Not to read my probably worthless manuscript. But come and have tea, and then join me in a trout-hunt, will you?'

'Yes, I will.'

'Good. I've got some old stale cake I want eaten up. What time shall we say?'

'Four o'clock?'

'That's a date. I'll rig up a fishing-rod for you.'

'No, don't bother. I've got one at the house, and I'll bring it with me.'

Barrington dropped her at the Hall, and then drove back to the cottage, where he ransacked the larder, only to discover that he had precious little in the way of 'eats' suitable for afternoon tea. So he drove into the village, and bought some crumpets and a dozen assorted pastries.

Instone was little more than a hamlet, but in addition to its attractive little old-time shops it boasted a beautiful church and a most attractive inn, with the ubiquitous name of the Jolly Farmer. The inn was exactly opposite the cakeshop, and Barrington, being thirsty, was drawn to it. He entered the saloon bar, and found it empty, but mine host was soon on the spot, smiling affably at his customer.

'I'll have a tankard of bitter,' said Barrington.

'Surely. Lovely morning.'

'Gorgeous, but then, all the mornings lately have been the same.'

'Aye, and we deserve it. At Easter it rained for a fortnight without stopping.'

'That ought to have pleased the farmers.'

'You can't ever please farmers. It's always too wet or too dry.'

He passed the pewter pot to Barrington, who tasted the beer and found it much to his liking.

'How old is this place?' asked Barrington, gazing up at the splendid oak beams.

'Some say three hundred years, and some four. My family have had it for over two hundred. When I took over them beams was all covered up by plaster, and so was that panelling. Can't think who was daft enough to have done that.'

'One of your ancestors, presumably,' laughed Barrington.

'I dare say. All right, I'm coming,' he called, as there came a rapping on the counter behind the glass screen. 'Excuse me, sir.'

He left Barrington to attend to a noisy party who had entered the four-ale bar on the other side of the screen. Barrington heard a good-natured quarrel going on as to who should stand treat, all in the broad, local dialect, which was not unpleasing to the ear.

'Eh, Joe,' said a voice. 'Can 'ee squeedge

a small gin in that there tankard o' mine.'

'Aye, just about,' responded the landlord.

'Then fill un up with ale,' retorted the voice, at which there was raucous laughter.

'I ought to have knowed you couldn't afford gin,' grunted the landlord.

'No, but I likes my pint full to runnin' over. Here's luck!'

'Why you chaps got yer best clothes on?' asked the landlord.

'Oh, we all a bin over to Darchester — to the inquest.'

At this Barrington pricked up his ears.

'Old man Grayling, you mean?'

'Aye. Old miser Grayling. Place was packed, and folks standing outside. Good as a cinema show it were.'

'Jim Farley, you ought to have more respect for the dead,' said the landlord reprovingly.

'What — me? If I knowed who done him in I'd buy the chap a drink, I would. Darned ole skinflint he were. Bad day it was when him and the old lady stole Strafford Park from Sir Robert — '

'Steady!' said the landlord.

'I know what I'm saying. Stealing it were, though some folk call it business.'

'Reckon Harry's right,' said another. 'I can remember the days when all the cottages at

Strafford were as bright as new pins, and look at them now. Wasn't no darned bailiff in those days. Sir Robert's father used to look after things himself. You could go and see him man to man and tell him what was wrong. He didn't believe in letting things fall to ruin.'

'Maybe he was a bit too soft-hearted,' said the landlord.

'He was a gentleman, if that's what you mean. It was a bad day when the Graylings came.'

'Maybe it was,' said the landlord. 'But if it hadn't been the Graylings, it would have been someone else. Anyway, what happened at the inquest?'

'Open verdict.'

'So he wasn't murdered?'

'It don't mean that. It means they b'aint clever enough to find out who done it.'

'Well, maybe things will be better now. Young Sir John may have a bit more power.'

'Not him. The old man didn't leave a will, so Lady Gertrude will get all the income. Can't see her doing anything for the likes of us, or letting Sir John have any say in matters. Proper autocrat she be.'

A few minutes later they left as suddenly as they had come, and the landlord came round to Barrington's side of the partition.

118

'Noisy lot,' he said apologetically. 'But they don't mean half they say. You're a stranger here, I suppose?'

'Yes.'

'Staying in the village?'

'Oh no — some way out.'

'They were talking about the inquest on a big property owner near here, who died in rather mysterious circumstances. Two of them are tenants so they are naturally interested.'

'And not particularly sympathetic,' said Barrington, with a smile.

'They have their reasons, or think they have. But I dare say there's an argument on the other side. Trouble is to get people to see there is another side.'

'How right you are,' said Barrington. 'Well, I must be on my way. Good morning!'

' 'Morning, sir.'

It was but another example of the bad feeling which had been created by the Graylings, and an indication of the intense interest which the local people were taking in the matter.

For the reception of his guest Barrington set up a rustic table on the lawn outside the window of the room where he worked, in such a position that it was shaded from the hot sun by the branch of a tree. At a quarter to four he put the crumpets under the gas grill, and prayed that Felicity would be on time. She arrived almost dead on the stroke of four, the first time he had ever known a woman to be punctual.

'Am I too early?' she asked.

'You are exactly right. I thought we'd have tea outside.'

'Two minds with but a single thought,' she replied. 'I find it terribly hot. Oh, that's where you disturb the grey matter.'

'That corner of the room is out of bounds. Everything is on the table outside, except the tea and the crumpets. I'll bring them in one minute.'

'But how did you know I love crumpets?'

'Perhaps it was a little bird, but more probably astonishing good luck. Be with you in a minute.'

Felicity passed through the casement window into the little garden and looked surprised at the well-laid table. She lifted a serviette and approved the small, thinly cut egg and cress sandwiches, and smiled at the attractive array of pastries. Then came her host with a teapot and a dish of crumpets on a tray, balanced on one hand.

'I'm sure you've been a waiter in your wandering years,' she said. 'Have you done all this yourself?'

120

'With my own fair hands. Would you like to be Mother for a change?'

'I certainly would. Where did you get that lovely silver teapot?'

'In the cupboard. This is the first time I have used it.'

'I didn't know John possessed such treasures. Oh, doesn't the lake look enchanting from here.'

'It looks enchanting from everywhere. You only need a few swans on it, and you might imagine yourself at the ballet.'

'There used to be swans long ago, and little cygnets every spring. I don't know what became of them. But do tell me about the book. What is its main theme?'

'Courage.'

'Physical or moral?'

'Both. I'm trying to show that with every man or woman there is a point at which they will fight to the death, defending what they hold dear with the ferocity of a tiger — a kind of instinct that flares up and takes possession of them when what they hold to be good is in danger.'

'Meaning you don't believe in cowards?'

'Exactly.'

'But men are shot for cowardice — in wartime, for example.'

'Only because they don't believe in what

121

they are supposed to be fighting for.'

'But they may believe in nothing but their own well-being.'

'Are there such persons? They may appear to be so because we, as mere observers, do not see the workings of their minds. We see them dodging trouble by all kinds of shifty devices. Lying because telling the truth may be to their disadvantage. But somewhere, deep inside them, is the citadel they will defend at all costs. In doing so the coward becomes transfigured.'

'Isn't that just stubborn idealism?'

'If you like to call it that.'

'But isn't it difficult to make a novel out of that? It sounds more like philosophy to me.'

'Every life has a philosophic content, or it would become mere existence, with no significance. The man in my story knows himself to be a physical coward, and he earned the contempt of all those who knew him, but there was one thing he loved more than his miserable life.'

'What?' asked Felicity.

'Music. In his younger days he had been a professional singer, and sang in most of the opera houses of Europe. He was an Italian and his name was Bruno, but his great success as a singer was cut short by a disease affecting his throat. When the Japs swept over Malaya Bruno was taken prisoner and put into a concentration camp. He tried to win his freedom by reason of his nationality, but as his wife was British the Japs just ignored his protests. Then one day the prisoners in the camp were taken aboard a Japanese ship, and moved to another place. With the many prisoners was a young boy, with a marvellous alto voice. Bruno was quick to recognize the untrained maestro, and from that moment he took the boy in hand. In a week or two they reached their new prison — a small sunbaked island in the Pacific. Here life was hell, and most of the party gave up hope. But Bruno had found a new and intense interest. His pupil was improving by leaps and bounds, and Bruno swore that one day he would be the finest singer in the world. The war dragged on, but at last the Japanese were in retreat. A Japanese warship came and took away the garrison, leaving the prisoners free, but almost without food. It was a fortnight before a small American ship came and took off the starving prisoners. Its accommodation was inadequate, and many of the prisoners were compelled to sleep on deck. To make matters worse a typhoon came tearing out of the blue. The vessel began to ship heavy seas, and one of these took the boy overboard. It was impossible to lower a boat and everyone believed that the boy was beyond help. But Bruno wasn't one of these. Flinging off his coat and shoes he rushed to the railing and dived into the raging sea. They saw him tossed about like a cork as he swam to where the boy had disappeared. The boat was put round in a wide circle; lifebuoys were thrown overboard, but neither Bruno nor his brilliant pupil was seen again, and finally the ship went on her course.'

Felicity had stopped sipping her tea during this brief but dramatic narration.

'There it is,' said Barrington. 'It happens again and again, not in the same manner, but in the same spirit.'

'But — but it sounded as if it were true,' said Felicity.

'It was true. It was told to me by a man who was on that ship, but in much more detail; a man who had called Bruno a 'wop' and had refused to admit that he was any use to himself or anyone else.'

Felicity, who had taken off her sun-hat, pushed back her abundant hair and sighed.

'No good?' asked Barrington, tackling a pastry.

'You know it's good — very good indeed. When are you going to let me read the manuscript itself?'

'Never perhaps — if it doesn't turn out right.'

'But it will — it must. How much have you done?'

'Not very much. Perhaps when all this trouble is over I'll be able to speed the thing up. But enough of that. Tell me about yourself. What are you going to do with your life?'

'I don't know.'

'John mentioned the stage.'

'How unwise of him. Nobody ever mentions the stage in our family. Mother thinks it is the lowest depth of depravity.'

'I'm surprised at that. She doesn't strike one as being so hopelessly old-fashioned. I understand that your grandfather was an actor in his earlier days.'

'He was — and a good one too, but he drank too much, and was apt to let the whole show down. I've got some photographs of him in Shakespearean parts. He was very handsome in those days. Poor grandpa — he never had a chance.'

'What do you mean by that?'

'He married too much money, and was naturally lazy. Grandma managed him as if he were a pet dog — so my father told me. She was a most dominating woman. Up to the day when she died she was undisputed

125

mistress of the household. The servants were scared of her, and so were we.'

'Not your mother, surely?'

'Yes, even she, and that's saying a lot. Philip, you've no parents living, have you?'

Barrington was surprised by the easy use of his Christian name, but it sounded much more friendly than the conventional 'mister' which hitherto she had consistently adopted.

'No,' he replied. 'My mother died when I was eleven years of age. My father less than a year ago.'

'Brothers?'

'No.'

'Sisters?'

'Unfortunately no.'

'Are you so sure that's a misfortune?'

'Yes. I am now, if not before.'

'Oh, so you're converted?'

'Yes.'

'Since when?'

'Since I've been meeting other people's sisters.'

'Tripe! I thought you were above flattery. Don't you think it's time we started fishing?'

'Perhaps it is. But did you bring that rod?'

'I left it in the porch. Oh, what about washing up?'

'That can wait.'

'Well, thanks for a beautiful tea. If writing fails you'll be able to run a small tea shop, with chintz curtains and bottle-glass windows.'

'It's an idea.'

Barrington enjoyed the fishing which followed, although the catch was inconsiderable. The cloud which had dampened the girl's spirits for the past few days seemed to vanish completely, and her laughter rang out occasionally, and was curiously echoed back by the big sheet of still water. Barrington, now able to examine her at leisure, found himself appraising her physical perfection, and her graceful movements, and at times she gave him a side-glance as if she were quite aware of his growing interest, and not in the least embarrassed.

Finally, after working their way round the lake, they came back in the twilight with their bag of five trout, three of which went to Felicity's credit. She sighed as she packed up her rod, and put on her discarded hat.

'I suppose this is where you start to burn the midnight oil?' she said.

'I shall do a spell of writing before I go to bed, but it will be much before midnight.'

'Curious way for a young man to live,' she ruminated. 'Don't you get bored to death?'

'Why should I? I've lived this sort of life

for years. If I found boredom creeping up on me I could go to the local pub and get drunk. But that's not likely to happen. What about getting home — shall I run you back in the car?'

'Oh no. I'll walk back across the park. Thank you, Philip, for rescuing me from the doldrums.'

'Thank you for making me feel young again.'

She gave a little laugh, waved her hand and was gone.

8

Three days later the mortal remains of Edward Grayling were interred with those of his dead wife in the beautiful churchyard at Instone. It was a very quiet ceremony attended mainly by the members of the family, but as the cortège passed through the village there was an air of insuppressible excitement. It was only when the coffin was being lowered into the grave that Lady Gertrude, who up to then had presented an unruffled appearance, felt for her handkerchief.

Brayton, the solicitor, went back to the hall and stayed to lunch. With no will to be read he explained the situation to the best of his ability. The usual advertisement had already appeared in the Press, asking for any information regarding any will which might have been made by the dead man, but he was in no doubt about the result.

'In due course you will be recognized as next of kin,' he said to Lady Gertrude. 'If, in the meantime, you should require any money, I should be happy to accommodate you. So far as I can gather there are few possible claims against the estate, and they should all be in shortly. Probate will naturally take some time, as there are innumerable valuations to be made.'

'I understand,' said Lady Gertrude.

'All the same, it is a pity your father died intestate. I think it is so much better that one should know positively the last wishes of a deceased person. Now there will be a trust set up, and your inheritance will be limited to the income from the estate, plus furniture and a small cash sum. But the income should be ample for your needs.'

'I shall behave as I am sure my poor father would wish me to,' said Lady Gertrude.

'I am sure you will.'

It was that evening, after a rather solemn meal, that Lady Gertrude called the family together in the lounge, but if any of them hoped she was going to discuss the future distribution of the dead man's property they were disappointed.

'John dear,' she said. 'I'm worried about the headstone for the grave, which the mason took away, to add grandpa's name at the bottom. I have given him the main lettering, to match up with that we used for grandma. But in her case we had an epitaph. Don't you think we ought to do the same for grandpa?'

John looked a little embarrassed. He remembered too well the epitaph chosen by his mother — 'I have done the work which Thou gavest me to do' — and considered it to be in very bad taste, especially in view of his grandmother's earthly record. But up to now he had kept his opinion to himself.

'Does it really matter, Mother?' he asked.

'I think it does. What do you think, Lucy?'

Lucy, looking up from her knitting, endeavoured to get a lead from her husband, but John gave her no hint as to what she should say.

'I really don't know, Mother,' she said, with a smile. 'I suppose a lot depends upon whether grandpa himself would have liked it.'

'I am sure he would.'

Felicity, who had been turning over the pages of a magazine, threw it aside with a savage expression.

'What were you saying, Felicity?' asked her mother.

'I wasn't saying anything.'

'You made some sort of rude noise.'

'I'm sorry.'

'I thought perhaps you had some practical suggestion to make.'

'The only suggestion I can make is that we leave just the bare facts on the stone — name, age and date of death. Grandpa wasn't in love with epitaphs. He often used to poke fun at grandma's.'

'How dare you say that, Felicity?'

'Because it's true. He used to say that the only — '

'That's quite enough. I will not tolerate irreverence at a moment like this. John dear, get the Bible. I'm sure we shall find something appropriate there. It can be brief and to the point.'

To Gertrude's great surprise John did not obey her command with his usual promptitude, but stood stroking his jaw reflectively.

'John — did you hear me?'

'Yes, Mother, but I think Felicity is right. Grandpa and the Bible do not mix. Oh, let's be honest with ourselves. Grandpa had no use for the Bible, nor for religion. You know how scathing he was about the Rector and the Church. To commemorate him by any epitaph which suggests he was a God-fearing man is quite needlessly hypocritical.'

The effect of this upon Gertrude was tremendous. For a moment she looked as if she would fly into one of her tantrums, but she steadied herself and looked at her children as if they had inflicted mortal injury upon her.

'To think that I should stand here and hear you speak ill of the dead,' she said. 'My own father, too! I'm ashamed of you both. Especially you, Felicity, whom he loved very much.'

'I loved him too,' said Felicity. 'But not because of his virtues. I admired him because he never pretended to be what he wasn't. He was kind to me, and sympathetic, but he wasn't so kind to other people. He didn't believe in anything — God or eternity, or the moral law — '

'That's enough!' snapped Gertrude. 'I had hoped that I could rely upon my kith and kin to help me when I needed help, but presumably I was wrong. I won't trouble you any more.'

She rose from her seat, spurning John's assistance, and walked majestically to the door.

'Wait, Mother,' begged John. 'Of course we want to help you, but — '

Gertrude did not wait for him to finish, but passed through the doorway, and closed the door behind her.

'Oh, damn!' said John. 'Why is she so touchy?'

'She's been through a lot,' said Lucy. 'The police enquiry, the inquest and now the funeral.'

'So have we all,' said Felicity. 'But what I can't stand is any attempt to whitewash grandpa now he is dead, and at peace. He lived a long life, and he died without suffering. If there is no such thing as a Last Judgment, then grandpa is lucky.'

John winced at this for he never could quite accommodate himself to his sister's irreverence, and Felicity, noticing this, caught him by the arm.

'Sorry, John,' she said. 'But we all know the truth about the less respectable side of our family. They gave father a very raw deal, and he, poor dear, knowing nothing about high finance, fell for it. Everyone has suffered in consequence. Now what about some fresh air — a walk round the park while there is still some light?'

John looked at Lucy, and Lucy begged them not to bother about her as she wanted to get on with her knitting.

'Well, we shan't be long,' said John.

He and Felicity then left the house by the terrace, descended some steps, and passed through the lower gardens, where the early summer blooms were rampant. Felicity drew the sweet, cool air into her lungs with a sigh of enjoyment, but her brother seemed completely absorbed by his thoughts.

'Wake up!' she said.

'I'm awake all right. Which way?'

'Any way. It's all the same to me.'

'Shall we look up Philip, and find out why he has been hiding himself away these past few days?'

'We know why — he's writing a masterpiece. But let's call, all the same.'

They walked for a time in silence and then Felicity put a question which she had wanted to ask for a long time.

'John, what is your private opinion about grandpa's death?'

'It isn't very private. The police have obviously reached the same conclusion, despite the open verdict at the coroner's inquest.'

'Murder?'

John nodded his head grimly.

'But who did it, and why?'

'Someone who calls himself Childe Roland, for a reason which we may never know.'

'Not — not someone in the house?'

John looked at his sister searchingly.

'Drive that idea out of your mind, Felicity,' he said. 'There's no one in the house capable of such a dreadful crime.'

'But it must have been someone who knew that grandpa always had that drink by his bedside — someone who knew that grandpa slept in that particular room.'

'What then? Do you suspect Susan, or cook, or poor little Ethel? Can you imagine one of them quoting an obscure passage from Shakespeare and addressing it to mother?'

'No, of course not.'

'Then it leaves only you and me and Lucy and mother.'

Felicity was silent, finding it impossible to admit the dreadful thought that was constantly at the back of her mind. Not yet was she satisfied with her mother's explanation of her late visit to the death-chamber, after her previous denial. Someone, she felt, must have stood to gain by her grandfather's death. It was horribly significant to realize that no one stood to gain so much as her mother, who all through her life had loved money, and the things that money could buy.

'It's all a hopeless mystery,' she said. 'I don't understand that message about the 'dark tower' nor what it was intended to convey to mother.'

'Don't try,' said John. 'Let the police try to unravel it — if they can.'

'You think they won't?'

'I think they're going to find it difficult. But there's one good thing which may come out of all this trouble. Mother is not likely to be so flint-hearted as her parents were.

It's disgraceful the way the farms and the cottages have been allowed to decay. I'm hoping that soon we shall be able to start some repair work. But to change the subject, what do you think of Philip?'

'I think he's very nice.'

'Nothing more than that?'

'No — just nice. That's more than one can say about quite a lot of people. Oh, did you see that?'

'See what?'

Felicity pointed away to the left, where there was a big expanse of rushes, at the head of the lake. John stared in the direction indicated, but saw nothing.

'A rare bird?' he asked.

'No — a man. He disappeared into the rushes, as if he had seen us and was scared.'

'It might have been Phil.'

'No. He was quite different. I'm sure it was someone I have never seen before.'

'Well, we'll soon find out. We'll go in that direction and up the farther side of the lake.'

'No — wait!'

'But why? If we hurry we may be able to cut him off, and find out what his business is. It may possibly be a quite innocent trespasser.'

'But it may not. Oh, John dear, be careful.'

'Well, you go straight for the cottage. Look — there's a light just appearing in the window. Evidently Phil is there. I'll go through the rushes and over the bridge.'

'No. I'm coming with you.'

'Good. Oh, this may give us courage.'

He went away to his right and picked up a thick cudgel of wood which was lying under an elm tree. Then he went forward to the entrance of the path which wound through the rushes, with Felicity bringing up the rear. It was now nearly dark, but not dark enough to hide a series of large footprints on the soggy ground — footprints so wide apart as to suggest the recent passage of a running person. John increased his pace, and finally came out on the rustic bridge, from which he gained an unobstructed view of the northern side of the lake. Not a living thing was to be seen, and there again was the bright light in the window of Deepwater Cottage.

'Curious!' he muttered, resting for a few moments.

'You mean — those big footprints?' asked Felicity.

'So you saw them?'

'Of course.'

'They might be Phil's or Weston's.'

'Yes, they might, but I can't imagine either

138

Phil or Weston running about the place at full pelt. Anyway, we can ask Philip when we see him.'

They resumed their walk to the cottage, John discarding the cudgel since it seemed that the intruder had managed to get clean away. Ten minutes later they were outside the cottage, ringing the bell. Barrington came to the door immediately, smiling with pleasure as he saw them.

'Come right in,' he said. 'You're just in time for some coffee. I've only just got back from Dorchester. Worked myself flat out yesterday, so decided to take the day off.'

A piercing whistle suddenly rent the air, and John pricked up his ears, while Felicity covered hers with her hands.

'My new acquisition,' explained Barrington. 'A whistling kettle. My lady of all work is inclined to let kettles boil dry, so I had to do something about it. I defy even Mrs. Sawyer to ignore that little fellow. I'll have to attend to it. Go in, and I'll bring the coffee instanter.'

The visitors passed into the lounge, and Felicity noticed that the typewriter was now covered up, and the manuscript neatly packed in a spring-backed case. Barrington was soon back with a tray, coffee-pot and accessories.

'Here we are,' said Barrington. 'Better help

yourselves and then you'll get the mixture as you like it. It's days since I saw you.'

'Whose fault is that?' asked Felicity.

'The spirits which lend a poor writer inspiration. I had to keep going while the mood was on me. Don't be afraid of the sugar. I've got a surplus.'

'How?' asked Felicity. 'We never have enough.'

'I use golden syrup for all other sweetening purposes.'

'The man's a genius,' said Felicity. 'So you've been to Dorchester?'

'Yes. Soon after breakfast. I spent the whole day there, and had a meal before I left. My chief object was to find a typist to retype a batch of manuscript which I had corrected rather heavily.'

'Why, I could have done that,' said Felicity.

'I had no idea you could typewrite.'

'I can not only typewrite, I can even spell correctly, which I am certain no author can.'

'How right you are. My spelling is abominable. All I can remember is that 'i' comes before 'e' except after 'c', and even that isn't invariable. But tell me the latest news. Is McLean still bothering you?'

'Haven't seen him in days,' replied John. 'But he's in the neighbourhood, and from what I can gather there's hardly a living soul within miles who hasn't been visited and questioned. I should imagine that the police have a history of our family that could be issued in three large volumes. But I can't think it will lead anywhere.'

'I'm not so sure,' said Barrington. 'McLean has the reputation of being the shrewdest investigator that the C.I.D. have produced. He isn't taking this mass of evidence for fun, or to kill time. If I had committed a murder I should hate to know that McLean was after me.'

'So should I,' agreed Felicity. 'Although he's rather handsome, and otherwise attractive. Perhaps already he has a definite clue. Weston told me that he was questioned and cross-questioned for over an hour, and it was all to do with the past, and not with the present at all.'

'You didn't tell me that,' said John.

'Well, I wasn't sure whether I should tell anyone, or whether Weston behaved correctly in telling me, but now the inquest is over I can't see that it makes any difference.'

'That certainly is a queer argument,' said John. 'If everyone acted on it the murderer might get some very useful guidance as to his

141

future behaviour. But what is all this about the past?'

'According to you I mustn't tell.'

John shrugged his shoulders, as he realized that he had been hoist with his own petard.

'You score there, Felicity,' he said. 'I suppose it is a natural weakness to want to know everything about any matter in which one is deeply concerned. I slipped up there badly.'

'But it is our business as much as McLean's,' protested Felicity. 'None of us will get any peace until we know the truth.'

'What is needed more than anything else is patience,' said Barrington. 'More coffee, Felicity?'

Felicity nodded and this time Barrington helped her, watching her narrowly as he passed her the cup. He had a gift for sensing situations, and he sensed one now — some new trouble shared by brother and sister.

'Why not tell me?' he asked.

'Tell you what?'

'Something that is worrying you both.'

'It's something Felicity saw,' explained John, with some reluctance. 'We were coming across the park, towards the clump of rushes near the bridge, when Felicity saw a man, who promptly made himself scarce. I thought it might have been imagination, but there were heavy footprints on the muddy track through the rushes — the footprints of a running man. When we reached the bridge we looked for him, but saw nothing. It was fairly dark, but Felicity is quite sure it was no one she has ever met before. I suppose the footprints couldn't have been yours?'

'Not if they indicated a running man. I am never in such a hurry that I resort to running. But of course any pedestrian could easily get into the grounds if he wanted to, without entering by the main drive.'

'Agreed. But why should he want to?'

'Mere curiosity perhaps.'

'Aren't you trying to play down the incident a little?' asked Felicity. 'What about the person who came here, and presumably wrote that curious message? He couldn't have been merely a curious pedestrian, could he?'

Barrington had no answer to this, but he found it difficult to believe that Felicity's shadowy personage was the same as he who had entered the cottage, and helped himself to the piece of manuscript paper, presuming he had anything to do with the murder. Surely no man would be so foolish, or daring, after the crime had been committed.

'I suppose the best thing to do is tell the police,' he said. 'Also to keep our eyes open, in case he should come again. What was he like, Felicity?'

'Fairly tall, with a rather wide-brimmed felt hat. I got the impression he was wearing a light-coloured pullover, with a rolled top. But I only saw him for a moment before he disappeared.'

'What about a little co-operation? Your bailiff is on the telephone, isn't he?'

'Yes,' replied John.

'Then tell him what has happened, and ask him to telephone both of us if he sees anyone snooping around. We'll both do likewise, and then start an organized search. We might get him that way.'

'It's an idea,' replied John. 'I'll speak to Weston in the morning, and we'll dig out a couple of shotguns, in case the fellow won't stop when he's told. But in any case, I'll tell the inspector when, and if, he calls again.'

'He'll call all right,' laughed Barrington. 'At this moment I expect he and that big sergeant are digesting the mass of depositions which have been made. I don't envy them their job.'

9

Barrington was very nearly correct in his random shot but not quite. For McLean had already 'digested' such evidence as had been taken, and was working out his next move in the game in a room put at his disposal by the chief constable. Sergeant Brook, who had been typing almost solidly for the past two days, was now in fine fettle, for in his opinion the worst of the work was over.

'Where do we go from here, sir?' he asked.

'To Breckton. That's over the Devon border.'

'Oh yes, that's in the evidence. The Grayling home before they came to Strafford Park.'

'I have made an appointment with the Rector of Breckton for tomorrow morning — ten o'clock.'

'More evidence?'

'Yes.'

'I'll have to get a bigger file.'

'I think that's quite possible.'

'I thought you were to play golf tomorrow.'

'I thought so too, but I've had to call it off.

It's good of the Rector to see me on a Sunday — the most inconvenient day for him.'

'Oh, he'll get a kick out of it. What's the position regarding the will?'

'No response at all to the advertisements. I think we can take it for granted there is no will. That was pretty obvious from the first. Nor have our colleagues been able to discover any chemist who may have dispensed, or lost, any considerable quantity of the poison which killed the old man.'

'Atropin.'

'Yes. Now I'm tired, and you must be too. Early beds are clearly indicated. We shall need to be away from here by nine o'clock tomorrow morning at the latest.'

They shut down the office and went back to the Bull where they indulged in a 'nightcap' and sought their rooms. Shortly before nine o'clock the next morning they were on the road, and moving through the beautiful scenery towards the Devon border. Breckton was little more than a hamlet tucked away in the folds of the hills in the wild country between Ilminster and Honiton, but it possessed a beautiful church and a long history, and the Rectory was one of the most delightful places McLean had ever seen. He and Brook were shown into the library where the Rector was waiting for them. He was a very old man, with scanty hair and wizened features, and McLean very quickly discovered that he was more than a trifle deaf.

'Do sit down, Inspector,' he said. 'And you, sir. Now, what can I do for you? I confess it is the first time I have been visited by Scotland Yard.'

'It's rather a serious matter,' said McLean. 'But there is no need for me to go into the details. Do you remember a Mr. and Mrs. Grayling who used to live in this parish?'

'Grayling — Grayling. Why yes, of course. Dear, dear. What a long time ago it was. Quite twenty years, I should say.'

'Much more. They left here thirty years ago.'

'As much as that. Yes, I recall them very well. He was a handsome man, and she was a dominating woman. Wasn't there a daughter too?'

'There was. Her name was Gertrude.'

'Gertrude Grayling, of course. What a curious thing the mind is. I had forgotten those people, and yet you had but to mention them and it all comes back in a flash. I remember the daughter better than her parents, because she was in the habit of attending church and they were not. I also prepared her for confirmation. She had all her father's good looks. Soon after they left here Gertrude married a man of title. I forget his name.'

'His name was Medding, but at the moment I want to talk about the Graylings. Where did they live?'

'Seething Manor. It's about three miles from here. A nice old house, with a lot of land.'

'Did they entertain much?'

'I don't think so. There was some trouble in the family. Mr. Grayling went away for a period, and there was a good deal of gossip about it.'

'What kind of gossip?'

'I scarcely like to repeat . . . '

'I respect your reticence, but both Grayling and his wife are now dead.'

'Well, it was said that the husband was a dipsomaniac, and his wife had him certified as insane. But later he came back to the Manor. I ceased calling at the house after paying one or two visits, because Grayling was most objectionable. He was a very, very difficult character. They appeared to have considerable means, for they kept a large number of servants, including Gertrude's old nurse. It was she who brought Gertrude to church. Otherwise I am sure she would never have come.'

'Do you know where any of the old servants can be found?'

'Dear — dear, that's very difficult. It's all so long ago. Oh, wait, their old gardener had a son who use to work with him. I think the son is still at the Manor, but his father has been dead many years. His name is Cudley — Tom Cudley.'

'And the nurse?'

'I don't know what became of her. She would be very old now. I can't even remember her name.'

'What was your impression of Gertrude, the daughter?'

The Rector reflected for a moment while he chose his words.

'Intelligent, and proud. Much better educated than her parents. They appeared to come from quite common stock, but were ambitious about the daughter's future, and had the means to send her to one of the most expensive schools. She was a highly emotional creature, impulsive to a degree, and not a little vain of her looks. A lot of the young men in the district paid attentions to her, but she appeared to be quite unapproachable.'

'Did you know anyone of the name of Roland who might have been a friend of the family?'

'No. I think, had there been anyone of

that name, I should remember it.'

'Who is living at the Manor now?'

'A Colonel Clifton. The property has changed hands several times since the Graylings left it, and portions of it have been sold off.'

'Does the gardener live on the estate?'

'He did six months ago, which was the last time I called. Alas I have to limit my visits these days, as I can no longer afford to run a car.'

'And you never saw the man whom Gertrude married?'

'No. I don't think he ever came to the Manor. Certainly not to my knowledge.'

'Can you think of any other servants who may still be in the district?'

'No. During the past twenty years there have been such changes in this neighbourhood. Many of the old cottages have been bought by townspeople as week-end places, and men have left the land to go into factories. I wish I could be of greater service to you.'

'You have been of great help. I am rather interested in the old nurse, and if you should hear anything of her whereabouts I wish you would communicate with me.'

'Most certainly I will.'

McLean handed him a card with a telephone number on it, and then walked with him through the lovely walled garden, to where he had left the car.

'Now, which is the way to the Manor?' he asked.

The Rector gave him most minute instructions, which appeared to be rather necessary since it involved about half a dozen different turns, and finished up by adding, 'You can't miss it.'

'It sounds as if I might,' laughed McLean. 'Well, good day, sir. And thank you again.'

The car moved through the hollow, undulating lanes, Brook making the turns as they presented themselves. All the country about them was densely wooded, and it was only at the summit of a long ascent that they were able to get a panoramic view.

'There it is,' said Brook. 'Dear old Devon at its best. Jove, I'd like one of those white-washed cottages to retire to in my dotage.'

'Not you,' replied McLean. 'The country lad who used to live in these parts is gone for ever. How would you like to walk six miles to the nearest pub?'

'I'd manage. Oh, look, there's a place which might be the Manor.'

McLean looked in the direction indicated, and saw an ancient half-timbered house, lying well back in a natural garden. The right fork of the road brought them to

151

a gate on which was a board inscribed 'Seething Manor'. It lay on a wide stretch of heathland and the low, containing wall seemed to extend for miles. Then suddenly McLean saw something which caused him to hold his breath. It was the top part of an old tower, projecting above heavy timber about half a mile west of the Manor.

'We may not have located Roland,' he said, 'but that might easily be the 'Dark Tower'.'

'You're not serious?' asked Brook.

'Not really. Luck of that kind seldom comes our way. I think we'll call at the house and inform the Colonel of our business. Probably the quickest way to contact Mr. Tom Cudley an' all.'

They entered the drive and pulled the car up close to the main entrance of the house, and in two minutes they were inside an oak-beamed room, where a middle-aged man was reclining, reading a Sunday newspaper. He was wearing a pair of old khaki trousers, and a tattered jersey.

'Must ask you to excuse my attire,' he said. 'Just been doing a spot of gardening. The police, I understand?'

'Yes.'

'Come to arrest me for working outside trade union hours?'

'Not quite,' laughed McLean. 'I am anxious to question a Mr. Tom Cudley about a certain matter. Is he still in your employ?'

'Yes. He goes with the property. Was here long before I came. I hope he hasn't been misbehaving himself?'

'Oh no. It's in connection with some people he knew in the past. Is he in the vicinity?'

'Yes. He lives at Rose Cottage. That's down the lane which goes off from the main road, about two hundred yards farther on. You can't miss it. It's the first cottage of a pair. I expect you'll find him at home. He usually spends Sunday morning attending to his own garden, which is a darn' sight better kept than mine. Still, he's a good fellow.'

'Nice place you have here,' said McLean. 'Have you had it long?'

'Only since my retirement — five years. Yes, it's nice enough, but there's always something wanting doing. But I've got a nice bit of rough shooting — nearly a hundred acres of woodland. Of course the house is too big, but there's nothing I can do about that, except to forget there's a top storey, and cellars like a labyrinth. My wife has trouble about domestic help, but so has everyone. No one wants to do any real chores these days.'

'Is that old tower in your holding?' asked McLean, pointing through the leaded window.

'Not now. I sold it off with an old villa and ten acres to a man named Fenton who runs a poultry farm. Very useful it is too, to have new laid eggs and poultry on my doorstep.'

'What was the tower?'

'Oh, there's a yarn about that. It is reputed to be a signal tower for the use of smugglers about two hundred years ago. There's no doubt that smuggling was rife along this coast in those days, and the story goes that the man who built the tower stocked his cellars with wine and brandy from France, which the Revenue officers never even smelt. But I'm inclined to think the story is just idle gossip. Looks more like an honest hunting tower, used by the owner of the Manor and his guests. There are quite a lot of such places in this country. Anyway, it's useful to the poultry farmer as a store shed.'

'I presume you didn't know the Graylings who used to own this property?'

'No, but I've heard about them, and not much to their credit. The man appears to have been an incurable drunkard, and his wife a scheming virago. But there again, it isn't always wise to pay attention to what one hears. From all accounts they were very rich, and very mean. But Cudley can tell you all about them. Oh, is that why — ?'

'Yes,' confessed McLean. 'Well, we must be getting along.'

They soon found Tom Cudley, doing exactly what the Colonel prognosticated. The little garden behind his cottage was as neat and tidy as any garden could be, and Tom, in breeches and shirt-sleeves, digging very early potatoes. He was a well-built man of about fifty years of age, with a weather-tanned face and muscular arms.

'Aye,' he said. 'I've never had any other job than at the big house. Began to help by father in the garden when I was fourteen year old. When my father died I did the whole job, with no help at all. The young mistress was about my age, but it wasn't long before she left to get married, and the place was sold at auction. I stayed on.'

'Tell me about the daughter — Gertrude. Did you get on well with her?'

'Oh yes. She was easy to get on with, when she was at home. But most of the time she was at school and only came home in the holidays until she left school and came home for good. But it wasn't so easy to get on with Mrs. Grayling.'

'Why not?'

'She interfered too much. Mr. Grayling would give me a job to do and then Madam would tell me not to do it. I never knew quite where I was.'

'There was an old nurse or governess, wasn't there?'

'Yes — a Miss Lansbury. The family always called her Bee, but I think her name was Beatrice. She was a grand woman — a real peace-maker when anything went wrong. Everyone loved her.'

'What became of her, after the family left?'

'I don't know. I never saw her again.'

'Do you know where her home was?'

'I think it was Exeter, because I used to post letters for her, and a lot of them were addressed to Exeter.'

'Can you remember any particular address in Exeter?'

'Yes. Quite regularly she wrote letters to a place called Summerlands. That's always stuck in my mind because of the unusual name.'

'Summerlands is a street,' interjected Brook.

'Yes, I know,' said McLean. 'Any particular number, Mr. Cudley?'

But Cudley had already stretched his good memory to its limits, and shook his head.

'Never mind,' said McLean. 'Now do you recall anyone with the name of Roland?'

'No, sir.'

'Think well. This is rather important.'

Tom scratched his head reflectively.

'Is it a Christian name, sir?' he asked.

'It might be either a Christian name or a surname.'

'No, sir,' said Tom, after a long pause, 'I can't say I've ever heard that name before.'

'Did you ever see the man Miss Gertrude married?'

'Yes, sir. He came to the Manor several times. He was a young soldier, wasn't he?'

'Yes.'

'I remember seeing him about the grounds with the young mistress, and then suddenly he went away — overseas, I think. I'm trying to think of his name.'

'It was Medding.'

'So it was. Someone told me he would be a lord one day.'

'Not quite that,' said McLean. 'Now, after Medding had gone overseas, can you remember how long it was before the Graylings left the Manor?'

'It would be about two years. Yes, just about two years. I was married that year — nineteen-eighteen.'

'Do you know anyone else who might

157

have courted Miss Gertrude before she was married?'

'There were several young men who used to call frequently, and she used to drive out with them or go shooting. But as for courting — how should I know?'

'No, I suppose you wouldn't. But tell me a little more about Miss Gertrude. What kind of a girl was she? Gay or serious?'

'A mixture of both. Sometimes she was very gay — ready for any bit of fun, but at other times she seemed to be in a dream. I've known her sit in the garden with a book for hours on end, and a servant, or her old nurse, would have to come and tell her that lunch was served.'

'Did you get the impression she wasn't really very happy?'

'Yes, I did. Several times I came across her in the garden crying. What the cause was I don't know, but servants in the house used to say that she didn't get on with her parents.'

'You still can't remember Roland?'

'No, sir,' said Tom with a grin. 'It's no use. If there was a Roland I never knew him.'

McLean thanked him and left him shortly afterwards. The information he had got was largely corroborative, but there were a few small additions to the picture he was building up of the Graylings. When the car was passing the Manor he directed Brook into the rough track which led to the poultry farm and the old tower.

'May as well have a look at it,' he said. 'But we'd better see the owner first.'

They passed the tower and finally came to a very dilapidated house, beyond which, in a clearing, were innumerable poultry houses, and many pullets running around searching for additional food. They left the car and McLean rang the bell at the door. A few moments passed and then a tall, wiry fellow, with an aggressive countenance, appeared and stared hard at the visitors.

'Sorry to trouble you,' said McLean, 'but I've just left Colonel Clifton. I'm interested in old towers, and wanted permission to look over the one yonder, but he told me it was no longer in his possession.'

'That's right. I bought the damned thing with a parcel of land. Want to look at it?'

'If it's quite convenient?'

'Go right ahead. Sorry I can't come with you, but I'm in the middle of a job. Those damned birds of mine keep me going twenty-four hours each day. Better not try the steps. They're none too safe. If you go along the fencing there you'll find a gate of sorts, but please close it when you leave. Nice car you have there.'

'Not too bad.'

'You ought to see mine. Genuine nineteen-twenty model. You may meet my dog furraging around. Just call him 'Bob' and he'll know you're okay.'

'Thanks!' said McLean. 'Trousers are expensive these days.'

McLean and Brook walked along the wire fencing, and soon came upon the gate. This led them across an acre or two of rough grass, and then into the pinewood where the tower lay. It was a massive construction when seen at close quarters. It was built of brick, with a facing of cement, and thick ivy grew over the lower portion, almost obliterating the slit windows. McLean mounted the few steps and pushed the heavy door full open. Inside was a large hexagonal room, now cluttered up with feeding troughs, rolls of wire netting, bits of hen coops and what not. To the right was a stone staircase, which clearly went spiralwise to the top of the tower. The plaster had come down from the ceiling, but the stout supporting oak beams still kept the old floorboards in place.

'Pouf!' said Brook. 'Smells like a pigsty that the pigs refused to live in. What did they do for heating here?'

'Went without. What was that?'

'Sounds like Bob, 'furraging' around. I don't like his voice.'

The deep horrible bays grew louder, and Brook picked up a heavy lump of timber.

'All you have to do is to call him 'Bob',' said McLean.

'I can think of other names.'

At that moment the dog came bursting into the place. He was a powerful Alsatian, and he stood with his hackles up, in a most threatening attitude.

'Hullo, Bob,' said McLean sweetly. 'Are there any more at home like you?'

The dog turned his head to one side, and looked a little less bloodthirsty. Then he came sheepishly to McLean and allowed himself to be petted.

'Wonderful example of the inferiority complex,' said McLean. 'He was scared to death.'

'You're telling me,' grumbled Brook. 'Why don't I behave like that when I'm scared?'

'You haven't seen yourself. Anyway, we're all friends now. You'd better go home, Bob. Go on — home, boy!'

The dog turned and went out of the place, whereupon Brook breathed with more ease, and threw aside his cudgel. McLean went to the staircase and looked up it.

'Doesn't look too bad,' he said. 'I think I'll have a look up there. If you're coming you'd better keep well behind to distribute the weight.'

'Better let me go first. If it will hold me it will hold you.'

But McLean was already on his way up the narrow, dark, twisting staircase. In places he could see that there really was danger of collapse, for there were long cracks in the outer wall, and gaps between the steps themselves. Soon he was in the first-floor room which was an exact replica of the lower one, and lighted by two narrow windows. Here there was nothing but fallen plaster, and a few names inscribed on what plaster remained. Brook came after him, puffing a little.

'That staircase was built for slim men,' he complained. 'Going up?'

'Yes.'

'Should get a good view from the top. How many storeys are there?'

'Three, I think.'

The next storey told the same tale. Damp and decay had done their work, and there were more initials in pencil, with dates going back over a century, also a very good drawing of a deer with splendid antlers drinking from a pool. This was undated.

'Funny thing how some people must write on blank walls,' commented Brook. 'Childish vanity, I call it.'

'It might be the artistic spirit expressing itself. There's not a great gulf between writing one's name and drawing a deer. Well, up we go!'

The next part of the ascent was tricky for some bricks from the inner wall had broken away, and obstructed the much steeper passage. But McLean clambered over them while Brook, just visible round the bend, waited, and gasped for breath.

'All right,' called McLean, and became lost to view.

They met in the third-floor room, and now the top branches of the highest trees were below them, and they had an uninterrupted view across the beautiful landscape to the south.

'The sea!' said McLean.

'By Jove, it is!' said Brook. 'Blue as the Mediterranean. What a sight!'

The spiral staircase had now ended, but in the corner of the room there was a straight narrow flight of steps, and an open trap at the top.

'That obviously leads to the gallery,' said McLean. 'We may as well do the whole thing.'

These steps were in very fair condition, and they were soon out in the open air, in a circular gallery, surrounded by a four-feet parapet.

'There's the Manor,' said Brook, pointing with his finger. 'And the road we came by. This is worth the climb. I wonder the poultry farmer doesn't open it up to the public at a tanner a time. Might be more profitable than rearing poultry.'

A little later they descended the steps, and McLean gazed around the walls at the various initials and names. Suddenly he gave a little hiss of surprise and moved closer to an inscription which, unlike the rest, had been scratched into the plaster by a sharp implement.

'Just look at that,' he said.

Brook read the inscription aloud:

OLIVER AND GERTRUDE
May, 1917

'Doesn't it ring any bell?' asked McLean. 'Well, there's Gertrude, but that isn't a very uncommon name.'

'My dear Brook, you are a marvel! This inscription has quite shaken me. Remember that this tower was once in the grounds of the Manor, and Gertrude might easily be

Gertrude Grayling as she was at that date.'

'Yes — but Oliver?'

'Roland and Oliver are associated names. Haven't you ever heard of the expression, 'A Roland for an Oliver'?'

'Can't say I have.'

'If you had you couldn't be so casual. We have spent a lot of time looking for a Roland, and now we have found an Oliver. This is the 'Dark Tower' to which the writer of that message was referring. His name was Oliver, but he believed that the recipient would understand the transposition.'

'But she didn't.'

'She said she didn't.'

'You think she was lying?'

'I don't know, but this journey today, which looked as if it had been rather fruitless, has yielded something of the very deepest importance. The next step lies back at Strafford Park.'

10

In the meantime Lady Gertrude had settled
the contentious matter of the epitaph. Much
as she would have liked to cull some neat
little text from the Bible, her children's
stubborn opposition restrained her. But she
was determined that her wild-living father
should not go to the gates of Paradise
without some kind of passport, and so she
decided upon a phrase which could be
interpreted according to one's knowledge of
the deceased. At least it would not open her
to ridicule. Yes, John was right about that.

'Here it is,' she said to the stone-mason. 'It
can be in small lettering. Nothing obtrusive,
you understand?'

'Yes, my Lady.'

'And I want the headstone back at the
grave as soon as possible.'

'In a couple of days, my Lady. The other
carving is all done.'

She drove back to the house in her large
but rather dilapidated car, which she had got
to hate. Thank goodness that soon she would
be able to buy something more suitable to
her social position. For the first time in her

life she would be able to indulge her taste for nice and expensive things, a taste which she had not inherited from either of her parents, who worshipped money for its own sake.

Arriving at the house she saw a long, black saloon car parked outside, and recognized it at once as McLean's car — the sort of car she herself meant to possess shortly. John opened the front door of the house before she could reach it.

'I've been trying to find you, Mother,' he said. 'The police are here again, and the inspector has been asking for you.'

'I guessed as much,' she said. 'Oh, dear, what a nuisance they are. Well, I must go to my room first. You might tell the inspector I am back and will see him shortly.'

'I will.'

It was a quarter of an hour later when she deigned to knock on the door of the morning-room, and was invited in. McLean was sitting at the table with various documents before him, and he and Brook rose politely as she entered.

'I'm sorry to have kept you waiting, Inspector,' she said.

'Not at all,' replied McLean. 'There was no great hurry.'

She sat down in the chair opposite him, looking remarkably composed. McLean toyed with his papers for a few moments, while Brook got his note-book ready.

'I'm sorry to have to ask you some more questions,' said McLean. 'But since I last saw you there have been a few interesting developments that call for further elucidation. I am hoping you may be able to help me.'

'I will if I can.'

'I'm sure you will. I am going to ask you to take your mind back to the time when you lived at Seething Manor in Devon.'

'That is not difficult,' she said, with a smile.

'Do you remember the date when you left the Manor?'

'I think it must have been early in 1918.'

'You were engaged to be married then, were you not?'

'Yes.'

'How long had you been engaged at that date?'

'Almost two years. My husband — I mean my fiancé — went overseas in 1916. We became engaged just before he sailed.'

'Where did he go?'

'To France. There he was taken prisoner by the Germans, after being seriously wounded. In 1918 there was an exchange of badly wounded prisoners of war and he was repatriated. We were married soon after his arrival in England.'

McLean nodded while Brook wrote furiously.

'In 1917 did you meet a man named Oliver?'

'Oliver what?'

'I don't know his surname.'

'I'm not sure,' she said slowly, but not convincingly.

'I want you to try to remember that man. Perhaps I can assist your memory. He called at Seething Manor, and you and he went to the old tower there. One of you appears to have made an inscription there — on the wall of the top room. Do you remember that occasion?'

Some of Gertrude's former composure seemed to have leaked away, but she met McLean's direct gaze boldly enough.

'I'm not sure that I do,' she replied. 'I often went to the tower with young officers who came to us under a hospitality scheme. Most of them were Dominion troops.'

'But your name, coupled with another, only appears once.'

'It may have been done without my knowledge. But in any case, I fail to see where this is leading.'

'You must permit me to decide whether

it is likely to lead anywhere. You are sure you do not remember anyone of the name of Oliver?'

'Quite sure.'

'But you do remember going to the tower with young officers at that time?'

'Yes. It was in our property, and was naturally of interest to men coming from abroad. Most of them were keen about old houses and towers — things they scarcely ever saw in their own countries.'

'I can appreciate that. You were born at the Manor, were you not?'

'Yes.'

'So the old tower must have been a familiar feature to you?'

'Of course.'

'And when that curious message was received by you, did you not instinctively recall the tower?'

'No, I can't say that I did.'

'You mean that despite your having spent all your childhood in the shadow of an old tower, it never occurred to you for a moment that that message might possibly have had reference to that same tower.'

'I never gave it a moment's thought, because many things can happen in thirty years. Besides, the message said Roland — '

McLean took her up in a flash.

'Would it have made any difference had the message said Oliver?' he asked.

'None at all,' she replied. 'Since neither name had any significance for me. If there is such an inscription, as you say there is, and which I am bound to believe, it can have no reference to me.'

McLean switched his gaze from her to his papers. He had not quite expected this denial, since she had nothing much to lose by admitting knowledge of the incident, and lightly laughing it off. But she had lied once before, and he believed she was lying now.

'Do you remember Beatrice — your old nursery governess?' he asked suddenly.

'Yes, of course.'

'She was very devoted to you, I believe?'

'Yes, and I to her.'

'Did she leave you shortly before your marriage?'

'Yes.'

'How long before?'

'About three months.'

'Do you know where she went?'

'No.'

'Do you mean you have never seen her or heard from her since your marriage?'

'Oh no. I meant I didn't know where she went immediately after she left us. I had one or two letters from her after that, from

171

different addresses.'

'You mean from where she was employed?'

'Yes, I think so. But after a few years we ceased to correspond. I imagine she must be dead by now.'

'Why?'

'She was twenty-five years older than me.'

'That wouldn't make her so old as to presume she must be dead. Did her family once live in Exeter?'

'Yes, I think they did. Your information is very extensive, Inspector.'

'It needs to be — at times. Well, I think that is all. I'm sorry to have taken up so much of your time.'

'Thank you, but I'm getting used to this sort of thing now. All the same, I shall be glad when it is no longer necessary. Now may I ask you something?'

'Certainly, but in the circumstances I can't promise you a ready and truthful answer.'

'I understand. Well, here's the question. Do I strike you as being the sort of woman who might possibly poison her own father for personal gain?'

McLean let his glance rove over her still admirable figure, and her clean-cut excellent features.

'Madam,' he said. 'I should be a disgrace to my profession if I allowed my judgment to be influenced by the good or bad looks of witnesses. I have met persons who looked like angels and behaved like devils, also vice versa.'

Gertrude laughed as she rose to her feet, and made for the door which Brook hastened to open for her. At the door she hesitated for a moment, and then sighed and passed through it.

'Nothing worth a rap,' said Brook, as he came back to the table.

'Nothing positive, but she doesn't like this delving into her past, and least of all she liked the mention of her old nurse. How quick she was to assume the death of that lady, without the slightest reasonable ground. It looks as if we shall have to go to Exeter and try to locate that important witness.'

'You think there was an Oliver?'

'I'm certain there was.'

'Then why didn't she admit it?'

'There are two possible reasons — one is that she really has forgotten all about him, and the other is that had she said she remembered him, and their visit to the tower, her former claim that that message had no significance for her would have appeared lame. She's an educated woman, and must be well aware of the historical association of Roland and Oliver. I think that Beatrice, the nurse, may have a better memory, unless she too may have reason to pretend otherwise.'

A few minutes later there was a rap on the door and John entered the room.

'I'm sorry to interrupt you, Inspector,' he said. 'But I have been wanting to see you. We had an intruder in the grounds two nights ago.'

'Indeed! Who was he?'

'That's the point. He got away before we could question him.'

'I should like to know the details.'

John told him all the circumstances, and McLean furrowed his brows.

'Might be some ambitious reporter from the Press,' he ruminated. 'But on the other hand — '

He stopped and John waited for him to finish, but McLean did not complete the sentence.

'You were saying — ' said John.

'I'll look into it. Unfortunately we are very short of men, or I would put a couple on night duty here. I'll speak to the chief constable, and see what can be done.'

'So you think there is danger?'

'Not necessarily. Are the ladies nervous?'

'None of them know, except my sister. I thought it best to leave them in ignorance.'

'Quite right. It may be nothing at all. The place has been much in the news, and there are all sorts of idiotic, but quite harmless, persons about.'

'Such as the person who poisoned my grandfather?'

'Even he is not to be ruled out, but I scarcely dare hope that he will put in an appearance.'

John looked at him sharply.

'Am I to take it you have a clue?' he asked.

'No, but the solution is not entirely without hope. Oh, while you are here — did you ever chance to meet your mother's old nurse — Beatrice?'

'No. Mother often spoke of her in the past, but I think she left the family when mother was married.'

'That's all, thank you.'

Brook looked at McLean when John had gone.

'A bit queer, isn't it?' he asked.

'The intruder? It might have been anybody. I don't feel justified in posting a man here, unless there are more substantial grounds for doing so. Our next obvious task is to find Beatrice, or some near relative who may be able to tell us something about her. We'll go over to Exeter in the morning.'

175

On the following day Barrington awoke to find a veritable deluge descending from the leaden skies. It was the first rain since he had come to Deepwater Cottage, and it was making up for lost time. It lashed through the heavy foliage of the trees and churned up the water in the lake. It over-flowed the guttering, and fell in noisy cascades on the sun-baked land beneath. Mrs. Sawyer arrived at her usual time, with water streaming from her hat and the cycle covered with mud.

'Lor'!' she ejaculated. 'I've had to ride through rivers. My husband says it will keep on for days, and he's a jolly good weather prophet.'

'Well, I hope he's wrong for once,' said Barrington.

'Oh, but the land needs it, he says. Can't do anything but good just now. Nice job he had this morning, driving the cows in for milking. Wet to the skin he was when he came home to breakfast.'

'So were the cows, I imagine.'

'Oh, them. They don't seem to care whether it rains or not. Silly things cows — almost as daft as chickens. Would you like a bit of a fire this morning in the sitting-room?'

'Good heavens, no. I'm almost boiled as it is.'

'But a fire's such a comfort on a rainy day. Brightens up the world, so to speak.'

Barrington knew that if he lingered she would never stop talking so he went into the sitting-room and sat down at the typewriter. Within a minute or two he had caught up the threads of his story, and after that everything else was swept into oblivion, until Mrs. Sawyer came in with his breakfast on a tray. This and the morning newspapers kept him engaged for nearly an hour, after which he went back to the typewriter, quite resolved to put in a full day's work, and to forget the weather.

But this good intention was rudely interrupted at eleven o'clock by Felicity, who arrived looking like a drowned rat. Mrs. Sawyer let her in and she stood making puddles on the floor, while Barrington stared at her in amazement, for she was gasping for breath as if she had been running.

'Anything wrong?' he asked.

'No. I felt I wanted a walk, but I didn't quite realize how hard it was raining. I'm interrupting your work.'

'That doesn't matter. You'd better get that raincoat off and get Mrs. Sawyer to hang it before the stove. Here, I'll help you.'

He rose and helped her off with her saturated garments, only to notice that

177

her shoes and stockings were in no better condition than her coat and hat.

'You'd better take those off too,' he said. 'I can lend you a pair of slippers. I usually have a cup of coffee at this time, so perhaps you'll join me.'

'Are you sure I'm not in the way?'

'Quite sure. I'll get the slippers. Better still, go up to my room, and dry yourself off. You'll find some slippers in the wardrobe.'

'I will. Which room is it?'

'The one to the right of the stairs. I hope Mrs. Sawyer has had time to straighten it.'

When she had gone Barrington took the coat and hat into the kitchen, where he found one of Mrs. Sawyer's usual roaring stoves. She certainly believed in a bit of comfort.

'Miss Felicity has got herself wet through,' he said. 'Will you try to get these dry, also her shoes and stockings, which she'll bring you in a minute or two. And we should like some coffee.'

'I was just making the coffee. The rain has come right through this coat. That's the way to catch your death of cold. I was only laid up for a whole month that way. Good thing I've got a nice fire.'

Barrington went back to the sitting-room, and then noticed that in the chair

178

across which Felicity had laid the raincoat temporarily there was a small bottle which obviously must have fallen from one of the pockets. He picked it up, and found that it was empty. There had been a label on it, but the top part of this had vanished. On the remaining part was faint handwriting, and only part of it was legible:

‘ . . . *onna. Eye drops*’.

He uttered a little hiss of astonishment, then removed the cork and smelt. Reflectively he put the bottle on the low table, and paced up and down the room. Mrs. Sawyer came in with the coffee.

‘Oh, put it down there,’ he said, and Mrs. Sawyer dumped the tray by the side of the small bottle.

‘Shall I take this away?’ she asked, indicating the bottle.

‘No. Leave it there.’

Some minutes passed before Felicity came down, with her hair freshly brushed, and her bare legs terminating in a pair of slippers many sizes too large.

‘I’ve left the shoes and stockings with Mrs. Sawyer,’ she said. ‘Coffee! How lovely!’

Then suddenly she saw the bottle and

179

looked up at Barrington.

'I think it must have rolled out of your raincoat,' he said.

'Yes — it did.'

They both sat down and Barrington served the coffee. The bottle seemed to trouble Felicity as much as it did him, for she glanced at it once or twice as she sipped the hot coffee.

'I thought eye drops were something out of the past,' said Barrington.

'Yes, they are. I've read about them in books, but have never known anyone to use them. Victorian ladies used to make use of them to make their eye pupils lovely and large in bright light, didn't they?'

'So I understand. But your eyes need no such treatment. At the moment they are as large and lustrous as — '

He stopped as Felicity winced and turned her eyes away.

'Don't joke, Phil,' she said. 'This is a serious matter.'

'Yes, I rather think it is,' he replied. 'That bottle once contained Belladonna. What are you doing with it?'

'It isn't mine. I found it by accident this morning.'

'Where?'

'In the house. I was looking for something

180

else, and suddenly came across it. We had a good chemistry lab. at school, and I seem to remember that there is some connection between Belladonna and Atropin — the stuff that was found in grandpa's body.'

'It's practically the same thing. Have you forgotten your botany? The plant from which it is made is called Atropa Belladonna — the Deadly Nightshade.'

'Yes — of course. Oh, Phil, this is dreadful.'

'Have you any idea who owned the bottle?'

'No.'

'But you found the bottle. That should help you to draw some conclusion. Where did you find it?'

Felicity hesitated for a few moments.

'Well, you needn't tell me if you prefer not to,' said Barrington. 'I've no right to ask you.'

'But I will tell you. I must tell somebody. I found it at the back of a drawer in Lucy's bedroom. She had a bad headache, and as I was going upstairs she asked me to get her two aspirin tablets which she said were in the top drawer of her dressing-chest. I looked in the top drawer and couldn't find them, so I tried a lower drawer. There I found that bottle. A little later I found the aspirins elsewhere.'

181

'You didn't mention the Belladonna to her?'

'No. My mind was in a whirl. I didn't know what to do, except get out of the house. If I mention it to Lucy it will look as if I suspected her, which would be sheer nonsense. Oh, tell me what I am to do.'

Barrington inwardly cursed this luckless find, with its inevitable implications, and probably groundless suspicions. He had not seen a great deal of Lucy, but what he had seen was enough to cause him to believe she was a gentle and godfearing woman.

'I wish I knew what to say,' he replied. 'It's no use trying to minimize the importance of this discovery. The police have tried very hard to find the source of the poison which killed your grandfather, and now this turns up. We could of course throw it in the lake and forget all about it.'

'Are you advising me to do that?'

'No. You'd never have a moment's peace of mind afterwards, and you know it, don't you?'

'Yes I do. But I can't bear to think of Lucy being closely questioned, as she is bound to be. This whole business has worried her tremendously, although she has been marvellously self-controlled.'

'But you haven't the slightest doubt about

182

her innocence, have you?'

'No.'

'Then I think she would be the first to want the police to be informed. The bottle is obviously very old, and in all probability she may be ignorant of its existence. Half the label has been worn, or torn away, and what remains bears neither the name of the purchaser or the chemist from whom it was obtained. It may have been at the back of that drawer long before Lucy came into the family. It may indeed be just a coincidence. Why not make a clean breast of it to Lucy, before you give it to the police? It would at least give her a chance to explain the matter.'

'But she's not at all well.'

'Then try John. At least do something.'

Felicity was silent for a few moments, and then Barrington, watching every movement of her face, knew that she had come to a decision.

'I'll speak to John first,' she said. 'He's so understanding. I'm sorry, Phil, to force our family troubles upon you. I wouldn't have said a word if the beastly bottle hadn't fallen from the raincoat. I didn't mean to come here at all, but the rain drove me in. Now I've interrupted your work, and probably spoilt the flow of ideas.'

'Nonsense! You know I'm always glad to see you. To prove it I'll make a suggestion, and I have an excellent excuse. Come out with me to dinner tonight, to some place where there is music and dancing. The excuse is that it happens to be my birthday, but the real reason is that you need a break, and so do I. To hell with work, and police inspectors, and all the dismal things that make one prematurely old. Will you come?'

'Yes. I should like to very much. But where could we go?'

'Leave that to me. I have a telephone and a local newspaper. I can't manage a dinner-jacket, but I promise not to wear corduroy trousers. You'd better tell your mother, but if I don't hear from you by lunchtime I'll know it is a date, and I'll call for you at seven o'clock. Okay?'

'Yes. Oh, I must wish you many happy returns.'

'Thank you. Now have some more coffee. Plenty of time. Your clothes can't be anywhere near dry yet.'

'Why don't you go on working?' she asked. 'I can amuse myself — reading the newspapers, or better still the first part of your book.'

Barrington laughed.

'How keen you are to dissect my poor little

unborn baby. Do you really think you could stand the strain?'

'You try me.'

'All right. You've asked for it, so don't blame me afterwards.'

He rose and brought to her the first part of the story. It bore no title and consisted of about a hundred pages of manuscript.

'This isn't the corrected copy,' he said. 'That is being re-typed, but it's straight enough for you to get an idea of what I'm driving at, if it's intelligible at all. Help yourself to the coffee before it gets cold. I'll go back on the job.'

'Okay. Forget all about me.'

But Barrington found this last piece of advice extremely difficult to put into practice. From where he sat, tapping the keys, Felicity's face was in profile, and every few minutes he found himself tapping wrong keys, and generally getting out of his stride. It was rather a shock to his boasted powers of concentration. It was Felicity who was concentrated. She really did look and behave as if she were unconscious of his presence, and the pages of the manuscript were turned with the regularity of a pendulum, as she read on and on.

It was no use attempting to delude himself. That distracting bare-legged nymph was a deadly threat to his creative powers. He knew he was writing rubbish, and that its early destination was the wide-mouthed waste-paper basket. He had even been careless enough to write 'Felicity' in place of the name of his fictitious girl in the story, and he blocked it out savagely with a series of Xs. With the most laudable object he had invited her out that evening, but now he strongly suspected his subconscious motive. Not very altruistic after all. This habit of regarding her as a rather lonely girl was mere stupidity. She was a woman, with all the guile, allure and mystery of her sex. Had he been annoyed when she had come dripping like a wet umbrella into his room to interrupt his work? Not a bit of it. His heart had given quite a little bound of pleasure. Why seek to deny it? Every time he saw her his innermost reaction to her youth and beauty increased.

It was no use going on, wasting good paper. He stopped and lighted a cigarette, reflectively blowing rings towards the window which framed the tormented lake. Felicity, still immersed in the manuscript, continued to turn the pages. Then suddenly she seemed to be aware of the dead silence, and looked up.

'Oh!' she said. 'Have you finished?'

'Yes. I've got as far as I want to go — for

the moment. I think the rain is easing off just a little.'

'Rain! Oh yes.'

'Wake up,' he said. 'I believe you are nearly asleep.' Her wide, lustrous eyes regarded him strangely.

'I can't believe you wrote this,' she said.

'Why not?'

'It's not like you — not like the way you speak. It's beautiful — wonderful.'

'Oh, come!'

'But it is. Now I can understand how you can live here alone, and be contented. You make your own world — your own people, and live in them. You've no need for the other world — my world. It holds nothing for you. You have this blessed means of escape, and how I envy you.'

'I wish it were true. No, I don't even wish it. Your world as you call it has much to recommend it. The artist merely interferes with the real world. He doesn't abolish it. He uses it as a model, but if he destroyed it he would destroy himself as well.'

'I think I can understand that. Phil, may I keep the manuscript — just until tonight. I promise to give it back to you when you call for me.'

'How can I refuse my one and only fan — so far?'

Felicity laughed in her lilting fashion, and searched round for a piece of wrapping paper. She was wrapping up the manuscript when Mrs. Sawyer knocked and came into the room, carrying the raincoat, and other articles.

'There you are, miss. Dry as a bone. Rain's leaving off a bit now, so you won't get wet going home.'

Felicity thanked her and, kicking off Barrington's slippers, commenced to roll the nylon stockings up her shapely legs, while her host pretended not to notice. Help in that respect being out of the question he reserved his assistance for the raincoat, and finally picked up the small bottle from where it lay.

'And there's this,' he said.

'Back to earth with a bump,' she sighed. 'I wish I had never gone for those aspirins. I won't go back by the lake, or I shall be tempted to throw the bottle into it. Nice of you to put up with me.'

In another minute she was gone, and Barrington paced round the room like a caged animal, wondering mightily.

11

It was after lunch that Felicity carried out her resolution. Both Lady Gertrude and Lucy had retired to their rooms, and Felicity and her brother were left alone in the lounge.

'Mother tells me you are going out with Philip,' said John, turning from the window.

'Yes. It happens to be his birthday.'

'The devil it is. He didn't tell me. Well, don't let the family down, young woman.'

'I couldn't let it more down than it is. John, I've got something I want to show you.'

'What is it?'

Felicity reached for her handbag and took out the small bottle. She handed it to her brother who took it, read the indistinct writing and looked at her.

'I don't get it,' he said. 'Why am I supposed to be interested in this?'

'It once contained poison — the same poison as that which killed grandpa.'

John gave an involuntary start, and scanned the label again.

'It says 'eye drops'.'

'Yes — Belladonna eye drops. From

Belladonna you get Atropin.'

'Who — who told you that?'

'I happened to find out.'

'But — but where did you get this bottle?'

'I found it in the second drawer of Lucy's dressing-chest this morning.'

John's expression was now one of deep resentment.

'You mean you went to Lucy's room and searched — ?'

'Wait, John, please. I went there to get some aspirins for Lucy, who had a headache. She asked me to go. I was searching for aspirins, not this.'

'But it's an old bottle — years old. The writing is all faded, and Lucy has only been here two years. What's more, she had never used eye drops. No one does in these times. What are you trying to say, Felicity? What is in your mind?'

'Nothing against Lucy. Do you think I'm crazy enough to believe that Lucy would knowingly harm anyone. But here's the poison that killed grandpa, and found in this house. I couldn't go to Lucy, and ask her about it, but I've got to do something, haven't I?'

John put his arm on her shoulder, and smiled an apology.

'One thing after another — no end to it

190

all,' he said. 'I suppose there is no doubt about the poison?'

'None. Phil told me — '

'Phil! You surely haven't told — ?'

'He found the bottle, after it had fallen out of my raincoat when I took refuge at Deepwater from the rainstorm. There was no way out of it. I simply had to tell him.'

'And what did Phil say?'

'He said it was a matter for the police, but suggested that Lucy should not be kept in the dark.'

'Phil was right. I'm going to ask Lucy to come down.'

'Oh, must you?'

'Yes. This thing must be thrashed out, no matter what it costs.'

John was back again in a few minutes, and Felicity was discomfitted to see her mother with him as well as Lucy. Lady Gertrude appeared to be in a bad mood, which was invariably the case when her siesta was interrupted.

'Now, what is it, John?' she asked. 'You are most irritatingly mysterious. Surely the matter could have waited, whatever it is.'

'No, Mother. In my opinion it's a very important matter, and the time to deal with it is now. Do please sit down.'

Lady Gertrude sank into a chair, but Lucy

remained standing, regarding her husband querulously.

'Lucy darling,' he said. 'Here's a small bottle. Look at it and tell me if you've ever seen it before?'

Lucy took the bottle from his fingers, scanned it interestedly and shook her head.

'Never,' she said.

'You are quite sure?'

'Quite sure. What are eye drops?'

'In this case they were Belladonna eye drops, to enlarge the pupil of the eye, and make women look beautiful. This bottle, Lucy, was found in your dressing-chest.'

Lucy expressed her astonishment.

'It must have been well-hidden,' she said. 'For I have never seen it. But mother had my bedroom before I came here. Don't you remember?'

'No. I had forgotten.'

John turned to Lady Gertrude, his face lined with anxiety.

'Did you use that dressing-chest, Mother?' he asked.

'Of course I did. Let me look at that bottle.'

John handed it to her. She took one glance at the label, and then laughed.

'All this fuss about a bottle,' she said. 'It's mine, and I must have overlooked it when I turned out the chest. It's ten years old, at least. I don't think you can buy the stuff now. Don't look at me like that. Why shouldn't I do something to offset a natural defect. My eyes were always supersensitive to bright light. The pupils used to contract almost to pin points. It made me look like a cat in brilliant sunshine.'

'Mother, you don't understand,' said John. 'Grandpa was poisoned by Atropin, and Atropin and Belladonna are almost the same.'

'What!'

'Didn't you know?'

'Of course I didn't know. I'm not an encyclopaedia, or a medical reference book.' Her eyes grew very hard and she stared at John with an intensity which caused him to wince. 'But one thing I do know. Again I am under suspicion. You have brought me down here to question me as if you were a police inspector.'

'Mother, be reasonable,' begged John. 'I had no idea that this bottle belonged to you?'

'Did you not? Then perhaps it was Lucy you suspected — Lucy, your own wife.'

'No, God forbid. I wanted Lucy to explain how she came to have that bottle in her dressing-chest. I knew she would have a satisfactory explanation, and she had.'

'And now you are quite satisfied that she did not poison my father?'

'Mother, don't talk like that.'

'Why not, indeed? Isn't that why we are here, to discover which of us is a murderer? My father's death was convenient to all of us, wasn't it? He was old and frail, but he might have lingered on for years, clinging like a miser to all the money he possessed. We shall all benefit by his death, I more than anyone, I presume. Well, here's the bottle which might have killed him, had there been anything in it, but there wasn't. Do you believe that?'

'Yes,' said John, 'of course I believe it.'

'Then what are you going to do about it — hand it over to the police, and add fuel to their silly suspicions?'

'It's our plain duty,' said John stubbornly.

'Duty to whom?'

'To society. Somewhere there is a murderer, and it's our duty to withhold nothing which might possibly serve the cause of justice.'

'Even at that risk of causing increased suspicion to fall upon innocent persons?'

'Even at that risk.'

Gertrude gave a hard metallic laugh.

'Duty to society at large, but none to members of your own family.'

Felicity, witnessing her brother's misery,

thought it time to say something.

'You must know in your heart, Mother, that John is right,' she said. 'Lying, or acting a lie, is horrible. I tried it once and paid for it. You say there was nothing in that bottle, and we believe you. The inspector may be able to substantiate that by having the bottle expertly analysed. They have wonderful means of proving such things.'

Lady Gertrude shrugged her shoulders.

'I have yet to be convinced that the police are so infallible,' she said.

'But there's another point,' said Felicity, now warming up to her argument. 'Would anyone but an idiot poison someone and then keep the bottle where it might easily be found, when there are drains by the dozen and a large pond within a few minutes' walk?'

'That's true,' said Lucy. 'I think there is everything to be gained by being honest, for what murderer would go to the chief investigator of the crime, and hand him an exhibit — if that is the word — which might be used in evidence against him? No one but an idiot, as Felicity has said.'

'He might not be an idiot. He might, in fact, be a very shrewd and clever person. All I know is that I am tired of being questioned. I don't believe this bottle will help the police at all. I am certain it has nothing whatever to do with my father's death. Why should I be humiliated again? Haven't I suffered enough?'

'So you are against our giving this bottle to the police?' asked John.

'No. Do what you like. It was Felicity who found the bottle. Let her do what she thinks is her social duty. Now I am going back to rest, and please do not disturb me again.'

She rose from her chair, spurning John's assistance, and then walked majestically to the door, and vanished. John gave a little sigh and gazed from Felicity to his wife.

'She simply won't co-operate,' he complained. 'Oh, Felicity, why did you have to find that bottle?'

'Yes, why? Tell me what to do, John dear.'

'There's only one decent thing to do, and that is what we have already agreed upon.'

'The police?'

'Yes. It's McLean's headache. Let him deal with it. Shall I try to get him on the telephone?'

Felicity nodded her head and John went to the telephone. He spent a few minutes there and then came back to the two girls.

'No luck,' he said. 'The inspector is not available, and they couldn't — or wouldn't — say when he would be. I expect we shall hear from him the moment he knows I have telephoned him. Felicity, you had better keep the bottle for the time being. Lucy dear, you're looking very tired. I'm sorry to have dragged you from your rest.'

'And I feel mean to have found the bottle and not told you,' said Felicity. 'I — I wanted time to think things over.'

'Of course. I quite understand. Well, I think I'll go and get the remainder of my forty winks.'

Barrington, having heard nothing from Felicity, kept his appointment that evening, and found Felicity quite ready, and looking fresh and lovely. While he had a drink with John in the study Felicity slipped a small parcel into the car, and shortly afterwards they drove away.

'This is lovely,' said Felicity. 'Where are we going?'

'You'll find out. This is a mystery drive. Thank goodness the rain has stopped.'

'Did John tell you about the family meeting?'

'Yes. But no more about that — not tonight. I refuse to have my birthday ruined by any melancholy dissertations about poison bottles. I'm going to spend the whole evening eating and drinking and treading on your toes. That was very potent sherry which John gave me. It's gone to my head.'

'I don't mind so long as it doesn't go to your feet. Oh, do you hear a noise in the car?'

Barrington laughed.

'You haven't heard anything yet,' he said. 'Wait till she gets hot, and all the big ends start jazzing. I have to put in a quart of oil every twenty miles. Fortunately this place we're bound for is only six miles away, so with any luck we ought to get there, unless I take a wrong turning and end up in a farmyard.'

But this never happened and about a quarter of an hour later they entered the grounds of Colton Priory, about which Barrington had heard very good reports. The lighted sign gave Felicity food for reflection.

'Why, this is Lord Somebody's place,' she said, as the car snorted up the drive.

'You are two years out of date. It is now a private hotel, with a drink licence, a good wine cellar, and a beautiful dance floor.'

'Oh, what a shame!'

'That's a nice thing to say, after all the trouble I have gone to.'

'I mean what a shame it had to come to this. It used to be one of the best country houses in England.'

'What would you do if you had a house with fifty bedrooms and income tax at about nineteen shillings in the pound? Pity the poor rich.'

The big mansion soon came to view, with bright lights shining from its many windows. It looked very romantic in its setting of thick timber, and when they reached the car park they found quite a number of luxurious limousines parked there.

'Looks like a full evening-dress affair,' said Barrington. 'But I was assured it wasn't. Best of being a woman you can go half and half. None of that for the poor male. Hullo, what's this parcel in the back?'

'Oh, that's mine. It's just a small birthday present — for you.'

'You shouldn't have done that.'

'It's of no value — just something I did in a moment of desperation.'

'Something you made?'

'Well — yes.'

'May I open it?'

'You might embarrass me.'

'When you tickle my curiosity like that you can't expect me to be patient. Here goes!'

He opened the small parcel and brought to view an attractive little sketch in water colours. It was the view down the lake at eventide, showing Deepwater Cottage, all golden in the sunlight, and the trees heavy with foliage.

'You mean you did this yourself?' asked Barrington.

'Yes.'

'But it's lovely — quite professional. I had no idea you were such an artist.'

'Just a dabbler. But I'm glad you like it.'

'I do — immensely. You couldn't have given me anything more pleasing. I suppose I had better leave it here. Come on, Mrs. Michelangelo.'

The dinner was quite well attended, and later there came many other couples, for dancing only. It was a great relief to Barrington to observe that at least half the throng were as unconventionally dressed as he was himself. Felicity wore a charming frock just off the shoulder, and seemed completely at her ease. Music was provided by a small but excellent string orchestra, and the whole thing went with a swing from the very start.

'I feel rather like a bull in a china shop,' said Barrington. 'Haven't danced in years.'

'You're doing very well indeed. Oh, this is wonderful!'

Barrington was of the same opinion. In the Paul Jones he danced with a number of partners, obtained by hazard and not from choice, and it was with a sigh of great relief that he eventually regained his previous monopoly of the light-footed Felicity, whose eyes were as bright as the scintillating chandeliers overhead.

'Enjoying yourself?' he asked.

'Yes — rapturously. Phil, it was good of you to bring me here.'

'It was good of you to take pity on a crusty old bachelor like me.'

'Old! Why, you aren't much older than me.'

'Oh yes, I am, and feeling the weight of my years.'

She laughed merrily, and seemed almost to draw herself closer to him, so that her flushed cheeks came close to his own. Then suddenly her expression became very serious.

'How much do you like me, Phil?' she whispered.

'Good heavens! What a question.'

'Yes, it is a question — how much?'

'I refuse to tell you.'

'Why?'

'It might not be good for you — nor for me.'

'What do you mean by that?'

'I mean that you are a most explosive piece of dynamite, my dear, to be handled with the greatest care if one is to avoid being blown sky-high. Now I have really trodden on your toes, and it's all your fault. I can't dance and be subjected to a soul-searching quiz at the same time.'

'I ask you a simple question, and you start throwing off literary metaphors about dynamite. You're either a plain coward, Mr. Philip Barrington, or a cheap dissembler.'

'All right — you shall have the horrible truth. I like you slightly better than castor oil, toothache, a pain in the neck, and the English winter.'

'And less than what?'

Barrington, bewitched by her lovely young eyes, and her gleaming teeth, pressed her closely to him.

'Less than nothing,' he said in a whisper. 'Felicity, what are you doing to me?'

'What have you done to me?' she asked. 'A little while ago I didn't know what happiness was. You were like a person in a story — a story told by my brother. He said you were the bravest and noblest — '

Barrington put his finger on her lips.

'For heaven's sake — !' he protested.

'All right. I'll spare you the details. But bless you for coming to Strafford Park, and opening a new window on the world — for me.'

Later, driving home in the moonlight, with Felicity by his side, Barrington was dazed by what had taken place. He had taken Felicity out for the evening, with no other object than to give her a respite from the domestic tragedy, the essence of which still hung heavily over her and her family, and here he was caught up in the toils of a romance. Old-fashioned in his ideas about women, Felicity's behaviour staggered him. With the utmost ease she had in one stride crossed a bridge which to him had appeared quite formidable, and the result was that, to his surprise, he felt like a man whose feet are no longer on the earth. When he left her at the door of Strafford Park that astonishing young woman lifted her face to his in a manner which left no room for misinterpretation, and he felt that soft, lingering kiss long after he had reached Deepwater Cottage, and had gone to bed.

12

Inspector McLean's trip to Exeter was made in most unfavourable weather conditions, for they drove in the teeth of a violent rainstorm which never let up for a moment, and which reduced visibility to about fifty yards. Small rivulets were turned into torrents, and floods in road depressions were so serious that they threatened a complete hold-up, but Sergeant Brook, who knew this country well, saved the situation by making a long detour over the high land between the main road and the sea. McLean, who had not visited the city since it was blitzed by the Luftwaffe, was appalled at the devastated area in its centre, and Brook groaned as he passed a piece of open land where once had stood his famous 'pub'.

'It'll never be the same again,' he complained. 'Many a tankard of beer I've had just about where that red car is parked. What a crazy world I was born into.'

McLean could understand this nostalgia for the past, for he too had the pleasantest memories of the Exeter that was. Where noble buildings had stood were huge lakes of water on the blasted red earth, and complete desolation was only saved by the presence of the lovely cathedral, which had withstood the holocaust most wonderfully.

It was still pelting with rain when they reached police headquarters, and here McLean looked up an old colleague, named Reynolds, to whom he made known his requirements.

'Summerlands,' said Reynolds. 'You must mean Summerlands Terrace?'

'Yes, of course. I remember now.'

'It's gone — only one house left standing.'

'You mean in the blitz?'

'Yes. A clean burn-out. What house are you interested in?'

'I don't know. But the woman's name is Beatrice Lansbury, and she had either friends or relatives in that terrace. But that was a long time ago — thirty years in fact.'

'That certainly is going back a bit. I'll see what directories we have in the library.'

A search of the old directories revealed that a Mr. Edgar Lansbury occupied a house in the terrace as recently as 1939, but it was one of the houses that were now non-existent. The enquiry was subsequently switched to the postmaster, and this gentleman was most helpful. He did not know what had become of Mr. Lansbury after his home was destroyed, but he was able to give McLean the name and address of an old lady who had lived in the next house, and who was living just outside the city. McLean saw this old lady an hour later in a small cottage at Ide. Her name was Mrs. Merrit, and she was a widow.

'Oh yes, I remember Mr. Lansbury quite well,' she said. 'He was my neighbour for over twenty years. He had a wife during the first two years, but she died of double pneumonia, poor dear.'

'Had Mr. Lansbury a daughter?'

'No. They had no children.'

'A sister perhaps?'

'Yes, he had a younger sister, who used to come and see him sometimes.'

'Can you remember her Christian name?'

The old lady thought for a moment, and then shook her head.

'Might it have been Beatrice?'

'Yes. That's right — it was Beatrice. A well-built young woman she was too. I think she was a nurse.'

'She was a children's nurse.'

'I think she told me that once.'

'Can you remember when it was that you last saw her?'

'No. It was a long time before the war, but how long I don't know.'

'And Mr. Lansbury. Have you any idea where he is now?'

'It's funny you should ask me that, because a week or two ago I had a letter from an old neighbour of mine who went to live at Exmouth. He told me that he had met Mr. Lansbury quite by accident and had had a long chat with him.'

'Did he say where he was living?'

'I think he did, but I can't remember where it was.'

'Have you still got the letter?'

'I think I have — somewhere in the house. Shall I try to find it?'

'Please do.'

The old lady's very long search was finally rewarded. She came down from her bedroom, with her spectacles half-way down her thin nose, waving a sheet of paper.

'I put it between the window sashes to stop them from rattling,' she gasped. 'Such a lot of wind here. My friend says that Mr. Lansbury lives in a small bungalow at Longdown. That's about two miles from here on the Mortonhampstead Road.'

'I know it,' said Brook.

'Does he give the name of the cottage?' asked McLean.

'No, but bless you, everybody knows everybody up there.'

McLean thanked her and got back into the car with Brook.

'Nice little village this,' commented Brook. 'Hasn't changed in a hundred years. They still draw their water from a public pump, and don't even know what main drainage means. There's a short cut to Longdown through that watersplash — if we can get through.'

'We aren't doing so badly,' said McLean. 'It's possible that Beatrice Lansbury may be living with her brother. If not, he is almost certain to know where she is.'

At Longdown the first person they asked was able to direct them to Mr. Lansbury's cottage, which was within a couple of hundred yards, and from which could be seen — veiled a little by the curtain of rain — one of the finest views imaginable. McLean had to ring three times before there was a response, then the door was opened by a bent old man, with a very bald head, who peered at them queerly.

'Are you Mr. Lansbury?' asked McLean.

'Yes.'

'We are police officers, and I should be obliged if you would give me a few minutes of your time.'

'Surely — surely. Please come inside, and shut out this awful weather. Police officers!

It's the first time any police officer has ever called on me.'

He led them to a very small room, cluttered up with old bits of furniture, books, a large radio, and scattered newspapers, and begged them to be seated.

'You are Mr. Edgar Lansbury, who once lived at Exeter?' asked McLean.

'Yes, I lost my lovely house there. I shall never forget the terrible night when the German bombers came.'

'I don't suppose you will,' said McLean sympathetically. 'Have you a sister named Beatrice?'

'I had,' said the old man sorrowfully. 'But I lost her two years ago.'

'You mean she's dead?'

'Yes.'

Brook saw from McLean's face that this was a bitter disappointment to him. With Beatrice Lansbury dead the trail which McLean had been following seemed to vanish into the blue.

'I'm sorry,' said McLean. 'I had hoped to get from her some valuable information. It concerns a family for whom she once worked as nursery governess — a family named Grayling who lived at a place called Seething Manor.'

'Oh yes, she was with them a long

time — best part of twenty years. She left when Miss Grayling got married.'

'Did she come to live with you after that?'

'No. The Grayling family treated her very well, gave her a pension for life, and she wanted to live on her own. I heard from her after a long silence — from a place in Scotland. To my surprise she had got married, and was expecting a baby. Not a bad effort for a woman of forty-five. Then, some years later, she wrote and told me that her husband was dead, and that she was feeling very lonely. I was lonely, too, having lost my dear wife, so I invited her and her baby to come and share my house in Exeter. Within two years the baby boy died. He was a pretty little boy, with fair hair and sky-blue eyes, but was always frail. We didn't realize that he was tuberculous, until it was too late to do much. It nearly broke her heart, and she was never the same afterwards. She lived with me until two years ago, and then she went to a nursing home, and underwent a serious operation. She — she never recovered.'

He wiped away a tear which had come to his eye, and turned his head away for a moment.

'Whom did she marry?' asked McLean.

'A man named Galbraith. I don't think it

was a very happy marriage, because when she came back she never seemed keen to talk about her husband. I think he was a commercial traveller.'

'I suppose your sister used to talk about the Graylings?'

'Oh yes. She was devoted to Miss Grayling, whom she had nursed as a baby, but she never really liked the parents.'

'Did she ever mention a young man named Oliver?'

'You don't mean her son?'

'Was his name Oliver?' asked McLean, with a glance at Brook.

'Yes.'

'I was thinking of another person — someone who was friendly with Miss Grayling.'

'No. There was no other Oliver to my knowledge.'

'Which nursing home did your sister go to?'

'Clapford House — just outside Exeter. She was there under observation for a long time.'

'From what you have said I take it that your sister was here with you at the time she went into the nursing home?'

'Yes.'

'Did she get her pension direct from the Graylings?'

'No. It was paid into her bank account every quarter.'

'How much was it?'

'Fifty pounds a quarter.'

'Did your sister leave anything in the nature of snapshots or photographs?'

'Yes. She had a nice little camera. I've sold that, but I still have two large albums of snapshots.'

'I should very much like to see them.'

'I'll get them. I keep them in my bedroom.'

After he had shambled out Brook looked keenly at McLean, and McLean knew what was agitating his mind.

'Oliver again,' he said. 'In most unexpected circumstances. Was that merely a random choice, or did she know the other Oliver? What a pity she isn't alive to explain much which needs explanation.'

The old man came back carrying two large albums, which he was rubbing with a duster. He handed them to McLean with an apology for their condition.

'I've no servant here to keep things clean,' he complained.

McLean opened one of the volumes, and was soon interested in what he saw. There were hundreds of snapshots, all bearing captions in neat handwriting, and the second

212

volume seemed to be equally packed.

'Mr. Lansbury,' he said. 'Might I borrow these for a few days? I will be responsible for their safe-keeping.'

The old man was agreeable, and a little later McLean and Brook entered the car and drove back to Exeter. There they had a belated lunch, and afterwards adjourned to a room at police headquarters where the two photograph albums were closely examined. They were interesting exhibits since they showed the Grayling family at home in the distant past, with Gertrude in most of the pictures, from infancy to womanhood, alone or with groups of other persons.

'And here's the old tower,' said McLean. 'Looking much the same as it does now. Enter the bridegroom — the late baronet. Fine looking man, and rather like his son. I wish Miss Lansbury had put dates to the snapshots. It would help considerably. Oh, just look at this. The old tower again, and Gertrude standing on the steps. Quite a grown-up woman. The caption says 'Gertrude and O' but the girl is alone.'

Brook scanned the snapshot.

'It's been trimmed down the side — since the caption was written,' he said.

'Yes, and pasted down again at the top corners.'

"'O' for Oliver,' said Brook.

'Yes, and 'O' for onions, but I think you're right, Brook. For some reason or other Miss Lansbury decided to take 'O' out of the picture. Apparently he was standing just a little way to the left of the girl. I wonder why she did that?'

'Perhaps 'O' wasn't very welcome at the Manor, and Miss Lansbury thought the snapshot might be seen by Mr. or Mrs. Grayling.'

'I think that's possible, since Gertrude lied so outrageously when I last questioned her. She couldn't remember any Oliver, or going to the tower with him, yet here she is with him at that very tower — if our conclusions are correct. And there's something even more damning against her. She didn't want us to go searching for Beatrice, and was quick to assume that she was dead. If she did really know that Beatrice was dead she was equally reticent about where she had died, and when. But she and her family must have known where Beatrice had been living for a long period, because she had been in receipt of a family pension, and the pension must have stopped when Beatrice died. As for the pension — it is ringed around with mystery.'

'Why?'

'Look at all the evidence we have collected respecting the Graylings. They were rich, but notoriously mean. They hated parting with money, and yet they paid Beatrice a largish pension for years and years. Even generously minded people would have considered two hundred pounds a year grossly excessive in the case of a servant who was well able to earn her own living. I mistrust Lady Gertrude's evidence. She tells the truth when it suits her, and lies when it doesn't. There are several photographs here which I want copied, so I think we had better stay over the night. When we return the albums I must find out where Beatrice kept her banking account, and attempt to track down the actual source of her pension so-called.'

The next morning turned out fine and sunny, and McLean got the copies of the photographs he needed, and took the albums back to Mr. Lansbury. On mentioning the matter of the pensions McLean was informed that it had always been paid into his sister's account in an Exeter bank, and gave him the name of the bank.

Half an hour later McLean was talking to the manager of the bank, and that gentleman had the records looked up, and was able to tell McLean that the money had been paid on a standing order from the banking account of Mrs. Maud Grayling, such order being cancelled at the time of Mrs. Galbraith's death, two years before.

'What date was that?' asked McLean.

'April the tenth.'

'Three weeks before the death of Mrs. Grayling herself,' mused McLean. 'That's all I wish to know. Thank you very much.'

'That seems to be everything,' said Brook. 'We ought to have a nice journey back.'

But McLean was not yet quite ready to return to Dorchester. He thought it might be possible to learn something at the nursing home where Mrs. Galbraith had died, and so Brook was instructed to drive to Clapford House, which lay between Exeter and Sidmouth. Here McLean saw the matron, who remembered very well her unfortunate patient.

'It was a sad case,' she said. 'Long neglected cancer of the liver. There were some doubts about the success of the operation, but in any case she could not have lived another six months. She was warned of the danger of the operation, but consented to have it performed.'

'She was here for some time, I think?'

'Five weeks in all.'

'Had she any special friend among your staff?'

'Yes — Nurse Wright. Mrs. Galbraith had known Nurse Wright's mother many years ago.'

McLean asked if he might see Nurse Wright, and a little later the meeting took place in a private room. The proficient-looking nurse remembered the case quite well.

'Did you talk much about her past?' asked McLean.

'Yes, a great deal, when she was not in pain. She suffered a lot and was very brave about it.'

'Did she ever mention her husband?'

'Oh yes. I gathered that her married life was very brief, and not particularly happy. There was a baby boy, but he had died early in life. She seemed to mourn the boy rather than her husband.'

'What persons came to see her while she was here?'

'Only her brother so far as I can remember. He came fairly frequently. She seemed to know that she would never get through the operation, and just before it was due to take place she gave me a letter which she asked me to post in the event of her death.'

'Can you remember to whom it was addressed?'

'Yes, because it was obviously to some

relative — a Mr. Galbraith who I assumed was either her father-in-law or brother-in-law.'

'Where was the letter addressed to?'

'I'm afraid I can't remember.'

'Did she live long after the operation?'

'Only ten hours, and she never regained consciousness.'

McLean had no more questions to ask, but all the way back to Dorchester he was so immersed in his thoughts that Sergeant Brook was unable to get a word out of him.

13

On the morning after the dance Sir John noted a remarkable change in his unpredictable sister. He came down to breakfast to find her eating like a horse, and as full of life as a hive of bees.

' 'Morning!' she said. 'Eggs and ham this morning. Things are certainly looking up. I've had a three-mile walk, and I'm hungry.'

'So it appears. Was it a sleep walk?'

'No. I looked out and saw the sun shining, so I decided to turn over a new leaf, and earn my breakfast. You should try it one day, and reduce that waistline.'

John, pouring himself out some coffee, gazed at her over the coffee-pot.

'I never know whether you're serious or not,' he said. 'But you were very late last night.'

'Late? I was in bed before midnight.'

'Well anyway — how did the dance go off?'

'Marvellously. I've never enjoyed myself so much in my life. Phil took me to Colton Priory. I had no idea the place had been turned into a private hotel. The food was splendid — everything was splendid. Pass me the marmalade, please.'

'I had no idea Phil was a dancing man.'

'Phil has all sorts of secret vices — as well as virtues.'

John laughed.

'Why, you've only known him five minutes.'

'I feel I've known him all my life. Aren't you going to eat anything?'

'I don't think so, I can't forget about yesterday.'

'Yesterday? Oh, that wretched bottle.'

'Had you forgotten it?'

'No, but I've been trying to. I can't believe that it has anything to do with grandpa's death. But the sooner the police have it the better. Do eat something, John. It's no use worrying over something which can't be helped. Or do you believe that the police will find some connection between the bottle and — '

'Of course not. I'm worrying about mother. You saw how she was yesterday afternoon, and when you had gone off with Philip last night she would scarcely speak to me or Lucy. She takes it all so personally, as if we enjoyed seeing her placed in an embarrassing position — '

At that moment Gertrude entered the room in her usual grandiose manner, and responded to their morning greeting with something that was little more than a grunt. John, from long habit, arranged a chair for her, and went back to his coffee and slice of dry toast.

'You were very late last night, Felicity,' said Gertrude.

'I'm sorry, Mother,' replied Felicity, as a peace gesture. 'But time seemed to pass so quickly.'

'I think Mr. Barrington should have known better. I permitted him to take you because I believed he had a sense of responsibility. It seems I was wrong.'

Felicity's mood changed instantly.

'You nearly always are wrong, Mother,' she said.

'How dare you speak to me like that?'

'How dare you speak of Philip like that? I am not going to argue with you, Mother — not on a lovely morning like this.'

With this Felicity rose and hurried out of the room, leaving her mother almost speechless with anger. Up in her bedroom the beautiful vista of the rain-washed park and gardens had the effect of cooling her off, and she sighed as she made her bed, and reflected upon the ever-increasing disharmony, the end of which she could not foresee, unless it lay in leaving Strafford Park for ever.

On the bedside table was Barrington's manuscript which she had forgotten to return overnight as she had promised. She had read it through again after her return from the dance, and was completely captivated by the personality of the writer with which every sentence — every line — was charged. And this was the man her mother charged with irresponsibility! Of course she hadn't meant it. It had been said out of spite, because of the finding of the bottle and the squabble which had followed. Her gaze went to her dressing-table, and she blinked with surprise to notice that the bottle was no longer where she had left it.

Thinking it possible that one of the maids might have slipped it into one of the drawers, she went across to the table and opened the drawers. There was no sign of the bottle, and her amazement and suspicions grew apace. Outside the daily girl was hoovering the carpet. On being questioned she denied having been in the bedroom that morning. Felicity had no reason to doubt her word, and went back into the bedroom, with her heart thumping almost painfully.

Undoubtedly someone had taken the bottle away since she had gone downstairs to breakfast, and who could it have been but her mother who had a definite reason for not wanting it to get into the hands of the police. She had expressed her repugnance at being questioned again, but was it merely the questioning she didn't like, or what might emerge from it?

At any moment Inspector McLean might ring up, to ask John the reason for his telephone call. Obviously John must be told at once. She hurried down to the library, and there, to her great joy, she found her brother reading the morning newspapers.

'Something's happened!' she gasped.

'What do you mean?'

'The bottle — it's gone.'

John put down the newspaper, and stared at her incredulously.

'Where did you leave it?' he asked.

'On my dressing-table. I saw it there before I left the room this morning.'

'That's extraordinary!' he muttered. 'I suppose you are quite sure it isn't anywhere in the room?'

'Absolutely certain.'

'But it's fantastic. Who would want to — ?'

He stopped as he saw the expression on Felicity's face.

'It wasn't you or I, or the maids, and Lucy is having her breakfast in bed,' said Felicity.

'And that leaves only mother,' he said heavily.

'Can you think of anyone else?'

He turned his head away, and bent his shoulders in an attitude of complete distress. Felicity went to him and caught his arm.

'What are we to do about it, John?' she asked tenderly. 'If McLean rings up — as he is bound to, what are we going to tell him?'

'I don't know. To tell him that the bottle has been stolen is worse than merely handing it to him. I must speak to mother. If she has been foolish enough to take it she must give it back.'

'You had better see her alone,' said Felicity. 'I am in disgrace at the moment.'

'I'll do it now. If the police should ring tell them I am not available.'

The subsequent interview between John and his mother lasted only a few minutes. He came back to the library with his face flushed and his hands clenched.

'This is the last straw,' he muttered.

'What happened?'

'She confessed. She took the bottle because she was sick of being questioned.'

'Has she got it now?'

'No. She smashed it to pieces and put the debris into the stove before she came in to breakfast.'

'She's acting as if she were guilty.'

'Oh no. I'll never believe that. It's her stiff-necked pride which drives her to childish acts, and she doesn't seem to realize that in doing this stupid thing she is forcing us to engage in deception.'

Felicity looked at him sharply.

'You mean you aren't going to tell the police?'

'How can I? What is the use of telling them about a bottle that doesn't exist any longer? Could we blame them if they took the view that only a person who had much to hide would behave in such a way?'

Felicity was silent. She could appreciate the argument as John had put it, but she could not forget that it was John who had hitherto been most emphatic about the need to keep nothing from the police which might serve as a clue. Now, here he was, advising a completely opposite course.

'You're forgetting Philip,' she said at last. 'He knows all about the bottle.'

'Yes, I had forgotten. There's only one thing to do, and that is to tell Phil just what happened. I'll run across and see him.'

'No, let me,' begged Felicity. 'I'm certain that he'll see things our way. I've got to go to Deepwater anyway, to take back some manuscript which I promised to return.'

'As you wish.'

'But what about McLean — if he telephones, or calls?'

'I'll be here to deal with him. You run along while I think up some plausible explanation. I detest the whole business, but what else can one do?'

When Felicity reached the cottage she found Barrington tinkering with the engine of his car. He did not see her until she pushed the manuscript into his back, causing him to start and turn round.

'Oh, good morning!' he said. 'You're about early. What about all those chores you told me you did at the house?'

'I've done them — at least some of them. What's wrong with the bus?'

'Filthy plugs. I've got to run into the village, and she wouldn't start. But she's all right now. Like to come with me? You can help me choose suitable food for my delicate stomach.'

'Yes, I'll come.'

'Then give me a few minutes to clean myself up. Oh, is that my manuscript?'

'Yes, I forgot to give it to you last night.'

'It didn't really matter. Put it on my desk, will you, and I'll be with you in a jiffy. What a glorious day after all that rain, which Mrs. Sawyer assured me was going to last for a week. She's quite disappointed about it.'

Later, in the car, Felicity told him what had transpired since she had last seen him, and Barrington listened attentively. When she had finished he shook his head slowly.

'You — you think we are acting wrongly?' she asked.

'No. The circumstances are different. While you had an exhibit, so to speak, it was your plain duty to hand it over, but now it exists no longer, and there seems to me no reason why you should have it on your conscience.'

'That's a relief,' sighed Felicity. 'Now I want to talk about the book — your book.'

'All criticism gratefully received.'

'There's nothing to criticize. I've read it twice, and loved it even better the second time. I'm aching to see how it goes on.'

'You shall.'

When they reached the village the place seemed unusually lively. Round about the churchyard were little groups of people, talking together, and in the churchyard itself were many more. Then the Rector was seen hurrying from the Rectory.

'A wedding or a funeral,' said Barrington.

He parked the car in the little square, and Felicity accompanied him to the grocery store.

'What are you buying?' she asked.

'Mostly things in tins, but I want some cheese off the ration, and some vegetables.'

'But why don't you have the things delivered as we do?'

'I like to see what I'm buying.'

They waited a little while in a short queue, and then Barrington received attention. Felicity had never been in the shop before and was surprised at the vast variety of goods it had to offer, which included cigarettes, of which Barrington bought a large quantity.

'You'll smoke yourself to death,' she complained.

'There are worse ways of dying.'

By the time Barrington had filled his grocery bag, and collected one-and-fourpence worth of meat from the butcher, in the shape of lamb chops, the inn was open.

'Ever been in there?' asked Barrington.

'No, but I've often wanted to.'

'Then come on.'

They entered the private bar, and the landlord greeted them cheerily. Barrington ordered his usual tankard of ale, but Felicity needed time to make up her mind.

'I think I'll have a sherry,' she said finally.

From where they sat they could see the church through the side window, and the throng of people were still coming and going.

'Is it a wedding or a funeral?' asked Barrington of the landlord.

'Neither, sir. A bit too early in the morning for weddings, and we haven't had a funeral since old Mr. Grayling died. That's the cause of all the trouble.'

Felicity gave a start but the landlord seemed not to notice it, and was obviously unaware of her identity.

'What trouble?' asked Barrington.

The landlord was about to explain when two men came into the bar, convulsed with laughter. One of them ordered two drinks, which the landlord drew with great solemnity.

'Just been up to the churchyard,' said the customer, as he paid. 'Best joke I've heard in a long time.'

'Yes, a real corker,' said his companion.

'I don't know,' said the landlord. 'I call it a pretty poor joke. When a man's dead it's time to forget his faults. Why can't people let him rest in peace?'

'Maybe people would in the ordinary way. It was the epitaph that did it. Asking for trouble it was. Poor old Rector! He didn't know what to do. He wouldn't have it painted out until the police had seen it.'

229

The landlord, noticing the rapt attention of his two other customers, considered it time to explain.

'It's the trouble I was mentioning,' he said. 'Someone monkeyed about with old Mr. Grayling's tombstone during the night. It was only replaced yesterday, after it had been removed for Mr. Grayling's name to be added to that of his wife. There was an epitaph at the bottom. It read 'HE DID HIS BEST'. Some joker thought it wanted finishing, so he added the word 'FRIENDS' in black paint. Vandalism I call it.'

Again the two men guffawed, but stopped when they realized that neither Barrington nor Felicity appeared to be in any way amused. A few moments later Barrington and Felicity were back in the car.

'I'm sorry I took you in there,' said Barrington.

'Why should you be? Mother was asking for trouble when she chose that phrase. Actually I didn't know what she had chosen. We had a fearful squabble about it. She wanted to use a text from the Bible but we protested, so she went off in a huff and said she would deal with the matter herself. This is the unhappy sequel. I wish it could be kept from mother, but she is bound to get to know.'

When they passed the church the crowd was still there, and a little farther on they encountered a uniformed policeman, riding a bicycle and looking very hot and flustered. Barrington could not repress a smile as he noticed what appeared to be a pot of paint hanging from the handlebar of the machine.

14

The next few days passed without incident, and another spell of lovely sunny weather made outdoor life most enjoyable. McLean had telephoned Sir John regarding the latter's telephone call, and John made his excuses and said it was no longer of any interest. Then from McLean's direction came dead silence.

Lady Gertrude, having largely recovered from the shock of the defilement of her father's grave, and freed from the hateful repetition of being questioned, recovered her habitual equanimity. Moreover she seemed to be conscious of having behaved rather badly, and surprised the younger members of the family, almost as much as she did Barrington, by calling on the latter one afternoon, just as he was finishing a long spell of writing. He was knocked almost breathless to see her standing in the porch, after a long double ring of the bell.

'Good afternoon, Lady Gertrude!' he said, turning down his shirt-sleeves. 'Please excuse my appearance. But it's been so hot and oppressive — '

'I hope I'm not interrupting your work,' she said, with a sunny smile.

'Not at all. I've just finished what I was doing. Won't you come in?'

'Thank you. Incredible as it may sound, I haven't been in here for ten years. It's really quite a nice little place. What a perfect view up the lake.'

'Yes, and it's even better round about sunset. But may I offer you some tea? It's quite ready. Mrs. Sawyer always lays a tray before she leaves. All I have to do is boil a kettle, and I put that on a few minutes ago.'

'I should love to. How is the book going?'

'Fairly well. Oh, there goes the kettle.'

'That whistle?'

'Yes, it's an economy idea and it works wonderfully. Even Mrs. Sawyer is compelled to turn off the gas before she suffers damage to her ear-drums. Excuse me!'

In the kitchen he slipped on his coat, combed his hair and replaced his tie. It took but a minute or two to make the tea and add another cup and saucer, and some extra cakes. When he returned to the sitting-room Lady Gertrude was immersed in a book which she had taken from the bookcase.

'All ready,' he said. 'But did you walk here?'

'Yes. I don't often walk, but I couldn't resist the sunshine. You're very domesticated, Mr. Barrington.'

'I've had to be. Sugar and milk?'

'Milk yes. Sugar definitely no. I've reached an age when sugar has disastrous effects upon my waistline.'

Barrington found that hard to believe, for her figure was as perfect as a young woman's. It was indeed amazing to reflect that she was the mother of John. But why had she called? Somewhere, he thought, there must be a well-concealed ulterior motive.

Despite the tabu in regard to sugar Gertrude seemed to be extremely vulnerable to rich pastry, consuming a quantity of the sweetest things with quite obvious gusto. She admired the room, and John's furniture which had recently replaced the vulgar stuff which her bailiff had introduced into the cottage while he lodged there.

'A most excellent man,' she said. 'But with no taste at all. I am afraid my own people were rather like that. They filled my old home with the most repellent articles. It was a great relief to me to come to Strafford with my husband, and enjoy the beautiful things which his forbears had collected over the centuries. It was a good thing that my mother was able to save Strafford, although in doing so her motive was misinterpreted by certain people, as you may have heard.'

'I know there has been a lot of vulgar gossip.'

'More than gossip. That disgraceful act of vandalism in the village churchyard is another example of bad feeling and bad breeding. My poor father had his faults, but they were not such as to arouse so deep an animosity.'

Barrington now saw the proverbial cat coming out of the bag. This was an exculpatory mission on behalf of her anathematized parents, masquerading as a social visit, and it seemed absurd that she should care what he had gleaned from the local gossip, or what his personal opinion was, but that she did care became more and more evident as she warmed to her task. Her mother was perhaps a little to blame, for she had been slow to recognize her responsibilities to her numerous tenants, and she was a strong-willed woman not willing to listen to good advice. Her father had inherited the estate at a time when he was incapable of understanding what was needed. But now it was going to be different. There would be a trust under the intestacy, and she proposed having plans drawn up to deal with the long overdue improvements. Also, under the trust, the estate would, in due course, come back to the Meddings, which was only right and just. In the meantime she wanted John to turn down any post which might be offered by the Foreign Office, and to stay on at Strafford Park, and run the whole thing as if it were already his own. As for Felicity — she had certain plans regarding her future, which she hoped Felicity would be sensible enough to approve.

This last remark caused Barrington to gaze at her, and hope that she would be a little more forthright, for he read in it a definite warning to any plan which he himself might conceivably have in a certain direction. But Lady Gertrude had said her piece, and switched to other and less contentious matters.

'Oh,' she said, as she was leaving. 'There's one thing I almost forgot. Would you care to make up a bridge four tomorrow evening? I have a guest coming for a day or two, and Lucy is none too well these days.'

'I should be pleased. At what time shall I come?'

'About eight-thirty.'

'I'll be there.'

'Splendid! Thank you for a very nice tea.'

When she had gone Barrington pondered over her various remarks, and felt not a little uncomfortable. Here was the born planner planning Felicity's future, as doubtless her parents had planned hers. Did the anonymous guest come into those plans, and was Gertrude intent upon his meeting this guest to suit her own schemes? He rang up Felicity later, and subsequently met her in the park.

'I entertained your mother to tea this afternoon,' he said.

Felicity opened her eyes wide.

'She never told me,' she said. 'You are especially honoured, Phil, for mother is most careful with whom she has tea. What did she have to say?'

'Quite a lot. I gather that she intends to make the estate an earthly Paradise. Incidentally she invited me over to bridge tomorrow evening. I understand she is to have a guest.'

'That's right. I didn't know until this morning. He's an awful bore and I'm supposed to entertain him. He's bridge mad and horse mad, so you and I share the honours.'

'Who is he?'

'The Honorable Arthur Poynings, eldest son of Lord Ravelling, who was a great friend of my father.'

'Do you like him — the son, I mean?'

'Yes — in a way.'

'What sort of way?'

'He can be entertaining, when he isn't talking bridge or horses and he's very manageable.'

'Marriageable?'

'I said manageable. But why all this excitement?'

'I'm not excited, but your mother, having intimated that she had plans for your future, is clearly keen that I should meet the young man who, I strongly suspect, is chosen to raise the family's social status. Tell me if I'm wrong.'

'No, Phil, you are dead right. It's been mother's not very secret desire for a long time, but now she has come out into the open. In the event of my marrying someone of whom she approves — meaning dear Arthur — she will settle a thousand a year upon me. Makes a girl think, doesn't it?'

Barrington took her two hands and held them firmly in his.

'What is this particular girl thinking?' he asked.

'Would you really like to know?'

'Yes.'

Felicity shook her head.

'You know already, Phil,' she said. 'You know, but you won't accept it. Do you doubt your ability to make me happy? Do you imagine that I want dressing up like a doll, or putting into a glass case as a kind of exhibit? What is it that holds you back? Tell me, and trust me to understand.'

'I'll tell you. It's poverty — with a capital P. I've scarcely anything but the clothes I stand in, and a typewriter. It may be years before I make any sort of a name. I've nothing to offer you but an almighty struggle for existence, not even a home that is worthy of the name. When I leave the luxurious cottage, which John so kindly lent me, I go back to Grub Street — two rooms and a wash-up on the third floor, with wonderful views of the gasworks, and a perpetual smell of fish and chips from a shop below me. Could you face that prospect?'

'You haven't even asked me?'

'I'm asking you now. Will you marry me?'

'The answer is yes — a thousand times yes. Now kiss me, and tell me you love me. I'm old-fashioned enough to want to be told that.'

Barrington pressed her closely to him, and kissed the red inviting lips again and again.

'I love you,' he said. 'Not only at times like this, but at every living moment of the day. But I must warn you that being Mrs.

Barrington is going to be a bit different from being — eventually — Viscountess Ravelling.'

'That could never have happened, for my heart was already given to you, for weal or woe as the poets say. But where do we go from here?'

Barrington looked across at the majestic house.

'There, I think — to your mother.'

'No, not yet, darling. Let her have her bridge party tomorrow. She'll enjoy that anyway. Oh dear, it's going to be difficult telling her. You see, she guessed what was going on, and struck the strategical idea of presenting you to my chosen husband, to warn you off. Of course, I shall have to be nice to Arthur.'

'Not too nice,' said Barrington, wagging a finger.

'At least, I can't refuse to ride with him. That would break his heart.'

'I wouldn't care if it broke his neck — no, I don't mean that. You see, you have got me quite homicidal. Felicity, how old are you — I should say how young?'

'Twenty and a bit.'

'Still a minor. Suppose your mother objects?'

'She will.'

'That's going to complicate matters a bit, isn't it?'

'Not really. I have an answer to that.'

'Well, I haven't — except to wait another year.'

'That's no answer. I know mother, better than she thinks. Got any drink in your cottage?'

'Yes.'

'Then let's go and celebrate.'

★ ★ ★

On the following morning the Honourable Arthur arrived in a luxurious-looking car, and was warmly welcomed by his hostess. Later in the day Barrington, out for a stroll, saw the young pair mounted on hired hacks, cantering down one of the lanes, and Felicity managed to blow him a kiss without being seen by her fellow-rider who was slightly ahead of her. Barrington swore under his breath. Why did Felicity look so happy, anyway? Then he laughed at his own childish spleen, and went back to his work.

Going up to the Hall that evening was quite an experience. For some reason or other he felt unaccountably nervous, and before ringing the bell he had to wait and pull himself together. It was all due to the

Honourable Arthur. How could he be polite to the fellow in the circumstances, or to Lady Gertrude who was using him only to serve her own ambitious ends? But finally he found himself in the lounge, where the family and the Honourable Arthur were gathered.

'Oh, good evening, Mr. Barrington!' said Gertrude, beaming at him. 'So glad you were able to come. Arthur, this is Mr. Barrington who is staying at the cottage.'

Barrington found himself facing a young, well-built man with fair curly hair, and intensely blue eyes. Having made up his mind to dislike him it was a little embarrassing to find his hand gripped firmly and well-shaken. John, in the background arranging the card-table, looked very serious, but Felicity's expression was as inscrutable as that of the Sphinx.

'I've been wanting to meet you,' said Arthur. 'Felicity has told me so much about you.'

'Has she indeed?' replied Barrington. 'I hope it wasn't all true.'

Arthur laughed easily, and Lucy, who was quietly knitting, gave Barrington a smile as she met his gaze.

'There you are,' said John. 'All ready for battle, except for another straight-backed chair. Felicity, you will be far more

242

comfortable in the one behind you. Avaunt!'

Felicity got up and sat down on the couch beside Lucy. To Barrington she looked more beautiful and irresistible than ever, Arthur apparently thought so, too, for his gaze went to her several times before he finally sat down at the bridge table, and Barrington, to his own surprise, found himself sympathizing with the young man, for whom the bitterest disappointment was in store.

The game which ensued was remarkable for its card distribution. Time after time slams were bid and made, and Lady Gertrude was in her element. Barrington, who partnered Arthur through two rubbers, found him quite expert at the game, and exceedingly tolerant of Barrington's few mistakes. Lady Gertrude, on the other hand, insisted upon a friendly post-mortem every time she and John went down.

They had just started the third rubber, in which Barrington and John were partners, when the telephone bell rang, and a moment or two later Susan entered to say that Lady Gertrude was wanted. Lady Gertrude, whose 'hand' was full of aces and queens, glared at Susan.

'I told you we were not to be interrupted, Susan,' she said.

'Yes, my Lady, but the gentleman said it

was most important.'

'Did he give his name?'

'No, my Lady, I asked him that, but he said it was of no consequence, and that he had a message from Roland.'

Lady Gertrude seemed to give an involuntary start, and Felicity, who had been talking quietly to Lucy, suddenly stopped and gazed across at her mother.

'I think you'd better go, Mother,' said John.

'But — but I don't understand — '

'Let me go, Mother,' said Felicity. 'I can pretend I am you.'

'No — no. I'll go. Please excuse me.'

She rose and went to the telephone in the hall, closing the door behind her. John looked puzzled and disturbed, and the silence was so tense that Barrington thought he had better break it.

'I think I saw you and Felicity riding this morning,' he said to Arthur.

'Oh, did you? Yes, we had a most splendid time. I was foolish enough to challenge Felicity over the only bit of flat country I've seen round here, and she beat me by about three lengths.'

'I didn't,' retorted Felicity. 'You were mean enough to let me win. I don't like winning that way.'

'But I didn't. I nearly came a cropper over that ditch. You were ahead and you couldn't see. And I still owe you sixpence, or was it a bob?'

Lady Gertrude then returned, looking as pale as death.

'It — it was nothing,' she said, and picked up her cards. 'I'm so sorry to have held up the game. Your call, I think, Mr. Barrington.'

'I had called two spades,' said Barrington.

'Yes, of course.'

She fumbled her cards, dropped one on the floor, and generally displayed intense agitation. After that her game went to pieces. She seemed quite unable to concentrate, and time after time had to ask what were trumps. When the rubber was over John tactfully suggested that it was rather late to start a new one, and prevailed upon Felicity to play something on the piano.

Barrington enjoyed the music much more than the bridge, and the Honourable Arthur sat as if spellbound, although Barrington had the feeling that the spell had something physical about it. Finally Lady Gertrude retired with Lucy, and Arthur, seizing the opportunity, asked Felicity if she felt like playing a game of billiards. She looked as if she were about to decline, when she caught her brother's eye, which told her very clearly that he favoured the idea.

'All right,' she said. 'But last time we played you gave me a start of thirty.'

'I'll give you forty in a hundred, and play you double or quits for the sixpence I owe you.'

'A shilling.'

'All right — a shilling.'

Barrington's gaze followed them to the door, and then switched to John's serious face.

'Well, Phil, what do you make of it?' asked John.

'Of what?'

'The telephone message, of course. You saw mother's reaction. She seemed scared out of her life. I must talk about it. The whole thing is getting on my nerves.'

'Yes, I can appreciate that. This business about Roland is most mysterious. First that queer note, and now this message. It must have some significance for your mother, or she wouldn't have gone to the telephone.'

'No. Nor would she have come back in such a bewildered condition. It must mean — it can only mean — that there is a person named Roland whom she has reason to fear. Mother isn't normally an emotional woman — nor a cowardly one, yet she was as shaken tonight as if she had seen a ghost.'

'Or heard one.'

'Yes, but what can one do about it? When she was questioned before about Roland she denied all knowledge of any such person, but tonight her behaviour was quite inconsistent with that declaration.'

'All you can do is to ask her to tell you the truth.'

'I mean to do that, but I have no hope of success. There are so many things she hasn't explained satisfactorily. I cannot believe that she is in any way responsible for my grandfather's death. Such an idea is ridiculous, but why does she behave the way she does?'

'If we knew that the mystery would be nearer a solution. It may be that this further reference to Roland may induce her to be a bit more confidential. Obviously she couldn't say anything with us all present. But I'll tell you one thing — anything to do with this mysterious Roland should be told to Inspector McLean, because I am certain that Roland is his main line of enquiry.'

'But I thought he had dropped the case.'

Barrington gazed at him incredulously.

'You'll have to think again, John. McLean is no nearer to dropping this case than on the day he took it up. That he hasn't been here lately signifies nothing. He's probably collecting odd bits of evidence in some other direction. But we shall see him again before long.'

John nodded and then gave a long sigh.

'I'll have it out with her,' he said. 'We simply can't go on like this. While we are alone there's something else I want to ask you. It's rather personal and I hope you won't be offended.'

'Shoot!' said Barrington with a smile.

'Is there anything between you and Felicity?'

'Why do you ask that?'

'I've got eyes, and I know Felicity. She's been acting rather strangely of late. Until you came she was far from happy — always talking about going on the stage, or at least going away and getting some sort of a job. But she is different now — restless, but happy in a delirious sort of way. I can't think of anything which could cause that state of mind except that she is in love with someone.'

'Couldn't it be Arthur Poynings?'

'No. He's never meant anything to her, although mother prays every night that a miracle may happen. If I'm wrong, Phil, I apologize abjectly.'

'You aren't wrong.'

John's eyes brightened.

'I'm delighted,' he said. 'But there are obstacles.'

'You mean your mother won't consent?'

'Yes. It isn't that she has anything against you, Phil. As a matter of fact I think she likes you; but when she has set her heart upon any line of action wild horses won't drag her from it. She wants Felicity to make what she calls a 'fortunate' marriage and young Poynings has all the qualifications. As a friend, and a prospective relative, I must warn you that there are breakers ahead.'

'I know. Felicity wants me to keep silent until Arthur has left, so please regard this as confidential.'

'Of course. Now I'm going to have a few words with mother, if you'll excuse me. This matter can't wait.'

'I wish you luck,' said Barrington. 'I think I'll go and see how the billiards match is progressing.'

15

Lady Gertrude's preparation for slumber was always a prolonged business. She paid great attention to her fine head of hair, which was quite remarkable for a woman of her age, and a lot of time was employed in removing the powder from her skin with the aid of great quantities of cold cream. Usually she liked to survey her features in the mirror under the very kindly light of a rose-tinted electric lamp. But tonight the face she saw was not one that was calculated to feed her vanity, for the little lines about her eyes seemed deeper, and the eyes themselves anxious and restive. But it was not her slowly fading beauty that was discomfiting, but something far removed from it. With a little sigh she wiped away the cold cream, and then gave a start as there came a rap on the door.

'Who is it?' she called.

'It's me — John.'

'I'm just going to bed.'

'But I must see you, Mother.'

'Just a moment then.'

She coiled up her hair, gave her face a few more rubs, and slipped on a dressing-gown.

'You can come in,' she called.

John entered, and found his mother sitting facing him.

'What is it?' she asked. 'I'm very tired.'

'It's about the telephone call — the message from Roland. Don't you think you ought to explain that?'

'There's nothing to explain. When I went to the telephone there was no one on the line.'

'I see,' said John slowly.

'You don't believe me,' she said harshly.

'No, Mother. I'm sorry to say I don't. If there was no one on the line why did you stay so long?'

'I was trying to get the operator.'

'And did you?'

'Yes. She told me there was no check on incoming calls, and that the caller must have rung off.'

'But why should he, after giving Susan that message?'

'How should I know?' she asked angrily. 'John, I object very strongly to this constant questioning of my acts. Why should I have to explain every single thing I do?'

'Why should you constantly place us all in a most invidious position? You denied going into grandpa's room, until it was brought home to you. You deliberately destroyed that bottle which I intended to hand to the police. Now you have a conversation on the telephone about a message from Roland.'

'I have told you there was no conversation.'

'But you went to the telephone — expecting one.'

'Naturally. I wanted to know what it all meant.'

'You mean you really don't know?'

'I do not.'

John's expression, despite this assurance, was one of complete dissatisfaction. He could not believe that the anonymous caller had rung off, since his mother had gone to the telephone without any delay. And how could one account for her subsequent behaviour, if the facts were as stated. Gertrude, realizing that she had failed to convince him, now produced another weapon from her considerable armoury.

'So I am suspect by my own children,' she said, with a heavy sniff. 'Ever since that dreadful thing happened to grandpa you and Felicity have spied upon my movements — '

'Mother, don't talk such nonsense.'

'It isn't nonsense. You watch me like a cat watching a mouse, as if waiting for me to commit myself in some way or other. I was hoping that this shadow which has fallen over our home would slowly vanish, and that we could all live here together in harmony and happiness, but almost every day some new and distressing suspicion is born. I can't go on like this, and I won't. I think it's unspeakably cruel of you — unspeakably cruel.'

She opened one of the drawers, and took out a very small handkerchief with which she dabbed her eyes. But no longer was John affected by these antics.

'I think it has come to this, Mother,' he said. 'You and I can no longer live together.'

'John, what are you saying?'

'I believe that you are holding back information that may be of vital importance to the police in their investigation. If so it is not only foolish but criminal. I refuse to be a party to that, and so does Lucy. This morning I had a definite offer of a post in the diplomatic service. I have to decide in the next few days. It is in Chile.'

Gertrude stood up and faced her son, no longer wailing, but fiercely resentful.

'If you imagine I had anything to do with my father's death then go to Chile, and I pray I may never see you again. Now go — go — go!'

John went to the door, hesitated for a moment and then closed it behind him.

The next moment Gertrude flung herself on the bed and broke into torrents of real weeping. John could hear it as he passed along the corridor and down the broad staircase. Despite the stand he had made he felt more like the victim than the victor.

In the meantime Barrington had found the billiards match quite amusing, for the Honourable Arthur was as good at billiards as he was at bridge. Now and again he would make a brilliant 'break', and then leave an easy opening for Felicity, who speedily lost control of the balls, and let her opponent in again. It ended as it was bound to — running out in a nice unfinished break of thirty-five.

'That's wiped out my debt,' he said. 'Felicity, you played very well.'

'You know I didn't,' she retorted. 'I've no ideas about the silly game. Phil, you take him on.'

'Not I,' said Barrington. 'I don't know one end of the cue from the other.'

They walked back into the lounge where John was sitting, smoking reflectively.

'Who won?' he asked.

'Arthur, of course,' said Felicity. 'But he cheated.'

'Cheated!'

'He left me all sorts of easy shots, and I

254

missed most of them. He was just playing with me.'

'I assure you I wasn't,' protested Arthur.

Barrington, realizing that there was small chance of getting Felicity to himself in the circumstances, gazed at the clock.

'Getting near my bed-time,' he said. 'If you'll excuse me I think I'll be getting back.'

'In that case,' said John, 'I'll walk a bit of the way with you. I should enjoy some fresh air.'

'Do,' said Barrington.

As soon as they had left the house John satisfied Barrington's unvoiced curiosity.

'It was rather a bad scene,' he said. 'Mother lost her temper and so did I. She insists that nobody was on the telephone when she answered it. That's the position, Phil.'

'Perhaps that is true.'

'No. I think there was a message, but she is determined to trust no one. When I threatened to part company with her she flew into a rage and told me to go.'

'You weren't serious, were you?'

'Yes — quite serious. I had an offer from the Foreign Office this morning — a post in Chile. It's not a very good post, nor the sort of place to take Lucy to. I should have declined it but for this new fact, and now I am inclined to accept. At any rate I have a few days to think it over. That brings me to another matter, which concerns you.'

'Me?'

'Yes. Under the Trust now being set up, I shall ultimately enjoy the income from the estate, so my future is assured. Deepwater Cottage, and a parcel of land at that end of the lake, was left to me by my father, and is not included in the property under the Trust. I propose to make this over to Felicity on her wedding day. I mention this now because the need of a suitable home might induce you both to delay the wedding. I don't want it delayed. I want Felicity to feel, and be, independent. Also I want her to be happy, and I'm certain I can rely upon you for that.'

'That's most generous of you, John.'

'Nonsense! You've done more for me than you know, and there's no one in this world I would rather see married to my sister. Good luck to both of you.'

Barrington stopped and gripped his friend's hand. Later when they parted he laughed loudly at this totally unexpected piece of good fortune, for it had the effect of dispersing the one cloud on his mind.

The following day was one of continuous

work and great contentment of mind. It was almost impossible to realize that the 'Grub Street' days were over, and that this delightful retreat would soon be shared with Felicity. Even if the novel turned out to be a flop he believed himself capable of maintaining a wife in a modest way by less ambitious efforts.

It was late in the evening when, to his great joy, he heard a 'coo-ee' in the distance, and stared through the open window to see Felicity swinging down the side of the lake. He left his overworked typewriter, and hurried across the lawn to meet her. In a minute or two she was clasped in his arms.

'Thank heavens to have you alone!' he said. 'How did you manage to get away?'

'He's gone.'

'Gone! But I thought he was staying for a few days?'

'That was the programme, but I had to make it clear to him that I had other interests in life. Poor Arthur! He looked quite bewildered, as if he couldn't understand any woman throwing away a prospective viscount.'

'I hope you treated him gently?'

'Oh yes. I didn't actually tell him that there was someone else in the offing, but I think he guessed. Naturally mother was amazed, and annoyed.'

'Do you think she guesses — about us?'

'I don't know. Phil, darling, John told me about his plans regarding the cottage. I almost cried with joy, because although I was ready to be regaled with fish and chips, I've always loved Deepwater. It's quite big enough for two of us, and even for some possible additions, don't you think?'

Barrington was gazing at her happy flushed face.

'You're lovely, Felicity,' he said. 'A lovely thing in a lovely setting. Why has all this come to me? I've done nothing to deserve it. Hitherto I imagined that my *magnum opus* was the only thing which mattered, but now for two pins I'd tear it up and burn it.'

'I'll see that you don't,' replied Felicity. 'To make it a balanced work you'll have to introduce a love scene, and you can practice on me. Oh, dear, there's mother to be told. I keep trying to forget that.'

'Perhaps she won't be as antagonistic as you imagine.'

'She'll be worse — now that I've sent Arthur away so unceremoniously. She so hates to be thwarted in any project close to her heart, and that one was very close, although she spoke little about it.'

'You think she will oppose our marriage?'

'Yes. Last night John had a fearful quarrel with her. I expect he told you?'

'He did. Very curious — that telephone business.'

'Everything is curious, and mother is making it worse by her behaviour. If John takes that job in Chile, and you and I get married, she will be utterly alone.'

'You forget that we can't get married without her consent.'

'It's the last thing in the world I am likely to forget, but I think I can force her hand.'

'How?'

'By threatening to live with you — in sin, as they call it — until I can marry without anyone's consent.'

Barrington shook his head. Eager as he was to terminate his bachelorhood, this notion left a bad taste in his mouth.

'No, my darling,' he said. 'I can understand your resentment against anyone who opposes your freedom of action, but that solution to the problem is cheap and sordid. If your mother should choose to behave badly in this there's no reason why you should do the same. I can't bear to think of you in that role. Let's keep the party clean, even at the cost of some happiness.'

Felicity was glum for a few moments

and then she smiled and raised his hand to her lips.

'You're right, Phil,' she said. 'And I'm wrong. You see how like mother I am — wanting to jump in and hit back with everything I've got. We'll try sweet persuasion, and take what's coming.'

'We will, but when?'

'Tomorrow morning, when she's got over today's bitter disappointment. Now you get back to that typewriter, while I read the new chapters of the book. That's what I'm aching to do.'

They went into the sitting-room, and Felicity took the new batch of manuscript and made herself comfortable in an armchair. The best part of an hour passed, the silence broken only by the tapping of the typewriter, and then Felicity gave a little sigh and laid the manuscript on the table.

'Well?' asked Barrington. 'How bad is it?'

'You know how good it is. You couldn't help knowing. It's bound to be an enormous success. I'd stake my life on it.'

'You would be very foolish. Plenty of better books have been complete failures — economically. But if you like it I am well rewarded. At least I have a public of one.'

She came across to him and linked her arms round his neck.

'No more for today, dearest,' she crooned. 'I have to go back to dinner, but afterwards I'll sneak out. Let's go somewhere — in the old car — the place you took me to before, where I made love to you so shamelessly.'

'Did you?'

'You know I did, illustrious fibber, and you were scared out of your life.'

'You'd scare any man when you get going. I'd like to know just how you acquired that technique.'

'I inherited it on my mother's side. My father was rather like you — very unemotional until someone warmed him up. Well, now I must be going, but I'll be back about eight-thirty. Have that car ready, with all the loose bits firmly lashed together.'

They walked together by the side of the colourful lake, until they came to the humpbacked bridge, where Barrington kissed her warmly, and watched her until she disappeared from view.

16

During the past week McLean's dossier of the Grayling case had grown very considerably since his return from the West Country, and this was mainly due to a piece of evidence which arrived at Scotland Yard, having been forwarded to him by the Dorchester Constabulary who had received it from old Mr. Lansbury, following a letter from McLean. As he drew it from its envelope and read the short accompanying note, McLean gave a little sigh of pleasure.

'The missing link,' he said. 'I had a feeling it might exist.'

'What is it, sir?' asked Sergeant Brook.

'The negative of that snapshot in Lansbury's album, part of the print of which had been cut away.'

'The Tower print.'

'Yes. Lansbury found it with a lot of other negatives. It shows the figure which Miss Lansbury cut out — the one she designated as 'O'. See for yourself.'

Brook took the negative and held it up to the light. It was a very good negative, despite the passage of the years, and he could see clearly the unmistakable military uniform.

'Our man at last,' he said.

'I think so. I want an enlargement of this as quickly as possible.'

'The man only?'

'No. The whole thing.'

The enlargement was produced by the photographic department at remarkable speed, and McLean scrutinized the male figure. He was a tall, dark, handsome fellow of about twenty-five years of age, and fortunately he was standing slightly at an angle, which enabled McLean to read the badge on his shoulder, and to see the two 'pips' of his rank.

'Lieutenant Oliver something of the —— shires,' he said. 'That's a long distance on our way, but still a few steps from the target. Searching War Office records for thirty years back is not going to be easy, but it has to be done.'

Sergeant Brook was put in charge of this operation, and he was away from the office for three days, after which he came back with a smile on his broad countenance.

'I've got it, sir!' he said. 'But you're going to be surprised and disappointed.'

'Go on. What's the snag?'

'His full name is Oliver George Galbraith.'

'What!' gasped McLean.

'Yes, sir, the same name as the man whom Beatrice Lansbury is said to have married.'

'That's remarkable. And the snag?'

'The snag is he was killed in action in August 1917.'

'Are you sure?'

'I saw the entry in the casualty list, and I saw a deposition made by a brother officer who was near him when he was blown up.'

'Did you take that officer's name?'

'Yes — and his address.'

McLean frowned at this unexpected result. At first it looked like a set-back, but on reflection he was not so displeased.

'I was a little off the track,' he said. 'But this does make sense after all. Those Scottish enquiries failed to bring any information about Galbraith. No one where the alleged Mrs. Galbraith lived had ever seen her husband. Yes, I think we have moved yet another step forward. But I want to know the exact circumstances in which Galbraith was killed. Where does that fellow officer live?'

'At Woking. He has a motor business there.'

'We'll go and see him.'

Two hours later McLean was inside the office of the ex-officer. He was a solid-looking man with but one arm, and he looked at the two visitors with considerable interest.

'What can I do for you, Inspector?' he asked.

'You are Captain Wilton, late of the —— shires?'

'Very late indeed. I've had this business for twenty years.'

'Did you once know a man named Oliver Galbraith, who was in your regiment?'

'Yes.'

'Will you look at this photograph and tell me if he is the man depicted?'

Wilton gave a glance at the photograph.

'Yes, that's Galbraith.'

'I understand you were near him when he met his death?'

Wilton looked embarrassed, and was silent for a few moments, while McLean watched him narrowly.

'He wasn't killed,' said Wilton.

'But his name was in the casualty lists, and you made a declaration at the time.'

'That's true. The fact is, Inspector, I did a thing which has worried me ever since. That man disgraced the regiment, and our battalion in particular. He deserted on the eve of battle — only an hour or two before zero hour. The C.O. never knew, and we never meant him to know. The junior officers met together and decided we would spare the old man the real facts, which would have broken his heart, for the regiment had a most gallant record. After the war we tried to find him, but there was never a trace. Heaven knows what happened to him.'

'Had he no relatives?'

'I don't know. None of us knew much about him.'

'Did he ever mention a girl with whom he might have been in love?'

'If he did I've forgotten.'

'Were you ever stationed near Dorchester?'

'Oh yes — within a few miles.'

'Did you ever go to a place called Strafford Park?'

'I don't think so. No, it's too long ago to remember.'

'At least you can tell me what sort of a man Galbraith was.'

'He was a queer chap. Very moody at times, and lively at others. You never knew how he would react. While we were in England he was a damned good soldier, but when it came to the real test he let us down. That's the way it is, you can never tell what stuff a man is made of until he is called to face death. Galbraith just couldn't take it.'

'Is this a good photograph of him?'

'Excellent.'

McLean came away feeling that he was now set on an even course. But presuming that Galbraith was still alive, where and how could he be located? In thirty years he might have changed beyond all recognition. To advertise for him would be useless, since a man with his record would not be likely to respond, no matter how cunningly the advertisement was worded.

'I was wrong about the snag,' ruminated Brook. 'If he wasn't killed in France he could have married Miss Lansbury, couldn't he?'

'He could, but why should he? She had no money except her pension, and she was over twenty years older. No, I don't believe that. As I see it the only line open to us which is likely to produce quick results is to put pressure on Lady Gertrude. So far I have treated her very lightly, but I have some questions to put to her which may shake her considerably. I think we'll run down to Dorchester this evening, and pay our respects to her early tomorrow morning.'

This plan was put into effect, after McLean had telephoned the hotel where he had last stayed, and rather late in the evening they reached the Bull and enjoyed a belated meal. Later McLean decided to pay a visit to the chief constable, and Brook was left to enjoy himself as best he could.

McLean found his colleague at his private address, listening to a broadcast performance of an opera. He, too, had dined, and seemed more inclined for a talk than anything else.

'Anyway, I know that opera from the first note to the last,' he said. 'So you're back again on the trail?'

'I've never been off the trail. What about those two men who have been watching Strafford Park?'

'I had to take them off yesterday. During the week they were on duty they had nothing whatever to report, except that the writing fellow has fallen for Miss Medding. I couldn't keep them on the job any longer, as two other men fell sick. In any case it had to come to an end some time, unless there were more substantial grounds for believing that anyone was in danger at the house. You don't think that, do you?'

'I don't know. This is a curious case. Since I last saw you a good deal of new evidence has come to light, evidence which convinces me that Lady Gertrude is considerably involved.'

The chief constable raised his eyebrows.

'You surely don't mean in the actual murder?' he asked.

'No, but she knows the man who sent her

that anonymous note on the night of the murder, despite all her denials.'

'You mean Roland?'

'His real name is Oliver.'

'Oliver! A Roland for an Oliver.'

'Precisely. No doubt he thought she would understand the transposition.'

'I should have thought so, if she remembered Oliver.'

'That, too, she denies, but I can't believe her.'

'What about the 'dark tower' nonsense?'

'It wasn't nonsense. There is a dark tower. Would you like to see it?'

'I certainly should.'

McLean quickly produced the enlarged photograph, which was rolled up in his overcoat pocket, and the chief constable examined it with interest.

'Where is this place?' he asked.

'In what once were the grounds of the house where Lady Gertrude lived at the time, with her parents.'

'That was damned clever of you.'

'Not really. It was partly luck.'

'And this man in uniform?'

'Oliver.'

'Are you sure?'

'Quite sure. At the top of that old tower the names of Gertrude and Oliver are inscribed

269

together, with the date — May 1917. It's interesting to reflect that on that date the man to whom Gertrude was engaged, and whom she married later, was in France. So we find her consorting with this handsome fellow a few months after she was engaged, to the intense disapproval of her parents.'

'Is that a guess?'

'No. The person who took the original snapshot was her old nurse, and in the facsimile print the man was cut out of the picture. For what other reason than that the nurse feared it might be seen by the parents?'

'Yes, that's a fair deduction. But isn't it carrying things a bit far to assume that this man — Oliver — nursed a deep grievance for thirty years, and then came back and murdered one or both the parents?'

'Not on the evidence. This young man subsequently went abroad believing that the girl whom he loved would wait for him. But she didn't wait. Her parents were keen that she should marry the man with the title, and they won the day. That nonsensical message as you call it was intended to remind Gertrude about that visit to the tower, and I'm sure she must have remembered it. I think I know what happened in that tower, and why Gertrude is prepared to make false statements. I think I know why Oliver waited all those years to take his revenge, but that part is yet theoretical, and I hate to discuss theories. But tomorrow I am going to produce a few facts to Lady Gertrude, which may put an end to her present attitude.'

'I see. You think she may know where Oliver can be found?'

'That is my hope.'

'And if not?'

'Then I shall have to plod along by the more circuitous route.'

'What a tenacious fellow you are. I'm rather glad you haven't the task of investigating the dark areas of my life. But did you discover why Sir John rang up to give you a message, and later called it off?'

'No. I think I may have to go into that. But wouldn't you rather play a game of chess than talk shop?'

'Not a bad idea. Help yourself to my tobacco while I hunt up the chessmen.'

The preliminary orthodox opening moves having been made, McLean suddenly launched a most unexpected attack, which his opponent could only counter by an exchange of pieces. There seemed no method in this slaughter until suddenly the chief constable found his king in imminent danger, and the supporting pieces badly placed.

'That's interesting,' he mused. 'I must think this out.'

'Do. But you should never have taken that knight of mine.'

'Damn it — you flung him at me.'

McLean smiled and watched his friend puzzling over the dangerous situation. Then from outside there came the double ring of the telephone bell.

'May be the office,' said the chief constable. 'But I hope not. Now what the devil do I do here?'

A moment or two later there was a tap on the door and the buxom housekeeper entered.

'Excuse me, sir,' she said. 'It's Superintendent Rankin. He would like to speak to you.'

'Thank you, Mrs. Wren. I'll come at once.'

The chief constable sighed as he rose from his chair, took one look at the chessboard, and then, with an apology to McLean, went out to the telephone. He was absent for quite a long time, and when he returned McLean judged that the game of chess would remain unfinished for a while, for his friend's expression was one of great seriousness.

'Quite a coincidence,' he said. 'You've arrived here at a most opportune moment. A call has come from Sir John Medding. He says that his sister has been kidnapped, and Mr. Barrington attacked and injured. I told Rankin to hold his hand for a few minutes as you are here and would probably want to deal with it.'

'I certainly do,' said McLean. 'Where is Barrington?'

'At his cottage. They have sent for a doctor.'

'I'll go at once,' said McLean. 'Unfortunately I have little chance of finding Sergeant Brook. Will you get your people to search for him — someone who knows him by sight. He's probably in some pub.'

'I'll try. If I'm not successful shall I send you another man who can write shorthand?'

'Please. This is an amazing development, but it proves one thing — that Mr. Oliver Galbraith is not far away.'

McLean got into his car, which was parked outside the house, and in a few moments he was driving at great speed towards Strafford Park. It was pitch dark, and once out of the town there was no traffic to hinder his quick progress. Instead of going straight to the Hall he passed it and stopped his car outside Deepwater Cottage, where another car was also parked. When he rang the bell it was Sir John who opened the door.

'Inspector McLean!' he ejaculated.

'Yes. I happened to be with the chief constable when your message came. Is that the doctor's car?'

'Yes. He is with Barrington now.'

'Nothing serious I hope?'

'No. A scalp injury which knocked him out for a bit. I think it is being stitched up.'

'Tell me briefly what happened.'

'I know very little. My sister took her evening meal with us at the Hall, and at about eight-fifteen she left us. She did not say where she was going, but I rather suspected she might have made some appointment with Barrington, to whom she is more or less engaged. It was shortly after half-past eight that I heard the telephone ringing and answered it. I heard a curiously weak voice at the other end, and scarcely recognized it as Barrington's, until he told me that he had been attacked and was in a bad state. Then suddenly the line went dead. I hurried to the cottage and found him lying on the couch beside the telephone, with blood all over his hair and face. I rang up the doctor, who came along within a few minutes. I didn't worry Philip with questions because he did not seem to be in a state to answer them. That's all I know.'

McLean nodded and went to the lounge

274

where he found a middle-aged man fastening a bandage round Barrington's head. The patient was now sitting up on the settee, with his eyes wide open, and on a chair beside him was a bowl full of gory water. The doctor tied the bandage before he turned and saw the intruder.

'The police?' he asked.

'Yes. Inspector McLean. What's the damage?'

'Nothing serious, but he must stay quiet for a day or two. Bound to be a bit of concussion. Some bruises on his legs, but nothing broken there. I shouldn't bother him with too many questions just now.'

'That's nonsense,' protested Barrington. 'My head aches like hell, but my mind is clear enough. I'm fit to answer any questions, and the sooner the better.'

'It's rather necessary,' said McLean to the doctor. 'But I'll take care, and get him to bed.'

The doctor delved into his pocket and took out a card.

'You may like to have this,' he said. 'I'll come and see him again tomorrow, but I must hurry away now, as I have a maternity case on hand. As for you, Mr. Barrington, get all the sleep you can.'

'I will.'

When the doctor had gone Sir John entered the room.

'Any objection?' he asked McLean. 'I should like to hear what happened.'

'Naturally. Now Mr. Barrington, what happened?'

'I had a date with Felicity. She was to come here after she had had a meal, and we were going for a run out in my car. I had intended to have the car ready, but I did a spot of work and left things to the last moment. It was twenty minutes past eight when I went to the boat house which I use as a garage. The sun had set and it was not quite dark. As I opened the door I saw Felicity coming down the far side of the lake towards the cottage. I waved and shouted to her to attract her attention, so that she should know where I was, but she didn't hear and continued to walk on. I was about to shout again when, to my amazement, a man dashed from behind a clump of pines, just in her rear, and clapped a hand over her mouth. I saw something white in his hand — a handkerchief I think — and almost instantly Felicity ceased to struggle. Then he caught her up bodily, and hurried through the trees. I turned and ran as hard as I could towards the drive, hoping to intercept him, but as I reached it — just short of the cottage — a car appeared coming towards me at increasing speed. I stood slap in the centre of the road, and waved my hands. I could see a grim face through the windscreen, but not very clearly. The swine never swerved an inch, but came dead at me. At the last moment I realized he meant to run me down, and I made a wild leap for safety. But either the wing or the bumper must have caught me, for I was projected backwards or sideways and cracked my head on a tree. I think I must have lain on the ground for some time, bleeding like a pig, but finally I dragged myself into the cottage and rang up Sir John. He came very quickly, thank God, and telephoned for the doctor.'

'You did not see any car when you went to the boat house?' asked McLean.

'No. But if it had been there I shouldn't have seen it, for I went out by the back way.'

'Can you describe the man at all?'

'No. There was poor light, and from the boat house to the spot where the attack took place it is over a hundred yards across the water.'

'Can you say whether he was short or tall?'

'Tall — definitely, and powerful, for he lifted Felicity with the greatest ease, and actually ran with her in his arms.'

'What about clothing?'

'A dark suit of some sort, and I am fairly certain he was wearing no hat.'

'Did anyone else know that you were expecting Felicity at about that time?'

'I don't think so. I certainly told no one, and I'm fairly certain Felicity didn't.'

'No,' interjected John. 'She said nothing to any other member of the family.'

'Now, about the car — did you notice the number plate?'

'No. I was too intent on trying to see the face of the driver.'

'Was he clean-shaven?'

'I think so, but he was completely in the shadow.'

'You did not see any sign of Felicity?'

'No.'

'Can you describe the car at all?'

'It was a large saloon — dark paint. There was a lot of chromium plating at the front — rather like an American car. It came at me so fast I had no time to notice any details.'

'You think Felicity was doped into helplessness?'

'Yes. I'm sure there was a handkerchief, or white pad, in the man's hand. It all took place in a twinkling, while I stood there completely paralysed.'

'I don't wonder,' said McLean. 'This is a most audacious business, and I must confess I didn't quite expect such a thing.'

'But we told you about the man whom Felicity had seen in the park,' said Barrington. 'And you did nothing. I think you should have done something.'

'But I did,' said McLean, smiling. 'Until two days ago this estate was under observation by two experienced detectives. They were taken off only because there were other urgent calls.'

'But I didn't know,' said Barrington.

'They had instructions to keep out of sight.'

'I'm sorry,' said Barrington. 'I shouldn't have spoken like that, but you can imagine how I feel about this. Felicity and I had made plans to get married. It's ghastly to reflect how useless I was.'

'You've no need to reproach yourself.'

'But I have. I should never have let her cross the park alone so late in the evening. I should have gone to meet her. I have had two warnings and have disregarded them. Inspector, what do you make of it? Is she in danger?'

'She may not be.'

'That may mean equally that she may be.

But why is she in danger? What has she done to be treated like this?'

'I'm not omniscient,' said McLean. 'All I can tell you is that I have a very good idea who is behind these mysterious happenings. That's all I can say at the moment. I suggest that you now obey the doctor's orders, and try to get some sleep. Sir John, will you give him some assistance?'

'Of course I will.'

'Oh, there's just one point, Mr. Barrington,' said McLean. 'I should like to know the exact spot where you saw the man appear first.'

'It's on the north side of the lake, almost exactly opposite the boat house. You will find a group of Scotch pine. He was concealed behind one of them, and he came upon Felicity just as she was passing the last of them.'

'Thanks.'

McLean left the cottage and took a powerful electric torch from his car. It did not take him long to recognize the trees which Barrington had mentioned, and he began to search the almost bare ground in their vicinity, for anything which might serve as a clue. He was thus engaged when he heard a car arrive outside the cottage, and saw the glare of headlights. A minute or two later a vague form, behind an electric torch, came towards him, and very soon he was able to make out Brook's large silhouette.

'Good for you, Brook!' he called.

Brook joined him, breathing deeply.

'I had a bit of a pub crawl,' he said, 'and then went back to the hotel. I found a message there, and rang up headquarters who sent a car round. This is a bit of a corker, isn't it?'

'Depends upon what you mean by 'corker'. This is where the attacker was hiding. No chance of footprints, but we may find something. Look for cigarette-ends, anything that is likely to help. You start from the other end.'

The search went on in silence, until at last the two searchers came together, with nothing to reward them for their pains. Then McLean moved out to the worn path close to the water's edge.

'Somewhere about here the fellow came up behind his victim. Ah, this looks like it!'

The ray from the torch fell on a disturbed patch of earth. There were no actual footprints, but there were a few clustered impressions of a small heel, which could only have been made in such circumstances as existed. They were all within a square yard.

'Nothing here but the disturbance, sir,' said Brook.

'No. From here she was carried bodily to a waiting car. I suspect that the car was driven off the drive to a spot where there was cover. We may be able to find wheeltracks or oil drips where the car stood. You take that line, I'll take this.'

Their line of advance took them away from the cottage, and to the left of the termination of the drive. They were very close to the drive when Brook stopped and called McLean.

'Wheeltracks here, sir, and oil,' he said. 'Well out of sight of the cottage, too.'

McLean saw the oil and the tracks, and was satisfied. He went round the site, with the ray of the torch lighting up the ground, and then stooped and picked up a very small object, which he examined with interest.

'A sweet?' asked Brook, as he saw what lay in McLean's palm.

'Some sort of lozenge, I think — half-sucked. It was probably spat out by the car-driver when he left the car. It couldn't have been the girl because she was unconscious. Keep that, and I'll have it analysed.'

Later they moved on down the drive, and had no difficulty in finding the spot where Barrington sustained his injury. There was blood on the base of a large elm tree, and much more on the drive itself. But nowhere was there anything which might have fallen from the car at the time of the impact.

'That seems to be all,' said McLean. 'Where the car went to is anybody's guess. We'll make another search in daylight, but I have small hope of any better result. Let's get back to the cottage and see what is happening there.'

When they reached the cottage Barrington was in bed, and Sir John tidying up the lounge. He looked at McLean questioningly, and McLean shook his head.

'No clue at all?' asked Sir John.

'Nothing worth talking about. Is Mr. Barrington comfortable?'

'Yes. I suggested staying here for the night, but he won't hear of it. Says he'll be up and about tomorrow.'

'That would be very unwise, but young men in love are difficult to restrain, and in such circumstances as these I'm not surprised that he wants to be up and doing — if indeed there is anything he can do. I presume it was a great shock to Lady Gertrude?'

'My mother doesn't know yet,' replied John. 'I came straight here on getting Barrington's message.'

'Then I think it would be as well to tell her without further delay. Perhaps I can run you back to the Hall?'

'I should be glad.'

A few minutes later they all entered McLean's car, and made the short journey to the Hall.

17

'If you have no objection, Sir John, I should like to be present when you tell your mother the bad news,' said McLean, when they were about to enter the house.

John gave him a quick glance.

'Very well, Inspector,' he said. 'But I'm afraid she will take it badly.'

'Naturally, but I want to ask her a few questions — afterwards.'

They all entered the big lounge, to find Lady Gertrude sitting alone under a standard lamp, reading a book.

'Oh, John!' she exclaimed. 'Where have you — ?'

She stopped abruptly as she realized that her son was not alone, and glanced from McLean to Sergeant Brook in the rear.

'Good evening, Inspector,' she said. 'What is all this, John? You look as pale as a sheet. Is something wrong?'

'Yes, Mother. I've bad news.'

Lady Gertrude laid the book on the table beside her chair.

'Go on,' she said, 'tell me. I'm used to bad news.'

'It's Felicity — she has been kidnapped.'

'Kidnapped!' she gasped. 'You can't be serious.'

'She was overpowered near Barrington's cottage, and taken away in a car. Barrington tried to intercept the driver, and was knocked down by the car and injured. He managed to crawl to the cottage, and telephoned me to come at once. I didn't want to tell you until I had some more details.'

Lady Gertrude seemed completely stunned. Her lips moved but no sound came from them for a few moments. McLean, who was watching her closely, knew that this was no piece of acting. She was genuinely horror-stricken.

'I — I don't understand it,' she muttered. 'What was Felicity doing at the cottage? Why didn't she tell us she was going?'

'You would have known tomorrow morning,' said John. 'They are in love with each other, and Philip intended to see you tomorrow morning.'

'See me?'

'To get your consent to their marriage.'

'What nonsense is this? I have other plans for Felicity. But all this is beside the point. Felicity must be found at once Inspector, what are you going to do about this — what are you going to do?'

286

'In the first place I want to ask you a few questions,' said McLean.

'Questions! What good will questions do at such a moment?'

'They may help. I believe I know the person responsible, and I think you also know.'

Lady Gertrude stared at him with well-marked resentment.

'Just what are you suggesting, Inspector?' she asked.

'I suggest that there is a man who has struck at least once at your family before this incident. Would you like to see him?'

'See him? What do you mean?'

McLean produced the enlargement of the snapshot which he had shown the chief constable, and handed it to Lady Gertrude, who unrolled it, and stared at it fixedly. The hands which held it trembled visibly.

'Do you remember the day that photograph was taken?' asked McLean.

'No.'

'But you remember the scene it depicts, don't you?'

'Yes. It is our old garden at Seething Manor.'

'And do you not remember the soldier who is standing on your right?'

'No. I can't say I do.'

'Then I must aid your memory. His name is Oliver Galbraith. Does that help matters?'

'No. But I presume he was one of the many soldiers who accepted my parents' hospitality.'

'That is correct. Were you not on very friendly terms with that young officer?'

'I have told you I don't remember him, nor many of the others who came to our house.'

'I'm sorry I can't accept that. In that room at the top of the tower your two names are linked together. It was your old nurse who took that snapshot, but when she made the small print she was careful to cut off the soldier. Why, do you think, did she do that?'

'How can I say?'

'Was it because your parents objected to him — and his attentions to you at a time when you were engaged to a man of title?'

'You have no right to suggest that.'

McLean gazed at her fixedly.

'In view of what has happened here recently, and tonight, I have every right to ask you such questions, if they are likely to help me locate a cold-blooded murderer and kidnapper. Won't you grant me that?'

'Yes — yes, of course. Anything to find my daughter.'

'Good! Now will you admit that this man made violent love to you?'

Lady Gertrude looked at her son, whose grim face looked as if it were carved in white marble.

'Why must I have all that revived?' she asked emotionally. 'I was young and impulsive, and it was wartime. Oliver was killed in action, and that makes all your suspicions wrong.'

'You believe he was killed — even after you received a note which should have convinced you to the contrary. That note which said, 'Childe Roland to the dark tower came'. Didn't you connect that with Oliver and the tower in your old garden?'

'No — not at first.'

'But you did afterwards?'

'Yes, but I thought it came from someone who might have known Oliver. I didn't want the whole thing revived, when it happened so long ago. Anyway, he's dead, and that should close the matter.'

'But it doesn't, because he isn't dead, but very much alive.'

'That's impossible. His name was in the casualty list.'

'I know, but it wasn't true. Your Oliver

was a deserter, and his fellow officers, out of regard for the honour of their regiment, covered up his crime. Was there an understanding between you? Did you in fact promise to wait for him?'

'I — I may have done.'

'And did he come back — when the war was over?'

'No. I have never seen him since — since the last time he came to Seething, just before he went abroad.'

'Did you write to him after that?'

'Yes — a few times.'

'And later you were married, although you still loved the other man?'

'No, I didn't love him any longer.'

'Did you write and tell him so?'

'I can't remember.'

'Is it a fact that he was forbidden to come to the house, and that you saw him secretly?'

'Yes.'

'Then he must have hated your parents for their opposition?'

'Yes.'

'I presume from that photograph that your old nurse was in your confidence?'

'Yes.'

'You have said you have not seen Galbraith since he went abroad, but have you heard from him, apart from that note about 'Roland'?'

Gertrude was about to deny that she had when she saw John's eyes fixed on her relentlessly. She hesitated.

'You must tell him, Mother,' said John.

'I — I received a curious message two nights ago,' said Gertrude. 'It came through the parlourmaid who answered the telephone. She said someone wanted to speak to me, and that he had a message from Roland.'

'Did you go to the telephone?'

'Yes.'

'Well, what was the message?'

'There was nobody there. I rang up enquiries and tried to find out who the caller was, but they said they didn't know.'

'Why didn't you tell me that?' asked McLean. 'Did you imagine that was also a practical joke?'

'Yes — yes. I thought Oliver was dead. I told you so. I thought he was dead. I — I can't stand any more. I feel — '

She pressed her hand to her heart, and closed her eyes. John hurried to the chair and caught her just as she seemed about to fall off it. He looked at McLean appealingly, and McLean gave her the benefit of the doubt.

'I'm sorry,' he said. 'But those questions were imperative. There are still a few details

291

about which I am in doubt, but they can wait. Brook, ring that bell.'

Susan arrived in response to the ring. She looked aghast at the sight of her mistress in such straits. Sir John sent her for some water, and a few minutes later Lady Gertrude recovered her senses. She asked to be helped to her room, and her son and Susan ranged themselves on each side of her, and escorted her out of the room.

'Quite a different story now,' said Brook, as he put away his note-book. 'Had you finished with her?'

'No. She decided to finish with me. I don't doubt she was not feeling well, but I think the faint was a strategical move. She needs time to think, and I have no option than to concede it. Our next move is the same as it has been for some time — to find Mr. Oliver Galbraith, with the least possible delay.'

'I can see that, sir,' said Brook. 'But where do we start?'

McLean didn't know. A police appeal over the broadcasting system seemed to him to be useless, without many more details of the man and the car he had used. The old photograph of Galbraith would serve little purpose, for in thirty years a man could be changed beyond recognition. Advertising for Felicity was no more promising since the kidnapper would take great care that she was not seen by any other person. With nothing more to be done at the house he decided to get back to Dorchester, and sleep on the matter.

Sir John came back a few minutes later. He looked very disturbed, not to say embarrassed, and McLean felt very sorry for him in the circumstances.

'Your mother has been very indiscreet in this matter,' said McLean. 'To cover up a certain episode in her life she has denied facts in this case, which should have been told to me at the start.'

'I appreciate that,' replied Sir John. 'But I assure you they were facts outside my own knowledge. But even now there is much I don't understand. Is it natural for a bitter frustrated man to wait thirty years to avenge himself on the persons he held responsible for his own disappointment?'

'Not very natural. But there might be circumstances in which it could happen.'

'I don't follow.'

'When the frustrated man nurses his hate, until it overcomes his will to resist his subconscious desire, especially if something should happen, after many years, to upset the balance of his mind.'

Sir John shook his head.

'You leave me in the dark. Did something happen to this man — Galbraith — to set him off on a course of murder?'

'I think so, but I'd prefer not to discuss that at the moment, as I have no definite proof.'

'One question before you leave, Inspector. About my sister — is she in great danger?'

'I am inclined to think she isn't. But we are dealing with a man who is certainly not normal, and it is not safe to attempt to predict his next move.'

18

Felicity's experiences that night were such as she had never dreamed of in her wildest nightmares. She regained consciousness to be painfully aware of a dull headache, and a sensation of extreme chilliness. Then she realized that she was lying on a rather hard bed, in a room or chamber which had no windows of any kind, and that the illumination was due to two candles wedged into the tops of large bottles, which stood on a painted chest of drawers. Beside the bottles were a jug and a drinking glass, and reposing on a cheap kind of chair was her handbag.

It took her quite a little time to recall the sudden and violent attack which had been made upon her, and the application of that suffocating pad which had been clapped over her nose and mouth. So swiftly had it dulled her senses that she had never even seen the face of the person responsible. It seemed to have happened but a short time ago, but when she looked at her wrist-watch she found that hours had passed since then, for it was now a quarter past eleven. Three hours or fifteen, for she had no means of telling whether it was night or morning.

Apart from the bed, the table and the chair there were no other furnishings, except for a worn rug on the cement floor. Opposite the foot of the bed there was a stout-looking door, studded with nails, and equipped with an enormous lock, and behind the head of the bed there were signs that a similar door had been bricked up in the past, and white-washed.

Burning with thirst she dragged herself from the bed and staggered to the table. The jug, as she had hoped, was full of water, and she poured some into the glass and drank it with a great sense of relief. When she examined her handbag she found that nothing had been taken from it. Even the four pounds in notes were intact. Staring into the small mirror she was shocked at her dishevelled appearance, and she proceeded to do something to her hair with the comb which the bag contained.

With her brain now functioning normally, she pondered the meaning of this abduction, but she hadn't got very far along these lines before she was aware of approaching footsteps — footsteps that echoed curiously and increased in volume until suddenly they stopped and a key rattled noisily in the lock. Then the door opened, and a tall man entered the room, carrying a dish in one hand. All she could see of his face was a pair of dark penetrating eyes and a very high forehead, beyond which was scanty grey hair, for the rest of his features were covered by a handkerchief which had been folded from corner to corner, and the ends tied behind his head.

'So you're awake,' he said, as he placed the dish on the table. 'I've brought you some sandwiches. I expect you are hungry?'

Felicity made no reply to this civil remark, but edged away from him until she was close to the wall.

'Oh, there's no need to be scared,' he said. 'I want you to be as comfortable as possible in the circumstances.'

'Who are you?' she asked.

'Someone out of the past. You wouldn't understand.'

'But I want to understand. I'm not used to being drugged and abducted.'

'No, I suppose not. You're used to the soft life of the rich and privileged. No inconveniences for you, eh? No doubts about where the next meal is coming from. I could keep you on bread and water, and see how you liked it, but there's nothing sadistic about me. What's your name?'

'Does it matter?'

'No. All that matters is that you are Lady Gertrude's daughter. Aren't you going to eat? They're quite good sandwiches, cut thin enough for a princess.'

Felicity gave a glance at the dish and shook her head. The whole situation puzzled and terrified her, for there was something sinister in that dead level, rather hoarse, voice.

'Why have you done this?' she asked. 'So far as I am aware I have done you no harm.'

'That's true. But there's an old saying concerning the sins of the fathers, and that includes the other half of the marital pact.'

'I believe I know who you are. You're the man who sent my mother a note, on the night when my grandfather was poisoned.'

'So you know all about that?'

'Yes.'

'And your mother, of course, denied that she knew anything about Childe Roland, who came to the dark tower?'

'Yes.'

'Very astute of her. But I think her memory was equal to the occasion. I wonder if you know how like your mother you are — I mean as she was when she was your age? The same wonderful hair, the same bold and intriguing eyes. I could almost

298

swear the clock has been put back thirty years, and that I am again that lovesick swain, entranced by protestations of love and endless devotion. Yes, you're beautiful enough, and your mother must be proud of you. She is going to miss you quite a lot.'

'Is that why you kidnapped me — to avenge yourself on her for some imaginary wrong?'

'Imaginary!'

He gave a curiously hollow laugh, and Felicity went to the table and drank another glass of water. He stood where he was watching every movement.

'Why don't you eat?' he asked.

'I'm not hungry. This place is damp and cold. Is it night or morning?'

'Night. If you are cold I'd better get you another blanket.'

'There's no need. I shan't be here long.'

'What makes you think that?'

'Certain facts of which you know nothing. Hasn't it occurred to you that my mother, on knowing what has happened, will tell the police all about you?'

'She will not, unless she feels that you are in mortal danger, which is most unlikely.'

Felicity stared at the dark eyes behind the mask.

'You don't think much of my mother, do you?' she asked.

'No, I don't, nor of her blood-sucking parents, who swindled your own father out of his estate. Well, they have paid for their trickery, but your mother has yet to pay. Until that happens I regret you will not be very comfortable.'

'That's a silly threat to make when the police are already close on your heels. They believe that it was you who poisoned my grandfather.'

'Believing a thing and proving it are two very different operations,' he replied calmly. 'Perhaps they also believe I killed your grandmother?'

'Perhaps.'

'No. Her conscience killed her, very belatedly. I happened to be present when it took place. I don't know what brought her into the garden so late at night, but there she was, completely alone, standing on the edge of the lake, looking at the moonlight on the water. Then she seemed to be aware of my approach and suddenly turned round and saw me. She didn't recognize me and asked me who I was. I told her, and she stepped backwards and into the water. I watched her drown.'

'You let her drown!' gasped Felicity.

'Why not? I had no particular wish that she should go on living.'

'You're inhuman,' said Felicity passionately. 'Please go. I don't want to talk to you.'

'Quite a show of spirit. I'm not offended. I rather like young women with plenty of spirit. Your mother had plenty of that, but not enough to deal with her loathsome parents. But that's all over and done with, and the field is now clear for the next act in this little melodrama, the end of which I hope is not far off. In that act you may play a small part. Still unafraid?'

'Yes. The police will get you before you can harm my mother.'

'They would have to be very lucky.'

'You can't be so sure of yourself, or you wouldn't wear that mask.'

'Would you really like to see the face of the man behind it?'

'No. I dislike the faces of cowardly creatures.'

'Cowardly!' The word seemed to jerk him out of his composure. The dark eyes flashed angrily, and for a moment she regretted her impetuous utterance, for he took a step towards her, as if to lay hands on her. Then he stopped, shrugged his shoulders, and moved towards the door. She tried to see what was beyond the door, but was

301

prevented by the interposition of his body. The door clanged, and she heard the key being turned, and the sound of retreating footsteps, after which came dead silence.

She sat down on the bed, amazed and perturbed by the strangeness of the situation. It seemed to her that she was in no immediate danger, since he had provided her with food, and had more or less admitted that his fierce hatred did not extend to her personally. But there was that allusion to the old biblical text about the sins of the fathers — meaning, in this case, mothers.

Despite her recent denial of hunger she was famished, and the sandwiches looked delicious and innocuous. She picked up one of them and tasted a small portion. It was excellent, and she put aside her suspicion in that connection. Very soon she had emptied the dish, and felt much better for the repast.

Her thoughts turned to Philip, with whom this promising evening was to have been spent. By this time he must be racked with anxiety. But she thought it most unlikely that he could have the remotest idea of what really had happened. Certainly he would have rung up the house, and the police must have been informed. But what could they do in the circumstances? She had not the vaguest idea where she was, or how she had been transported to this queer underground prison, and there seemed nothing to be done but wait for the next move in this perplexing game.

She went to the door and tried to see through the keyhole, but either the key was still in the lock or it was intense darkness on the further side. Going back to the bed she stretched herself at full length, and pondered possible means of escape. There seemed to be but two. One was to wait until she heard his next approach and feign illness — on the floor, and then to outwit him and make a dash along the passage. The other was grimmer, and more repugnant. It involved the use of one of the heavy bottles as a bludgeon, and to wait in darkness behind the door until he appeared. He would probably be carrying some more food to keep her alive, and would be open to a sudden and savage attack.

Hating all forms of violence she shuddered as she visualized the details of such an operation, yet why should she hesitate in such circumstances? He had shown no compunction at drugging her into unconsciousness, and had boasted at having watched a very old woman being slowly drowned. In addition there were grounds for believing that he had deliberately poisoned her grandfather, and was planning at that moment to harm her mother in some way or another. Surely any weapon was good enough to beat a mad dog?

Real sleep was out of the question, but she dozed at intervals, awaking only to be confronted with the same obnoxious problem. The candles burnt lower in the two bottles, and the air grew damper and chillier. Instead of lying on the bed she now lay in it, and soon began to feel less numb and miserable. The two guttering candles became more and more a challenge to her reluctant mind. Had she the courage to face up to this situation, and strike a blow for freedom, or was she to lie there and allow her heartless captor to carry out his plan without let or hindrance?

The candles were almost at their last flicker when she made her decision for good or ill. Pulling aside the bed-clothes she went across to the chest and blew out what was left of one of the candles. Taking the bottle in her hand like an Indian club she swung it round her head, and tried to work herself up to a state of frenzy. The whole thing was nauseating, and she wished that her jailor would come at once and spare her time to reflect upon her intending desperate deed. The second candle was dying before her eyes. She went and stood by the door, and a few moments later was in utter darkness, in which the illuminated dial of her wrist-watch shone out most clearly. It gave the time as seven o'clock.

But another hour was to pass before she was called into action by the sound of footsteps along the passage. She picked up the bottle from her feet, and peered for a moment through the keyhole. Coming towards her was her captor, carrying a dish, and a small electric torch, and wearing the same mask over his lower face. She gripped the bottle tightly by the neck and stood pressing her back against the wall on the opening side of the door. Her heart pounded as the footsteps finally ceased, and the key was pushed into the lock. Then the door opened and the ray of the torch shone on the bed, rested there a moment and then moved to the chest, where stood the single bottle. Now she realized that the stratagem had failed. That single bottle told its own story, and the hope of a suitable target to hit at was forlorn. A hand came forward and all but closed the door.

'Hand me the two bottles, and then I'll bring you your breakfast,' said a voice. 'Hurry, or you'll get nothing today.'

She hesitated for a moment and then did

as she was told. Her jailor then entered the chamber, guided by the torch. He put the dish on the table, and lighted a candle which he took from his pocket, fastening the latter to the table by using its own wax.

'Planning to knock me out, eh?' he grunted.

'Why not? Wouldn't you try to escape if you were in my position?'

'I might, but I've not treated you badly, have I?'

'Do you call drugging me not treating me badly?'

'I could have done far worse things than that. Don't push me too far or I may yet seek to amuse myself in a way you wouldn't like.'

'You're just a beast, without a single redeeming feature so far as I know.'

'You'd better eat your breakfast while it's hot. I'll wait.'

'Why?'

'To take away the candle. If I had been less wary a nice mess you would have made of me. Perhaps a spell of darkness will bring you to a proper appreciation of your position. Go on, eat it, or I'll take it away.'

Believing this threat to be serious, she drew the chair round the table and lifted the lid from the dish. Inside were eggs and bacon, a piece of fried bread, and a knife and fork. She commenced to eat, while he stood in front of the door regarding her fixedly.

'How long is this going on?' she asked, when she had finished.

'That depends upon a number of things.'

'What things?'

'Your mother chiefly.'

'You mean I am up for ransom?'

'Make what you like of it.'

'And if she refuses?'

'She dare not. But if she should be so foolish she will live to regret it.'

'I see. And all this because presumably you were disappointed in love, so long ago that any normal person would have forgotten all about it. What sort of a man are you?'

'The sort of man who never forgets an injury. I want no more talk on this matter. It is the time for action, not words. Now I'll take that dish, and the candle.'

'Wait!' pleaded Felicity. 'Leave me the candle, or I think I shall go mad. There's really no reason why you should torture me whatever my mother may have done.'

'Then say you're sorry.'

'Very well — I'm sorry.'

'You don't say it as if you meant it.'

'I've done what you told me to do. Isn't that enough?'

'All right. But don't try any more tricks.'

Felicity said nothing, and watched him go out. On this occasion she was able to see a little way along the passage. To her surprise it was as dark as her cell.

19

Barrington spent one of the worst nights he had ever experienced, and this was not by any means due to his head injury, and his bruises. Tossing from side to side all through the long hours he felt an utter wreck when at last the morning light filtered into his bedroom. At eight o'clock Mrs. Sawyer arrived, blissfully ignorant of all that had taken place the previous evening. Finding the cottage apparently empty she tapped on the bedroom door and was invited in.

'Oh, good morning!' she said. 'My goodness, Mr. Barrington, have you had a fall or something?'

'I was knocked over by a car.'

'Isn't that a shame. It's nearly happened to me more than once. Cruel how some of them motorists' drive. Ought to be put in prison. I hope you got his number?'

'Unfortunately, no.'

Mrs. Sawyer looked at his pale face.

'You do look queer,' she said. 'I suppose you've seen the doctor?'

'Yes. He is calling again this morning. I shan't want any breakfast.'

'What, nothing at all?'

'Well, just a cup of tea — in here. I'm not supposed to get up until I've seen the doctor again.'

'I'll get it right away.'

Mrs. Sawyer brought the cup of tea with commendable speed, and seemed very disposed to talk, but Barrington neither wished, nor felt like going into details. All he could think about was Felicity and the plight she was in, and he cursed his muddle-headedness for not taking the number of the car when he had a chance. That was far more important than trying to see the face of the culprit.

The doctor called an hour or two later, and proceeded to take his temperature. He nodded his head with obvious satisfaction when he consulted the thermometer.

'Almost normal,' he said. 'That's a good sign. How are you feeling?'

'Murderous.'

'Yes, but I mean physically?'

'Damned tired. I can't sleep knowing what happened to Felicity.'

'No, it's pretty bad. How's the head?'

'Aches a bit, but not too badly.'

'There was bound to be a bit of concussion, but I think you'll be all right in a day or two. Keep to a simple diet, and no spirits of any kind. A few days in bed — '

'A few days! I can't lie here for days on end.'

'Why not? The police have the matter in hand. You can do no good by getting up. I'll come and see you in a couple of days. You don't want a nurse I suppose?'

'Good heavens, no! Mrs. Sawyer comes in every day, and I expect she'll come over in the evening if I ask her. By the way, I haven't told her exactly what happened. If I did everyone within ten miles would know in a few hours.'

'They'll know soon enough. The newspapers are bound to make a song and dance about it. Well, you just lie back and relax — '

'I'd like to see you lying back relaxing, if the girl you intended marrying was kidnapped under your very nose,' grumbled Barrington.

'All the same it's sound advice.'

When the doctor had gone Barrington managed to get a little sleep, which had the effect of easing his headache. From outside came the drone of a vacuum cleaner, and he looked at his watch to find it was half-past ten. Then Mrs. Sawyer tapped on the door and entered the room.

'Oh, you're awake,' she said. 'Would you like me to make the bed?'

'No, thank you. Has there been any telephone call?'

'There was a ring, but I couldn't hear anyone the other end. I think the line is out of order. It goes like that sometimes.'

'Well, will you try to ring the Hall, and ask if Sir John could come and see me?'

'Yes, sir.'

She was absent for a few minutes, after which she returned to say she couldn't get through. This was aggravating in the circumstances, for he wanted to know what news, if any, had come overnight.

'I'll go and have a shot,' he said.

'Oh, sir, you didn't oughter,' she protested. 'The doctor told me you was to be kept quiet.'

'I know. But I must speak to Sir John.'

She went back to her cleaning, and Barrington got out of bed, and tried his legs. There was a little stiffness round the knees, but not enough to incommode him. Slipping on a dressing-gown he went down to the telephone, and dialled the Hall number. Instead of hearing the double ring there was a drone rather like the engaged signal. He put back the receiver and tried again. To his surprise he heard a voice on the line — a deep and very incisive male voice. It said:

'I mean the little café just outside the town.

It's called? 'The Lilacs'.'

'Yes, I know.'

His heart thumped as he recognized the second voice. It was Lady Gertrude's — choked with emotion.

'Good. Be there in half an hour. The girl is all right — at the moment, but her future depends entirely upon you. You'd better get that clear.'

'I understand. I'll be there.'

'You'd better. And one thing more. You are to come alone, absolutely alone. One word to anyone and the whole thing is off. Is that perfectly plain?'

Lady Gertrude's voice came in a kind of sob.

'Quite plain. I'll leave at once.'

Then there came silence and the line went dead. Barrington stood for a moment transfixed. Undoubtedly the line had gone haywire, but at tremendous advantage to himself. The thing to do was get on to Inspector McLean without a moment's delay. He found the number of police headquarters, and dialled it. Nothing happened now — not even a buzz. Quickly he realized how imperative it was to get into action. Lady Gertrude intended leaving at once to keep this secret appointment. There wasn't an instant to spare. He put up the receiver, and hurried upstairs, at such a pace that Mrs. Sawyer stared at him in amazement.

'I've got to go out,' he said.

'But the doctor — !'

Barrington didn't wait to hear the rest of her objection. He got into his clothes in the minimum of time, put a scarf round his neck, jammed a hat on his head as he passed through the hall and hurried out to his car. In a couple of minutes he was racing out of the drive towards the main entrance to the Hall. He stopped the car short of the exit drive from the Hall, and prayed that he wasn't too late. A few minutes passed and his spirits began to fall, but suddenly a car emerged, and he got a momentary glimpse of Lady Gertrude at the driving wheel. She went off on the Dorchester road at a high rate of speed, and it was as much as he could do to keep her in sight. About two miles farther on the car left the main road and entered a secondary road which led he knew not where, but certainly not to Dorchester.

There were many twists in the road, and a number of crossings, and the danger was that Lady Gertrude might shoot off at one of the crossings and leave him stranded. But he managed always to keep her just in sight, and very soon he saw a signpost marked Weymouth — 6 miles. This was evidently her objective, for there was no other town of any size in that direction which she could have reached in half an hour from home.

On entering the outskirts of the port Lady Gertrude slowed down, and Barrington kept his distance. Finally his quarry stopped and drew in to the kerb. Barrington saw her leave the car and enter a small café abreast of it. He stopped his own car at the nearest possible place, and switched off the engine.

The question now was whether he should try to get on to McLean and tell him just what was taking place, but after a few moments' reflection he decided against it. The obvious thing was to stay where he was until Lady Gertrude's unknown telephone-caller appeared, and then make an attempt to find his hide-out. He lighted a cigarette, and never for a moment took his eyes off Lady Gertrude's car. About a quarter of an hour passed, and then Gertrude appeared, accompanied by a tall man. He went with her to the door of the car, opened it for her, and then stood and watched her drive away. She reversed the car at the next turning, and came back the way she had arrived. Barrington lowered his head as she passed.

The tall man went off in the other direction, and Barrington moved along the street at a slow pace. A little later the man crossed the street and entered a large, dark saloon car. Was it by accident that a crate on the luggage grid had a covering which just obscured the number-plate?

He watched the car get away, and did not attempt to move until he felt certain that he was outside the range of observation through a driving mirror. Once clear of the town traffic the big saloon increased its speed, keeping a westerly course. Barrington watched the needle of his speedometer creeping up towards the 'sixties' and wondered how long his ancient 'bus' would be able to stand this punishment. The blue sea on his left began to fade away, and soon the whole character of scenery changed. He was now in hilly country, for the most part heavily timbered, and steam began to appear from the cap of his radiator. He prayed that the comparatively straight road would come to an end, and give his overheated car a chance to cool down, and to his great relief this happened after a mile or two. The narrow, twisting lanes which followed made it impossible for even the fastest car to exceed thirty miles an hour, and on corners the big saloon was at a disadvantage. He made up his mind that should the saloon come to a stop he would go past it without hesitation, and turn the car in at the next crossing. But the driver of the saloon seemed to have no intention of stopping.

For over an hour the big car continued on its course, going more and more inland, and Barrington, failing to see any outside mirror on the saloon, calculated that the dash-board reflector was incapable of taking in any car at the distance he was keeping. Another short burst of speed started more steam from the radiator, and a lot of knocking from his engine. He believed the little car was going to crack up, but again he was given a respite in the sudden appearance of a corkscrew section. He was thanking the Fates for this when a sharp bend revealed a terrific hill, going up and up interminably. It was fairly wide, and the saloon made light of it, while Barrington, reduced to using his bottom gear, crawled up it in a cloud of steam. It looked like the end of the chase, for now he was losing ground every moment, and the top of the hill was not yet in sight.

Painfully the little car slogged on, and finally breasted the summit and came out on a comparatively flat heath. Barrington stared at the arrow-like road. He could see a clear mile of it, and it was absolutely deserted. He stopped the engine to give the boiling radiator a chance to cool down a bit, and got out of the car into the bright sunshine. It was no use going on, he thought. By this time the saloon car was probably miles ahead. Bitterly disappointed he lighted a cigarette and looked around him at the superb scenery. And then, suddenly, he saw something in the distance which caught his rapt attention. It was the top part of a tower projecting above the pine trees away to his right, and instantly he recalled the anonymous note, with its grim and rather sinister message — 'CHILDE ROLAND TO THE DARK TOWER CAME'.

Could it possibly mean that the chase had not been a complete failure after all, and that the tower was the objective of the man in the big saloon car? Of course it might be merely a coincidence, but it was surely worth investigating. When the water had ceased to boil he got into the driving seat, and went forward cautiously. A few minutes later he reached a large house standing in timbered grounds, and saw the tower away to his right. At this point there was a very rough track which appeared to go direct to the tower, so he turned the car into it, and began to bump over numerous potholes. Now he could see that the tower was fenced off from what appeared to be the boundary of the large house, and farther on he could see a much smaller house. He stopped the car short of the house and looked through the slats of the chestnut fencing. Scattered about were poultry houses of various kinds, and through the trees he could see the big base of the tower. He moved along the fence towards the house, where the chestnut fencing gave way to an ancient stone wall. It was where this junction took place that he saw something which caused his heart to beat faster. It was a large, black saloon car, standing at right angles to him, and on the back of it was the crate with its wrapping still obscuring the number-plate. It was the end of the quest, for he could see enough of the front of the car to recognize it as the vehicle which had run him down, and which undoubtedly had borne Felicity away. The next step lay with the police.

He turned back, elated with his success, and again he saw the tower — this time from a better viewpoint. The heavy arched door was partly open, and an irrepressible desire came to him to see what lay behind it. But he shook his head doubtfully and moved on until he came to the car. Then again came the urge to satisfy his enormous curiosity. For all he knew Felicity might be somewhere inside that gaunt column, suffering all the miseries of the damned. The fence was no great obstacle, for in places it had sagged a lot. A good vault and he would be over it, and between it and the house there was plenty of obscuring timber.

Opening the tool box of the car he took out the heaviest tyre-lifter and weighed it for a moment in his hand. The decision was made. He placed the implement on the ground close to the fencing and then chose his spot and vaulted over, wincing as his knee bruises complained. The tyre-lifter was pulled through the fence and he hurried across to the tower, mounted the few steps and peeped behind the door. There he saw all that McLean had seen only a few days earlier — feeding stuffs, wire netting and a mass of clutter. Peering through the door he saw no sign of anyone, so he went up the stone staircase, with his heart beating fast, and peered into every chamber, until at last he came to the turret itself, where he stood panting from his exertions, and admiring the view of the ocean across the hills in the dim distance. From there he could not see the house, because of the screen of timber in its near vicinity, but from not far away he could hear the barking of a dog.

It was a little disappointing, but it did not greatly effect the importance of his discovery. Wherever Felicity might be her kidnapper was most certainly close at hand. He came down the dangerous steps with but one idea fixed in his mind — to find his exact position, and to telephone McLean from the nearest telephone. But when he got to the bottom he suffered the rudest shock. The door through which he had come was no longer open! Thinking it might have swung to in the slight breeze he turned the heavy iron handle. The door remained fast. He was a prisoner.

Wet with perspiration he gazed up at the narrow grill, through which projected a few sprigs of green ivy from the heavy growth on the outer walls. Was it a trap, or just an accident? Had the poultry farmer come for some poultry feed, and on this occasion locked the door behind him? Or had he seen the waiting car and formed his own conclusions about its significance?

Whatever the truth of the matter the situation was desperate. To go to the top of the tower and attempt to draw someone's attention to his plight was hopeless, for the country round about was completely deserted, and the track down which he had driven the car seemed to be a dead end. The barred window was his next thought, but on examining it he was certain that by no means could he squeeze his body through it and descend by means of the ivy, even if he succeeded in breaking through the grill.

He went to the next floor, but found that the window was identical with the one below, and it was the same with the floors above. Again he descended and searched in the lower chamber for rope, in the hope that he might find enough to lower himself to the ground from the parapet at the top of the tower, but all he found was a piece about twenty feet long, which was as good as nothing at all. His head began to ache badly, probably from the intensity of his thoughts, and he sat down on a broken chair, trying to anticipate the future. If the poultry keeper had come for chicken feed, it looked as if he would not come again that day. That meant a night in this ghastly place, and a complete day wasted all because of his stupid and unforgivable curiosity.

Again he heard the dog barking, and as he listened the barking grew louder, until the animal was quite near the tower. Suddenly the dog was stilled by an angry ejaculation in a gruff voice. He stood up and listened at the door. Undoubtedly someone was approaching. He looked at the tyre-lifter, and made a swift decision. To be found with that in his hands would most certainly arouse suspicion as to his object. Far better to pose as an innocent trespasser in the first place. He slipped the cold implement inside his shirt, and buttoned up his coat. Then he banged on the door to keep up the pretence.

The door was unlocked and pushed inwards, letting a ray of sunshine into the dank and gloomy place. Standing outside, on the bottom step, was the tall man with a double-barrelled shotgun in his hands. On the ground behind him was the large, growling dog.

'Good morning!' said Barrington. 'I seem to have been locked in — accidentally.'

The deeply set dark eyes regarded him steadfastly.

'Did you get in here accidentally?'

'Well, no. I wanted to give my dog a run, and he managed to get through the fence. I thought he had come in here so I climbed over to bring him back. He wasn't here so I went up the tower. I'm sorry about this.'

'So am I, but I don't believe you. I've been losing too many chickens lately, and that's your car outside, isn't it?'

'Yes. But I had no designs on your poultry.'

'Come this way, and don't attempt to run, or I shall be compelled to shoot.'

'But this is nonsense.'

'Come down the steps, or I'll get the dog to assist you.'

Barrington walked past him down the stone steps, and saw the barrel of the gun follow him. The dog began to show his teeth but stopped and came to heel at a word from his master.

'Walk on,' said the tall man. 'Up the footpath to the house. I'm going to telephone the police.'

Barrington, fuming with frustration, did as he was told, and finally passed through an open door into a large beamed sitting-room. Here he turned round and found the barrel of the gun still in line with his body.

'Well,' he said, 'aren't you going to telephone the police?'

'Not yet. Take off your hat!'

'Why?'

'Take it off!'

Barrington, anxious to avoid displaying his bandage, stepped back a little, but the barrel of the gun swept up and sent his felt hat flying. The next moment it was close to his chest again.

'I thought so,' grunted the tall man. 'You're the writing fellow from Deepwater Cottage.'

'Yes,' said Barrington. 'And you're the man whom the police know as Childe Roland, the swine who drugged and carried away a helpless girl, and ran me down afterwards. I came to see what you had done with her, and the police whom you were so keen to ring up are on their way.'

'Do you take me for a fool?'

'I take you for worse. I take you for a murderer, and I'm not the only one.'

'You know nothing, nor the police. But if you wanted adventure, you've got it. What's the girl to you?'

'She's my future wife.'

'You're an optimist, but I'm all for a bit of romance. Like to see her?'

Barrington looked at him warily, for there was something sinister in his tone.

'If you've harmed her — ' he said fiercely.

'Why should I? I've no use for women — not now. At the best they're a cunning, contriving lot of bitches. Well, I am going to give you a chance of a premature honeymoon. You'll find it has certain drawbacks, but you've come all this way to see her, and I should hate to disappoint you. Go through that door into the passage.'

Barrington, leaving his hat where it was, passed through the doorway, and was pushed along a narrow passage by the gun barrel. At the end was a door, which he opened to order, and a flight of descending stone steps.

'Down there! Push down the light switch on your right.'

Barrington did this, and the darkness was illuminated. He descended about a score of steps and found himself in an extensive cellar. Through this he was directed by the man with the gun, and finally found himself up against some old wine-bins.

'Pull the end towards you!'

Barrington pulled on the bin, and found it was hinged, and came easily towards him. It covered an arch beyond which he could see nothing. The tall man produced a torch and directed the ray down a long arched passage. The floor was flagged and slippery, and here and there drops of water fell from the roof. Soon there appeared an arched door like the one he had come through. He reached it and halted.

'Yes, in there,' said his guide. 'Here's the key. Open it and leave the key in the lock.'

Barrington picked up the key from the floor where it had been thrown. He put it into the large lock, turned it and opened the door. Inside was a candle burning, and sitting on the bed behind it was Felicity.

'I've brought you your lover,' said the tall man. 'Make the most of him while you may, for it may be later than you think.'

Barrington, staring at Felicity, heard the

door slammed behind him. The next moment they were in each other's arms, Felicity laughing and weeping at the same time.

'Thank God!' said Barrington. 'At least I've found you.'

'I don't understand. How did you get here? And you're hurt. Oh, my darling, what happened to you?'

'I saw you struggling with that brute — from the boat house, where I was getting the car out. I ran round to the drive in the hope of cutting him off. He drove straight at me, and I didn't get away in time.'

'Then how did you get here?'

'That's a longer story, but you'd better hear it.'

While they sat on the bed side by side Barrington told her of his movements that morning, keeping nothing back. The mention of the part played by her mother caused her to utter a little cry of incredulity, and when he had finished she looked dejected and puzzled.

'Seeing you again is marvellous,' she said. 'But I rather wish you had not been so successful.'

'That's a nice thing to say,' he protested with a smile.

'You know what I mean. Roland, or whatever his real name is, is planning to

327

score off mother. He told me that much, and from what you have said it looks as if my mother is prepared to deal with him.'

'You mean a ransom?'

'Yes. I accused him of that, but although he wouldn't admit it he didn't deny it.'

'But what has he against your mother?'

'The same thing as he had against both her parents. He hated them all because he loved my mother in the past, and went off to the war believing that my mother would wait for him. Apparently he came back to find her already married, and he held her parents chiefly responsible. He even admitted watching my grandmother drown, without raising a finger to help her. He's horrible — quite unbalanced. I'm sure it was he who poisoned my grandfather.'

'But why should he wait all these years to avenge himself on your family?'

'That's what I don't understand. He seems so cocksure of himself, too.'

'He certainly is that. I tried to persuade him that the police were on their way here, but he wouldn't swallow that. It makes me mad with myself to reflect that if I hadn't gone looking for you in that old tower the police really would be on their way here by now. What a hash I've made of things through overplaying my part.'

'You think the police have no clue?'

'I don't know. McLean isn't the sort of man to confide in anyone. It's possible he may know a great deal more than we imagine, but this place is in the middle of nowhere. Why should anyone look here for two missing persons? He went all the way to Weymouth to keep the appointment with your mother, and waited until she drove away before he entered his car.'

'Where are we, anyway?'

'Somewhere between Dorset and Devon, perhaps even over the Devon border. We came by back lanes, and never passed through any town of size. Is there any water in that jug?'

'Yes. I'll get you a drink.'

Felicity poured some water into the drinking-glass and handed it to him, watching him closely as he drank it.

'You poor darling,' she said. 'You look completely exhausted, and I don't wonder. Why not try to get some sleep?'

'No. I'm all right. This is no time for sleeping. That candle isn't going to last another hour. Has the brute given you any food?'

'Yes. Excellent eggs and bacon.'

'That's one good mark to his list of black ones.'

'Yes, but I don't trust his nice behaviour. Suppose mother is playing a clever game of her own? Suppose, for example, she leads him up the garden path to the point where she says she is willing to hand over a large sum of money, and then brings in the police at the nick of time. He might in his anger refuse to give any information about us. I know mother. She hates to part with money.'

'That's a point,' he admitted. 'Obviously the best thing to do is not to trust to his good behaviour, or your mother, begging her pardon, and to get out of this hole in the ground as quickly as possible.'

'And how — exactly?'

Barrington delved behind his coat and produced the tyre-lifter.

'I tried something like that,' said Felicity, 'with a bottle which was here; but it didn't work. He had a gun when he came here just now, and if we see him again I'm willing to bet he'll still have it.'

'But now there are two of us. There must be something we can do — there must be.'

'Do try to sleep,' begged Felicity. 'If it's only for an hour. Perhaps an idea will come after that. I'll put the candle out, so that we can use it when we want it. But have you any matches?'

'I've a petrol lighter.'

'Good. Come on, do as I say.'

Barrington gave way, and stretched himself at full length on the bed. Felicity blew out the candle, and then sat quite close to him, with one hand resting on his. In a few moments his breathing rhythm changed and she knew that he was asleep.

20

The half-sucked lozenge which McLean had found, proved to be a throat pastille of a common kind and was useless as evidence. He had, in fact, already written it off as negligible, and was not greatly disappointed. Before going back to Strafford Park he had a conversation with the chief constable, who was now following the case with immense interest.

'What do we do now, Mac?' he asked. 'Use the B.B.C. or the Press?'

McLean shook his head, having spent the greater part of the previous night weighing up the situation.

'Advertising for Galbraith would be useless,' he said. 'He would not have dared come back to this country without changing his name.'

'But you have the photograph?'

'As he was thirty years ago. I'm certain he isn't like that now. No, Lady Gertrude is my main hope.'

'But if she had an idea where Galbraith is, surely she would have told you, when her daughter is in danger?'

'It may well be that she doesn't yet know

where Galbraith can be found, and she may not believe that the girl is in any immediate danger.'

'Then how can she help you?'

'I think it won't be long before she hears from Galbraith. If, as I suspect, he is out to relieve her of a large sum of money, there is only one place where she can get it.'

'The bank?'

'Yes. She could doubtless sell certain things, but that would take time. The bank is quicker, especially with a customer who has just inherited a substantial income. If she should go to the bank for a loan it will prove to my satisfaction that she and Galbraith have agreed terms, for the safe return of her daughter. That is where we can take a hand.'

'Yes, I think you're right. But I'm far from understanding the situation. Naturally, she wants her daughter back, but why the devil should she behave as she has been behaving? Mac, are you holding out on me? Is there something I don't know?'

'You've seen all the evidence,' replied McLean. 'That is all we can deal with. There are certain things I should have liked to establish beyond a shadow of doubt, and I haven't succeeded. But in a case like this a man is entitled to use his imagination up to a point. I have read through all that evidence a dozen times, and always I get the same result.'

'And what is the result?'

'That Lady Gertrude doesn't want her past delved into to any great extent. She dare not take any chances with Galbraith, who became the most ruthless and implacable enemy of her family two years ago.'

'Why two years ago?'

'Have another look at the evidence, especially that taken at the nursing home at Exeter. Now I think I'll get on with the job. If there's any message for me I shall be at Strafford Park.'

It was nearly noon when McLean reached Strafford Park. He and Sergeant Brook were let in by Susan, who seemed to McLean to be unduly agitated. It was when he was shown into the lounge that he knew the reason why. Sir John was standing by the fireplace, with his hair disordered, and his tie askew, which in a man of his habitual neatness was symptomatic of considerable distress.

'Thank goodness!' he exclaimed. 'I tried to get you on the telephone, but was told you were on your way here. Something quite extraordinary has happened.'

'Well?' asked McLean.

'Barrington has disappeared.'

'When?'

'About an hour ago. I went over to Deepwater to see how he was progressing and found him gone. Mrs. Sawyer told me he had been trying to get me on the telephone, but without success. She said he came back to his room in a great hurry, dressed very quickly, and went off in his car. She thought he was coming to see me, as he couldn't get me on the telephone, but he never called here.'

'Had the doctor already called?'

'Yes. He gave Mrs. Sawyer a good report, but told her that Barrington would need a few days complete rest. I don't understand it.'

'Why couldn't Barrington get you on the telephone?'

'I don't know. I've made one or two calls and had no trouble to get through.'

'Have you tried to ring the cottage?'

'No.'

'Will you try now?'

Sir John went to the telephone and dialled the number several times, without success.

'No good,' he said. 'There's a fault somewhere. But if he wanted to see me so urgently why didn't he come here?'

McLean had no immediate answer to

that question. That Barrington's mission was important there could be no doubt, since he had risen from a sick-bed and gone off like a shot.

'We can only assume that time was the great factor,' mused McLean. 'He learned something and was compelled to act with the greatest speed.'

'But surely he could have left a few words of explanation with Mrs. Sawyer?'

'The facts seem to argue that he couldn't. Is Lady Gertrude available?'

'No. She had to go into Dorchester, and she's not back yet.'

'At what time did she leave?'

'About eleven o'clock. She came into the study to tell me, and a little later I saw her leave in the car.'

'That would be about the time that Barrington left?'

'Yes, I suppose it would.'

'Did Lady Gertrude receive a telephone call before she left?'

'I don't know. I can't hear the telephone bell from the study. But Susan might know.'

At McLean's request Susan was rung for. Sir John put the question to her, but Susan said that at that time she was changing the linen in the bedrooms. McLean did not take the matter any further, but said he would like to have the use of the morning-room again, and to be informed when Lady Gertrude returned.

In the privacy of the small room Sergeant Brook expressed his personal feelings about the case, with no lack of emphasis. He was getting out of his depth, and felt the need of a helping hand.

'Can't see the wood for trees,' he said. 'We never come to this place without finding that someone has thrown a spanner into the works. No one does a darn' thing to help so far as I can see, and that's an understatement.'

'You're wrong, Brook. I've a strong notion that Barrington was trying to help. He couldn't ring us up because the telephone wasn't working.'

'But he could have left a note telling us where he was off to.'

'It's possible he didn't know. I'm intrigued by the fact that both he and Lady Gertrude went off in their respective cars about the same time. Doesn't that stir your imagination?'

'You mean he may have gone snooping after Lady Gertrude for some reason or other?'

'I think that's highly possible, but we may know more about that when he returns.

337

Better run down to the cottage, and leave a note there. If the daily woman has gone slip it under the front door.'

McLean scribbled a note, and Brook went off with it. He was back again in about a quarter of an hour.

'Just caught the woman as she was leaving,' he said. 'I left the note where Barrington is bound to see it. Is her Ladyship back yet?'

'Presumably not. I think I'll just see how the ground lies before I see her. Run outside and try to get me her bank manager on the telephone. You've got the number, I think?'

'Yes, sir.'

'Tell him I want to speak to him. Call me when you're through.'

Brook was absent only a minute or two, and then called McLean to the telephone. McLean got a reply to his question, and returned to the morning-room.

'I want you to run me into Dorchester,' he said. 'Lady Gertrude can wait for a bit. The pace is getting a little hotter. She has been to the bank, but the manager, quite rightly, is not disposed to discuss his customer's business over the telephone. We'll go immediately.'

In a very short time McLean and Brook were seated in the bank manager's office. It did not take him long to satisfy that worthy gentleman that he was the person he had purported himself to be.

'What is it you wish to know, Inspector?' he asked.

'Merely the nature of Lady Gertrude's business with you.'

'She was in need of a temporary loan.'

'What amount?'

'Five thousand pounds.'

'Were you able to accommodate her?'

'Yes. She was willing to make over to the bank certain industrial holdings as collateral.'

'Have you actually paid the money?'

'No. She wanted it in notes, and I told her she could have it tomorrow morning.'

'Did she indicate for what purpose she needed that large sum of money?'

'She said it was to discharge an old debt.'

'At what time did she call?'

'Just after mid-day.'

'That's all I want to know,' said McLean. 'You will, of course, regard this enquiry as strictly confidential?'

'Most certainly.'

McLean thanked him and got back into his car.

'Back to Strafford Park, Brook,' he said.

'This beats the band,' said Brook. 'What is it — blackmail?'

'Yes.'

'Time that lady was put in her place. What does she think she is?'

'At the moment I think she is a very scared woman, who wants her daughter back, without too many questions being asked. But her wish is not going to be gratified, for the time has come when I intend to play every card I hold. But I should like first to see what Barrington has to say.'

'You think he followed her in his car?'

'It looks very much like it, and in that case he may have seen a meeting between her and Galbraith. Alternatively Galbraith may have telephoned her and made known his terms.'

When they reached Strafford Hall, McLean was informed that Lady Gertrude was having lunch, and that there was no news for him from Barrington, so he and Brook took a walk round the park, and on their way back they called at the cottage. It was locked up, and the old boat house contained no car.

'Curious!' mused McLean. 'I shouldn't have thought he was in a state of health to go running round the country. I'll give him another half-hour and then go ahead.'

It was nearly three o'clock when McLean's patient wait came to an end.

'I don't like the look of things,' he said.

'We are up against a very astute scoundrel, and young Barrington may have overplayed his hand.'

'Just what I was thinking,' said Brook. 'Shall I ring the bell?'

'Yes.'

Brook pushed the bell and a few moments later Susan entered. McLean told her to ask Lady Gertrude if she would be good enough to come to the morning-room as soon as possible, and Susan went off on her mission. About a quarter of an hour passed, and then there was a tap on the door and Lady Gertrude entered.

'I'm sorry to disturb you,' said McLean. 'But there are a few points which were not cleared up when I saw you last night. Do sit down.'

Lady Gertrude sank wearily into the chair which she had occupied too many times for her liking.

'It concerns your daughter. I presume you have heard nothing from her?'

'Nothing. But you — ?'

'I have no news of any sort to give you. I thought it was possible that the kidnapper might have got in touch with you. If, as I suspect, his intention is to hold your daughter to ransom, sooner or later he will make known his terms.'

'Yes, I suppose he would.'

'And you have heard nothing direct from him?'

'No.'

McLean's expression grew grimmer, and Brook knew that the storm was about to break.

'What was your purpose in going into Dorchester this morning?' McLean asked.

'I had one or two items of shopping to do. But I don't understand — '

'Did you visit your bank?'

'Yes.'

'For what purpose?'

'Really, this is intolerable.'

'I, too, find it a little intolerable,' said McLean. 'I am investigating a murder, and this kidnapping business is but a side issue, but the kidnapper happens to be the man I want. You have planned to draw from the bank a large sum of money, and I must know for what purpose you require that money.'

'You have no right to ask me such questions. It is a private matter.'

'You are very much mistaken. This matter is well within the scope of my investigation, and your reluctance to answer my question compels me to draw the obvious deduction — that you have either seen, or heard from,

342

Oliver Galbraith. Just now you denied it. Do you still deny it?'

'Yes.'

McLean was a little surprised at her stupid obstinacy. But not yet had he finished with her.

'All along you have attempted to confuse the issue,' he said. 'There are certain facts about Galbraith which you have deliberately tried to conceal. There was some excuse so long as you believed that Galbraith was dead, and could not, therefore, have poisoned your father. But now you know that he is very much alive, and by shielding him you are making yourself an accessory after the fact.'

'How am I shielding him?'

'By denying that you have seen him or heard from him. You are hoping that by paying him five thousand pounds he will go out of your life for ever, and that what you have tried to conceal will never be known.'

'What have I to conceal? I admitted that he was in love with me and that I gave him to believe I would wait for him. All I am concerned about is the safety of my daughter.'

'I wish I could believe you. Isn't there something else which you regard as equally important?'

'I don't understand you.'

343

'Then let me explain. Two years ago your old nurse died in a nursing home at Exeter. She had to undergo a serious operation, and she left a letter to be posted in the event of her failing to survive that operation. That letter was posted after her death. Do you know to whom it was addressed?'

Lady Gertrude was incapable of saying anything at that moment.

'It was addressed to Oliver Galbraith — her alleged husband.'

Lady Gertrude's pained countenance now registered extreme surprise.

'But I'm sure it wasn't true. There is no evidence that she was ever married. The reason that she took on the name of Galbraith was that she wanted to account for a child which was in her care. She gave him the name of Oliver too, but he died in early youth. All through her life, after leaving your parents' employ, she was in receipt of a substantial pension, paid to her regularly by your mother. I think you knew why that pension was being paid. I think you know who is the mother of that child. I think you remember why 'Childe Roland Came To The Dark Tower', and why Galbraith reminded you of that night, when he left you the note, on the death of your father. In that letter which your old nurse sent to

Galbraith from her death-bed she told him the truth about his child, how it had been spirited away — '

McLean stopped as Lady Gertrude lowered her head into her hands and burst into tears. He waited, and still she sobbed bitterly. Many minutes passed before she could face McLean again.

'Shall we start afresh?' asked McLean.

Lady Gertrude nodded.

'When did you see Galbraith?'

'Yesterday morning. He telephoned first.'

'What did he say?'

'He said Felicity was safe with him, and that if I wanted to have her back I was to see him in half an hour at a place in Weymouth. He warned me that if I mentioned a word to anyone he would know how to deal with it.'

'What did he say when you saw him?'

'He — he said he knew all about the child — that he hated me almost as much as he had hated my parents. He said he must have five thousand pounds in treasury notes. Failing that he wouldn't be responsible for Felicity's welfare.'

'How were you to get the notes to him?'

'I am to wait for him at the old oak on Willington Down, at nine o'clock tomorrow night. It's about five miles from my old home, Seething Manor, and Galbraith and I used to go there on occasion.'

'Is he to bring your daughter?'

'No, but he swears he will release her within an hour afterwards.'

McLean asked Brook to get the large-scale road map, and when this was spread out on the table he asked Lady Gertrude to indicate the spot. This she did immediately. It was near the junction of four cross-roads.

'There's an old burnt-out cottage,' explained Lady Gertrude. 'The oak tree is only ten yards from the ruins. It is very large and almost completely decayed.'

McLean made a small ring round the spot indicated, and then folded up the map.

'I want you to keep that appointment,' he said. 'But not with the notes. I will provide you with substitute parcels, which you will place in a suitcase. We shall be near at hand when this meeting takes place, so you have nothing to fear.'

Lady Gertrude seemed to be of a different opinion, but she was now reduced to a condition of complete subjugation.

'Now tell me about Galbraith,' said McLean. 'Has he changed much since you knew him in the past?'

'Yes. I had to look at him several times before I recognized him. His hair, which used to be dark, is now completely grey, and his features are different. He told me that he was hurt in the war and had to have some skin grafted on to his face.'

'Any special facial characteristics?'

'No.'

'When you met him at Weymouth did you see his car?'

'No.'

'Did he give you any idea where he had come from?'

'No.'

'I think that's all,' said McLean. 'Tomorrow morning I will bring you the substitute packages, and give you final instructions. If Galbraith should telephone you in the meantime, give him to understand that you will keep the appointment and bring the money. Can I now rely upon your full co-operation?'

'Yes. But I'm afraid.'

'There's no need to be. If you will do exactly as I tell you you will soon have your daughter back, and I shall be in a position to bring this investigation to an end.'

When Lady Gertrude had left, McLean uttered a sigh of great relief. The air had been cleared of falsehood and make-belief, and the time for real action was at hand. The first thing to do was to survey the site where this final meeting between Galbraith and his last victim was to take place.

'We'll do that now,' he said to Brook. 'Barrington can wait for a bit. I want to see what assistance we shall need to cover all escape routes from that spot.'

Within a few minutes they were on the road, Brook driving and McLean directing him. It was an easy route to follow, and the car made excellent speed. When they were within half a mile of the place, McLean told Brook to put the car into a side lane, where there was good cover for it.

'We'll walk the rest,' he said, 'and behave like two ordinary pedestrians, in case Mr. Galbraith should have a look-out somewhere in the neighbourhood.'

Brook hated walking, but had to admit that there was sense in McLean's plan. The road now ascended to an extensive plateau, with open country in every direction, and when, finally, they came to the cross-roads the old cottage ruins and the neighbouring enormous oak tree were immediately visible.

'There's the rendezvous,' said McLean. 'Very cunningly chosen, too. Scarcely a bush to conceal a man, nor a ditch. Our nearest cover is half a mile distant. That's going to make things a bit difficult, for I want to get him as soon as Lady Gertrude hands him the suitcase. He's chosen an awkward time, too. At nine o'clock it will be nearly dark, and if the sky should be overcast, field-glasses won't help much.'

'If he opens the suitcase and finds nothing in it but bundles of plain paper, he'll smell a rat.'

'Precisely! We can't even assume that he will come by car and be restricted to main roads. He might have a motor-cycle concealed somewhere, and lead us a dance across open country. No, there's only one way to make sure of success.'

'What's that, sir?'

'To have one man hidden in Lady Gertrude's car, who will hold him up until the rest of us can join him. If Lady Gertrude's car is not suitable for that, we can lend her a car, with a particularly large luggage container at the back.'

'I think you've got something there,' said Brook.

'We'll explore these various roads and see what turnings there are to be covered, in case things don't go as we expect.'

They spent an hour doing this, with McLean making pencil marks on his map, and then they walked back to the car.

'I think that should do the trick,' said

McLean. 'I shall need two cars, three motor-cyclists, and the man who is to be concealed in the car.'

'What about me?' asked Brook. 'I should like that job.'

'You're a bit on the large side, Brook. But we'll have a look at Lady Gertrude's car first.'

'Shall I drive there now?'

'Yes, but we'll call at Deepwater Cottage on the way.'

On their arrival at Deepwater, McLean was surprised to find the cottage still locked up, and Brook, peering through the lounge window, was able to see the note which he had left in exactly the same position.

'What do you make of that?' he asked.

'I don't like it at all. Run and see if the car is in the boat house.'

Brook returned after a few minutes, shaking his head.

'That makes tomorrow's business even more critical,' said McLean. 'We've got to close that trap while we have the chance.'

'I'll say we have,' muttered Brook. 'The fellow's a hundred per center if ever there was one. Deserter, murderer, kidnapper, and probably everything else you can think of. Yes, sir, I'd like to be in that car.'

When later they examined Lady Gertrude's

car, it turned out to be quite excellent for the job on hand. In the back of it there was a 'boot' of considerable size, and when the fitted suitcases were removed Brook found he could squeeze his big form into it without too much suffering.

'Is it a deal, sir?' he asked.

'Yes, but you'll need a gun. I'm taking no chances with Mr. Galbraith. Now we'll get back to Dorchester, and complete our arrangements.'

21

In the confinement of their strange prison Barrington and Felicity were finding the passage of time a slow and discomfitting process. The lack of ventilation was the chief trouble, and with two of them now to make use of what air remained their condition slowly worsened. Barrington had benefited by two hours of sleep, but this was soon offset by the polluted air and the need of food. They had refrained from burning the last bit of candle, lest they should need it for some emergency, and in the darkness they sat together, trying to keep warm.

'By this time John must know that something has happened to me,' said Barrington. 'He'll probably ring up McLean.'

'I can't see what good it would do,' replied Felicity. 'Neither of them can have the slightest idea where we are. Nor can mother.'

'But it's queer, isn't it, that there should be an old tower in the grounds? That message which she received was all about a dark tower.'

'I was thinking about that while you were

asleep. But mother swore she knew nothing about a tower. I'll admit that mother isn't very truthful when it suits her purpose not to be. In any case, there's no reason why she should believe I might be here. We are not even in the tower.'

'I'm not so sure.'

'What do you mean?'

'That underground passage from the house is just about the same distance as from the tower to the house. We might easily be in a cellar under the tower.'

'But there's no entrance to this place except along that tunnel.'

'There was once. That bricked up portion seems to prove it. There's another thing, too. When the candle was alight I thought I saw an irregularity in the ceiling — as if there had been an opening which had been plastered up and then whitewashed. Let's light the candle for a few moments.'

This was done, and Barrington moved over to a dark corner and held the candle high above his head. Felicity, close to his side, saw the circular patch, which was of lighter colour than the surrounding area.

'You're right, Phil,' she said. 'There must have been a ladder here once.'

'There's one now — in the bottom room of the tower. I saw it lying on the floor against the wall. I'll bet anything we're actually in the tower. If we could only break through that patch we should stand a chance of getting away.'

'Not if the door were locked, as it was before.'

'I could go up to the top of the tower, and let myself down with an improvised rope, made from the blankets and the sheets. This wants thinking over.'

'But how can you hope to get through the ceiling?'

'It may be only soft plaster, and above that the original wooden or stone covering. I could have a go at the plaster with the tyre-lifter. It's fairly sharp at one end. You stand by the door and listen, while I see what the ceiling is like.'

Swiftly he moved the table under the square patch and then lifted the chair on to it. By standing on the chair he was able to jab at the plaster. Very soon a lump fell down.

'Just as I thought,' he muttered. 'Shall I carry on?'

'No, it's too early, and he may come and catch us in the act. Better to conserve our candle and wait until it's time for him to go to bed. If he should come we might beg another candle. I don't believe he intends to starve us.'

'Perhaps you're right.'

The table was put in its original position, and the big lump of plaster was hidden under the pillow of the bed. In both of them fresh hope was born, and Barrington was working out what length of 'rope' the bedclothes would make. He thought there would be enough even if he made the strips sufficiently wide to carry his weight with a fair margin of safety.

It was as well he did not proceed at once with his task, for about a quarter of an hour later footsteps were heard along the passage, and a little later the door was opened and Galbraith came to view, behind an electric torch. He carried the shotgun in the same hand, and from his free hand was suspended a flat basket. On this occasion he did not wear his mask, since now it would serve no purpose, Barrington having already seen him. Felicity saw his curious features for the first time, and liked not what she saw.

'Food,' he said, and put the basket on the floor.

'Thank you,' replied Felicity. 'But can't we have a candle? It's impossible to eat in the darkness.'

'I thought lovers liked the darkness. Anyway, you'll find two candles in the basket, and some matches.'

'How long is this going on?' asked Barrington.

'Long enough for me to complete certain plans. There is a lady — at least she calls herself a lady, with a capital 'L' — with whom I am to have a settlement tomorrow. Provided she keeps her promise, which I think she will, I shall be out of this place for ever within twenty-four hours, and shall never trouble you again.'

'You won't get away with it,' said Barrington.

'Indeed? What makes you think that?'

'Inspector McLean knows far too much about you. I believe that you are cornered like a rat in his own hole. The moment you put your nose out off comes your head.'

Galbraith gave an amused laugh.

'It would be a pity if that should occur,' he said. 'For what would then happen to my brace of sucking doves, with no one to bring them food or drink? I have no intention of setting you free until my own safety is assured. Then I shall send a telegram to the celebrated Inspector McLean, as a gesture of good faith to him and your prospective mother-in-law.'

'Good faith!' said Barrington scornfully. 'Don't make me laugh. You've about as much good faith as a boa constrictor. Leaving

356

out myself, whom you ran down coldly and deliberately, why should you take it out of Felicity because she happens to be the daughter of a woman you think you have good cause to hate?'

Galbraith's eyes blazed like those of a wild animal in the semi-darkness.

'Think I have cause!' he bellowed. 'She robbed me of a son. She sold him — like a beast at auction. Now I have robbed her of a daughter, but unlike my son her daughter is alive. Think over that, Mr. Barrington — think over that.'

He retreated, and slammed the door after him, not forgetting to lock it. Felicity, who had taken the basket, now found the candles and the matches, and lights soon appeared.

'Thank God!' said Barrington fervently.

Felicity looked at him with wide eyes.

'What did he mean by that?' she asked.

'Heaven knows. Perhaps he was lying.'

'No, he wasn't lying. He meant every word he said. He had a son, and mother — '

'Felicity!'

'It could only mean one thing. Can't you see that, Phil?'

'Let's eat,' begged Barrington, delving into the basket. 'I'm famished. Oh, there's a large bottle of milk here. Sandwiches, cheese. He's done us quite well.'

'Phil, this is horrible, isn't it?'

He went to her and took her in his arms. 'My dear, he's crazy — half a maniac. But if what he said is true, who are we to judge without knowing all the circumstances? It happened to two people long, long ago. What is horrible is that one of them should have nurtured hate through all those years — a hate so violent that even murder was not ruled out. Let's concentrate on immediate needs. First food, and then escape. Come, sit down.'

Felicity occupied the chair, and ate for a while in silence. Barrington, watching her, knew what was passing in her mind, but felt it was useless to try and divert her thoughts into less disturbing channels. But ultimately she looked at him and smiled, and from that he gathered that the worst was over.

'What's the time?' she asked. 'I think my watch has stopped.'

'It's half-past eight.'

'How long had we better wait before you start on the ceiling?'

'I'd like to make a start right now.'

'No. It would ruin everything if he heard the noise and came to see what was happening. We must be patient.'

'Yes, I know. But it's difficult to sit here, half stifled, when in an hour or so we might

358

be in some house telephoning the police.'

'It's better than risking being overheard and compelled to stay here for two further days. We ought to wait until midnight.'

'That seems years away.'

'Am I such a bore?'

He reached out and caught her hand.

'It's the only bright spot in this situation — that you and I are together. He might have kept us apart, and that would have been ghastly. I presume he hasn't any more safe lockups. What did you think of him?'

'He's terrifying — in some inexplicable way. There's something unnatural about his face, a kind of youthfulness which doesn't go with his grey hair and his voice. It might even be a mask.'

'It might, but it isn't. More like the result of plastic surgery. He's quite a case — suave and pleasant enough when things go his way, but a fiend when he gets out of balance. Like other such persons with split personalities he's so sure of himself, positive that he can outwit anyone. I sincerely hope he isn't proved right.'

'I wonder if his name really is Roland?'

'It need not be. I take it that that note was sent with the intention of reminding your — I'm sorry, Felicity. Let's not talk about that now. We have a lot to do if we are going to get out of this foul place. You ought to lie down and rest until we can make a start.'

'But I don't feel like resting.'

'Please!' he begged. 'I'll blow out one of the candles. We can't afford to burn two at the same time. Come on — I'll put you to bed.'

He lifted her up in his arms and conveyed her to the bed, where, despite her protests, she lay quietly.

'Just about three hours to zero hour,' he said. 'You can sleep if you try, or shall I sing you a lullaby?'

'I don't trust your musical powers,' she replied.

In a very short time she was asleep, and Barrington made himself as comfortable as possible in the chair, and strove to kill time by letting his fancy rove freely. From time to time he looked at his watch, to discover how slowly the hands moved round the dial, and the urge to get into action was almost irrepressible. It gave him the greatest joy to imagine their captor coming into the cell early the next morning and finding them gone, and his expected ransom not worth a tinker's cuss. With any real luck he might by that time be in the hands of the police.

He glanced at Felicity, to note how calm

and lovely she looked in complete repose, even in this grimy airless prison, and he thanked Providence for the overheard telephone conversation which had brought them together again, even in adversity. Cramped by the small chair he stood up and began to pace the chamber, walking softly on his toes.

At long last the hands of his watch became superimposed on the hour of midnight. He crept to the bed, and raised her rather cold hand to his lips. She opened her eyes and blinked at him.

'Midnight,' he whispered. 'This is where we do our stuff.'

'But it was only a few minutes ago — '

'A few years you mean. I've had time to solve all the world's pressing problems, in my mind, not excepting our present one. As a matter of fact the first part is a one man job, so you can stay where you are if you want to.'

'No. I've had a good sleep, and feel refreshed.'

Again Barrington put the table and chair into position, and climbed up on them, with his lone and somewhat clumsy tool in his hands. Having previously made an impression on the plaster, his renewed efforts produced quick result. Felicity, now holding the candle to prevent it being hit by the falling plaster, watched the steady rain of pieces, as they hit the table with a thud and bounced off it. The hole grew wider and deeper, Barrington resting only momentarily to brush the dust from his eyes and mouth.

'Easier than I thought,' he said. 'I'm in about six inches already.'

He gave a fierce jab with the tyre-lifter, and an enormous chunk of the plaster came away, missing his left shoulder by no more than a few inches, and crashing on to the frail table.

'Take care!' begged Felicity.

'Hold your breath. I'm nearly through — I think.'

In a minute or two the improvised chisel made a metallic noise and Barrington put the implement in a vertical position and pushed upwards with all his might.

'I'm up against metal,' he said. 'Looks like the old iron trap-door, but I can't move it.'

He drove the chisel in between the metal and the plaster and brought down more large chunks, until finally he exposed a small section of the circular trap-door. Then again he pressed upwards, and little beads of perspiration trickled down his forehead, until he was compelled by exhaustion to sit down in the chair. Felicity, staring at his grim face,

362

knew that his former high hopes were being dashed.

'Is the trap-door fixed down?' she asked.

'Yes. I can't make the slightest impression on it. I don't believe it's the old trap-door at all. Heavens, now I remember.'

'Remember what?'

'When I was in the lowest chamber of the old tower I noticed a big metal bin, full of chicken feed. It was just about in this position. I — I believe it was put there deliberately, to cover up the trap-door.'

'Then — we're done?'

'I'm afraid so. The original floor is far too solid to be penetrated. Our one chance was through the plaster.'

'Then come down — please.'

'No, let me — '

'Phil, there's blood on that bandage. You've pulled one of the stitches. Come down, please, please.'

Barrington threw the tyre-lifter on to the bed, with a grunt of displeasure, and made his way down, bringing the chair after him.

'I'm sorry, Felicity,' he said. 'I really believed — '

'Phil, you look dreadful. Are you all right?'

'Head aches a bit. Is there any milk left in that bottle?'

'Yes. Sit down, and I'll get it for you. Not in that filthy chair — on the bed.'

He staggered to the bed, and Felicity brought the half glass of milk to him. While he drank it she sat gazing at the debris, and at the gap in the ceiling.

'No hiding up what we've been doing,' she said. 'I wonder just what Roland will say about that?'

'I'm not going to give him much opportunity to say anything.'

'What do you mean?'

'Plan number one failed. There's still plan number two to be tried out.'

'What is plan number two exactly?'

'Assault and battery. We can't let him get away with it. He has already told us what he means to do — collect a large sum from your mother, and then clear out. To save his conscience he will wire the police telling them where to find us, but only when he feels himself to be safe. That might well be when he is in a foreign country. It isn't a question of our staying here another day or two, but of queering his pitch.'

'But how? We are helpless. He's got that gun and is mad enough to use it, if we attempt to attack him.'

'I don't intend to attack him — not openly.'

'What then is in your mind?'

'My head's bleeding a bit, isn't it?'

'Yes. What can I do about it? Shall I undo the bandage?'

'No, let it bleed. It will stop sooner or later. Suppose he were to come in and see me lying here, with blood all over my scalp? Suppose you were to tell him that that big piece of plaster fell on my head and knocked me out, and that you believe me to be dead, or dying? That would be likely to bring him to the bed, wouldn't it?'

'It — it might.'

'That's all I want. He doesn't know I've got any sort of weapon. I could have that tyre-lifter handy, and knock him cold.'

'Phil!'

'You don't like it much?'

'No. It's too risky. If you failed he might kill you.'

'It's up to me to see I don't fail. Even if he kept his head out of range I could knock that gun out of his hands, and then engage him while you got the gun. It's our only chance, and I think we ought to take it.'

Felicity winced as she saw the crimson stain extending on the soiled bandage. Sensing her fears he took her hand and squeezed it warmly.

'Don't worry,' he begged. 'I'm all right.

The wound isn't deep, and the bleeding won't last long. If it does we'll call the thing off. Is that a bargain?'

'Must I answer now?'

'No. We've got hours yet. Tell me later. What wouldn't I give for a hot bath, and a breath of really fresh air. Now come and relax.'

Felicity blew out the candle and nestled up close to him. She could well understand his burning desire to turn the tables on their jailor, but she had every cause to believe that Barrington was in no fit state to engage in a violent struggle, if his attempt to deliver a knock-out blow failed. She slept fitfully, as did her companion, and in the early hours she found the matches and took a look at him. The bleeding had apparently stopped, but he looked a terrible sight, with his hair clotted and the bandage now completely crimson on the side of the wound. He opened his eyes and blinked at the burning match.

'Oh, it's you,' he muttered. 'What the — Yes, of course — we're still here. What's the time?'

Felicity had just time to look at her watch before she threw away the match.

'Nearly five o'clock,' she said. 'How are you feeling?'

'Fine. The bleeding has stopped, hasn't it?'

'Yes.'

'Then what's the verdict?'

'We'll try out plan number two.'

'Good! Have you been asleep?'

'At intervals.'

'Then let's light up. I don't feel tired any longer — only filthy, and desperate. He's not likely to come yet, but we don't want to be taken unawares. Can I have a look at myself in your mirror?'

Felicity opened her handbag and gave him the mirror. He gazed into it, and uttered an exclamation of horror.

'If I were as bad as I look I'd be heading for the cemetery,' he said. 'But it suits the circumstances exactly. When you hear him coming you'd better start banging on the door, to add a note of realism. Know anything about shotguns?'

'Not much.'

'Well, if you get hold of the gun, stand well away from him. Don't give him a chance to grab the barrel. If you have to shoot don't do it while I'm behind him, or I'll get a packet, too, and aim at his legs. That will stop him in his tracks. But I hope it won't be necessary.'

'So do I,' said Felicity fervently.

It was half-past seven when their whispered conversation was interrupted by footsteps in the passage. Barrington, already on the bed, quickly got himself into position, with his gory head turned towards the door, and his right hand lying within an inch or two of the tyre-lifter. The candle on the table illumined the pallid face and the bloodstained bandage to good effect. Felicity moved across to the door and banged on it with the bottom of the empty milk bottle. The footsteps ceased, and there was a moment of hesitation before the key rattled in the lock. Then the door opened very slowly, to reveal Galbraith standing on the threshold, carrying a basket in one hand, and a pistol in the other. Instantly Felicity realized that the situation was different from that expected — much more hazardous. But Barrington, with eyes closed, was in a blissful state of ignorance, and she got no help from that direction. Then Galbraith saw the debris, and the big gap in the ceiling.

'What's all this?' he snarled. 'Trying to escape, eh?'

'He's injured,' said Felicity. 'Part of the ceiling fell on his head. He's dying . . . I've been trying to make you hear. You must do something — you must.'

Galbraith put down the basket, and drove Felicity away into the corner, by pointing the pistol at her. Then he approached the bed very cautiously, and suddenly extended his right arm and pushed the barrel of the pistol into Barrington's chest.

'Don't move,' he said, 'or it will be your last silly action. Ah!'

His free hand suddenly fell on the hard implement just under the bedclothes, and he dragged it out, and waved it triumphantly. Barrington, realizing that the plan had failed, now opened his eyes and sat up.

'Dying, are you?' sneered Galbraith. 'You don't look as if you're dying. Did you expect me to fall into such a clumsy trap? That hole in the ceiling wasn't made with a penknife. It was clear you had a tool somewhere; and you meant to use it — on me.'

'Why not?' asked Barrington. 'You're anybody's prey now. A man wanted for murder, and other things nearly as bad. I've a small personal debt, too.'

'You talk of debts to me. Haven't you any sense, either of you? Don't you realize that I could dispose of you both for ever and no one be any the wiser? Well, you'll have to pay for this. No more food, no more light. Tonight I shall be gone, but you shall stay here for another week, before I tell the police where to look for you. Perhaps that will give you a sense of proportion. I'll leave you the ration, as a farewell gesture.'

Backing to the door he locked it behind him, and they heard his footsteps echoing down the passage, until at last there came only silence.

'I'm sorry,' said Barrington. 'I didn't bargain for the pistol. It made all the difference. I've made an awful mess of things.'

'He's more cunning than we imagined,' said Felicity. 'I wonder if he means to carry out his threat?'

'We have to assume that he will.'

'Can we last out all that time, on the small amount of food which he left, and nothing to drink but a bottle of milk?'

Barrington shook his head and began to unpack the basket. It contained eight sandwiches, made from canned beef, a bottle of milk and two hunks of stale cake.

'Divide that by seven, and there's scarcely enough to keep a cat alive,' he muttered. 'It looks as if our future lies very much in the lap of Inspector McLean. I should like to know how far he's got by this time.'

'It doesn't seem possible for him to get far. The odds are all on Mr. Roland winning hands down. Phil dear, you aren't listening.'

Barrington wasn't. He had just remembered something, and he thumped his fist on the table in self-condemnation.

'I'm just a slow-witted idiot,' he said. 'I believe we could have got away if I had been less of an ass.'

'But how? You did all you could.'

'No. I told you that it was the corn-bin which was covering that outlet. If I had punched a few holes in the bottom of it the grain would have run out like water, and I might then have pushed the empty bin aside. Now Roland has taken the one tool available. I've got only a fifth-rate brain after all.'

'I, too,' said Felicity. 'For I never thought of that simple solution. What about the food? Dare we eat any of it?'

'One sandwich each, and a sip of milk.'

'Oh, dear!' sighed Felicity 'And to think that it may be a sunny day outside, with birds singing . . . '

Barrington put his arm round her, and drew her close to him.

'We'll see it all again very soon,' he said. 'At least we are together.'

'Yes, that's something,' she replied with a wan smile.

22

In the meantime McLean had found out the registration number of Barrington's car, and had circulated a full description of it through Scotland Yard. With his plans now complete he and Brook went to Strafford Park late in the afternoon, to learn, as he expected, that no news had come from Barrington. He brought with him some bundles of plain paper, and saw Lady Gertrude, who provided a small suitcase to hold the spurious notes. When told that Sergeant Brook was to be concealed in the luggage compartment she seemed a little relieved.

'It is most essential that you reach the rendezvous at precisely nine o'clock,' he said. 'As soon as you see Galbraith stop the car and switch off the engine, so that Sergeant Brook will be able to hear any conversation. At the moment you hand over the suitcase switch on the engine again. That will be the signal for Brook to act. Is that perfectly clear?'

'Yes.'

'I shall have the whole business under observation, and there should be no hitch.

If he does get away from Brook all the roads leading away from the spot will be covered by my assistants, and every person on those roads will be stopped.'

'Am I to ask him where my daughter is?'

'Yes, but he's not likely to tell you. He'll probably promise that she will be returned to you without much delay. But his promises are of no importance in the circumstances. I have every hope that we shall take him alive.'

Later McLean heard from headquarters that his assistants were all posted in the positions chosen, and as he himself was now ready to leave, he had a last word with Sergeant Brook, whose eyes were gleaming with excitement.

'Before you start make sure that the handle of the luggage boot is in the open position. When Lady Gertrude switches off the engine get your gun ready. The moment the engine starts nip out and hold him up. As soon as I see you I shall come forward in the car. Detective Andrews will be with me, mounted on a fast motor-cycle, in case of any possible trouble with the car. Anything you want to ask?'

'Only one thing, sir. Am I to shoot in emergency?'

'If he produces a gun — yes. But shoot low.'

When McLean started off in the car the sun had disappeared behind a cloudbank, and his hope of a fine, clear evening was largely dispelled. Visibility was a matter of prime importance to him for his observation point was over half a mile from the old oak tree, and there was no place of concealment in between. Within half an hour his worst fears were realized, for the sky became completely overcast, and in the distance he could see flashes of lightning. Then came great spots of rain on the windscreen, which quickly developed into a deluge.

When, finally, he reached the observation point, a first-class thunderstorm was in full operation, and looked like continuing for some time. Detective Andrews, from the County Constabulary, was already in position, with his motor-cycle propped against a tree. He looked like an ordinary civilian, and he saluted as McLean got out of the car, which was in a position where it could not be seen from the main road.

'Weather's against us, sir,' he said.

'Yes. But it may lift in time.'

'Hope so, sir. Can't even see the oak tree at the moment.'

McLean produced a pair of powerful binoculars and looked through them. The pelting rain was like a veil, but at intervals the enormous tree came to light. McLean looked at his watch. It gave the time as a quarter to nine.

'I am expecting Lady Gertrude's car to pass here at a few minutes before nine,' he said. 'When that happens start up your engine and I'll do the same. The moment I give the warning make for the oak tree as fast as you can.'

'Very good, sir.'

The slow minutes passed amid violent crashes of thunder and vivid lightning, but the rain eased off a little, and the oak tree was never completely obscured again. At five minutes to nine not a living soul was visible in its vicinity. McLean now found his nerves tingling. Then suddenly he heard the sound of a car engine, and he peered through the gap in the trees to the main road. The car came to view and he was able to see the driver. It was Lady Gertrude.

'There she goes,' he said.

He moved to the car and started the engine, while Andrews did the same with his motor-cycle, and sat astride it. McLean watched Lady Gertrude's car moving up the road towards the oak tree. His eyes were now glued to the binoculars, and he saw the car stop just abreast of the tree. Nothing happened for a few moments. But for the lone car the place was completely deserted. He could see the heavy rain splashing off the roof, but not a sign of the man he wanted.

'That's curious,' he said. 'I hope he hasn't funked it.'

'I can see something,' said Andrews.

McLean saw it, too. It was the tall figure of a man, clad in a mackintosh, which had suddenly appeared as if from the blue. He walked across to the waiting car, and loitered in the rear of it for a moment, then went to the window.

'Get ready!' called McLean.

Through the window of the car appeared the end of the suitcase. The man took it, opened it and closed it quickly, and then suddenly moved across the road, raised a motorcycle from the horizontal position, and got astride it. McLean realized in a twinkling what had happened. When Galbraith had loitered behind the car he had locked Brook in the luggage compartment. Now the motorcycle was moving not on the road but across the heath.

'Am I to go, sir?' asked Andrews.

'No. I must deal with this. Take the car along and get Sergeant Brook. Warn all patrols. Hurry!'

McLean took over the motor-cycle, and streaked down the road to the point where

Galbraith had escaped. He had no goggles and the rain drove into his face, and through his thin clothing. On a beaten track he could just see the tyremarks made by Galbraith's machine. They went on and on, right across the extensive heath, and never once did he get a sight of his quarry. When the heath finished the tracks continued in a narrow sunken lane, and then went off again across a common, which in the ordinary way no one would dream of crossing on a motor-cycle, for there were bushes and ditches and quagmires. All the time it rained and grew darker and darker. McLean switched on his headlight, and peered at the tracks as he bumped over hillocks, and swung the heavy machine round difficult corners. Skirting a copse he suddenly came to a pool which had formed in the bottom of a disused quarry, which had been driven into the side of a steep hill, and, to his surprise, the tracks went straight into the pool. He pulled up his machine for a moment, and stared at the rain-lashed surface of the water. Then he picked up a handy piece of rock and threw it into the water. By the volume of sound which came back he judged that the pool was of considerable depth, and the obvious deduction was that the escaping man had abandoned his machine. This conclusion was borne out by the presence of a few faint footprints going in the direction of the steep, wooded hill.

He stayed where he was, and reflected for a few moments. How clever the fellow was! Immediately upon his arrival at the rendezvous he had seen possibilities in that large luggage container, and had taken action accordingly, rendering Sergeant Brook completely helpless. He had foreseen the likelihood of treachery on the part of his victim, and in order to throw off any pursuit had put an end to the tell-tale tracks of his machine. In all probability the motor-cycle bore a faked number-plate, or had been stolen for this special occasion. Now he was on foot, with everything in his favour, except those bundles of valueless paper, which in his haste he had certainly no time to open and examine more closely. McLean smiled as he visualized the scene when those bundles were finally opened.

His machine now useless, he decided to continue on foot, in the hope of picking up further footprints, and he took from the pocket of his raincoat a small but powerful electric torch, and pressed the switch. It functioned perfectly despite its wet exterior. Propping the machine against a tree, he produced a card from his wallet, and wrote on it, 'Going up over the hill. R. M.' Then, after fixing this under the lamp, where it was sheltered to some extent from the rain, he switched off the headlight, and proceeded up the hill on foot.

It was eerie climbing up amid the thickening timber, with the rain cascading from the branches, and the lightning flashing every few moments. There was no beaten track, only a carpet of last year's leaves, and pine needles, and as he proceeded the gradient grew steeper, until he was breathing like a horse in distress. Already he reckoned he had climbed several hundred feet, and still the ascent went on and on.

He was convinced from the strenuousness of his own efforts that Galbraith could not be far ahead, for there were limits to the progress of a man on foot up that fierce gradient. At the top it might be possible to make fresh contact with him, always provided that he was going in the right direction. It was some minutes later when the gradient eased, and the timber began to thin out. Suddenly, from close at hand, an engine began to fire, and through the falling rain he saw the glow of a car's headlights, moving away from him. He cursed his bad luck as the darkness closed in on him again, and rested for a moment.

Here was the climax. Galbraith seemed to have beaten him at his own game. Already he must be outside the cordon which McLean had placed around the meeting place, and there appeared to be nothing to stop him from going anywhere he chose. Obviously the car had been left by Galbraith in a convenient place, and the motor-cycle used as a last link. The fellow had brains, and had used them to good effect. It was all bitterly disappointing, and it seemed quite useless to go on. He was about to retrace his footsteps when a vivid flash of lightning lit up the whole sky ahead of him, and showed every feature of the landscape for miles. He drew in his breath with a gasp of surprise as above the pine trees in the distance he saw the top part of a tower. He knew it at once as the old tower at Seething Manor — the place that he and Brook had visited, and where they had found the inscription on the wall!

That fact was significant enough to cause his heart to beat with new hope. Surely this could not be a mere coincidence? To a man like Galbraith, obsessed with the idea of vengeance, the remote tower, which held so many memories for him, might be an irresistible magnet. But to make use of it he would need to have easy access. Was it possible that the present owner of the Manor was none other than Galbraith? No, he was far too old. But there was the other man, who had rented the land on which the tower stood — Fenton, as he called himself. McLean recalled him as being tall and angular, with a rather curious type of face, not in the least like the early photograph of Galbraith. But Lady Gertrude had said that he had changed so much that she herself scarcely recognized him.

There was no going back now. He forgot his wretched condition, and went in the direction of the tower at increased speed, crossing a rough track which he believed Galbraith had used for the passage of the car. Another flash of lightning revealed the tower again. He was off the line a bit but now made a correction, and almost ran over the wet, springy turf.

A quarter of an hour later he stood outside the fence which surrounded the chicken farm, and thirty yards on the other side was the tower, lit up momentarily by the long ray of his pocket torch. He felt in his hip pocket and produced an automatic pistol. Like everything else in his possession it was wet. He extracted the magazine, dried the cartridges on his socks, and replaced them. Then he climbed over the fence, and crept towards the tower, with the torch directed on the ground.

On reaching it he found the door closed. He mounted the few steps and cautiously tried the handle. It turned but the door resisted his efforts to open it. Undoubtedly the place was locked up, but he thought he could hear faint tapping from inside. Putting his mouth close to the large keyhole he called out:

'Anyone there?'

Nothing came back but the queerest sort of echo, and now the tapping had ceased. He called again, but with no better result. The obvious thing to do was to get the key, and that was a matter calling for both caution and tact. If Galbraith was in the house he would by this time have discovered that he had been cheated out of his ransom, but although he had taken clever precautions against being followed, there was no reason to believe that he knew this had actually taken place — if indeed McLean was right in his deductions. Certainly there was danger, for not again could he plead merely an innocent interest in old towers, in the middle of a violent thunderstorm. The real reason for his visit could no longer be disguised. The time for a showdown had arrived. He now transferred the pistol to his overcoat pocket, and then climbed over the fence and made his way along the muddy road to the house. When he reached the front of it he looked for a car, but saw no sign of it, and the double gates which gave access to the garage were closed, as was the garage itself. The whole house seemed to be in darkness with the exception of a small light in the hall which cast a glow through an old-fashioned fanlight. After a few moments' hesitation he unlatched the small gate and walked up to the front door, where he pushed a bell button. Immediately there was a loud barking, which was suddenly silenced by a gruff voice. Then the light in the hall grew brighter, and the door was opened by the man he had seen before. He was clad in breeches and high boots, and McLean noticed that the boots were perfectly clean and dry. He stood for a moment gazing with surprise at his drenched visitor.

'Good evening!' said McLean. 'I don't suppose you remember me?'

'No, I can't say I do. Oh, wait — didn't you call some time ago with a friend, to see my old tower?'

'Correct. I'm still interested in that tower.'

'I don't get it.'

'I am a police officer, and am looking for a young lady named Felicity Medding, who disappeared some days ago.'

McLean was met with a steady incredulous stare.

'But what has the tower to do with a missing woman?' asked the tall man.

'Nothing — except that it is part of my duty to search all likely places in this area.'

'Well, I must say you have chosen a ghastly sort of night to do it. Better come inside while I get the key. Didn't you come by car?'

'Yes, but my asistants are farther along the road.'

McLean, now very much on the alert, followed the poultry farmer into a very untidy room at the back of the house.

'By the way, what is your name?' he asked.

'Fenton — James Fenton.'

'Oh yes. I remember someone telling me that. Been here long?'

'Just over two years. Now I'll get you the key, but it's a terrible waste of time. I was in the tower only a few hours ago, getting feeding stuffs for my poultry. Anyway, I suppose you won't be happy until you've had a look.'

'I shall certainly be glad to get home and have a bath,' replied McLean. 'Nice lot of books you have.'

The poultry farmer gave a glance at his

overflowing bookcase.

'Not much to do here but feed a lot of gluttonous pullets and to read books when I get a few minutes' leisure.'

While he was gone McLean got a brief look at the books, and noted a good collection of the poets, including Shakespeare and Robert Browning. In a very short time the owner of the books came back with a huge key.

'Here it is,' he said.

'I should like you to come, too,' said McLean.

'What earthly good will that do?'

'I should prefer it that way.'

'Very well — if you say so. Got a torch?'

'Yes.'

'Then I'll just get a mac and hat from the hall.'

McLean went to the door with him and watched him get the mackintosh and hat. Both of them were saturated with rain, a fact which did not pass McLean's notice. Finally they went out by the back door, McLean keeping his free hand in his overcoat pocket. They passed the poultry houses, and were very soon on the steps of the tower. McLean handed the key to his companion.

'Open it,' he said.

The lock was operated and the two men passed inside, McLean being last. The place was empty except for the general clutter and the big galvanized corn-bin.

'Satisfied?' asked Fenton.

'So far. Let's see what is upstairs.'

'There's nothing upstairs, except damp and mildew, and the whole damned place is likely to fall down at any moment.'

'We'll go up all the same. You first.'

As he made the ascent McLean became intensely interested in Fenton's back. The pockets of the mackintosh hung dead flat against him but there was a definite protuberance in the neighbourhood of his hip pocket which McLean had no intention of ignoring. Up they went, with McLean flashing the torch in each empty chamber as they came to it. Finally they reached the topmost room, and McLean flashed the torch round it, until it rested on the inscription which had been his first clue in this astonishing case.

'Oliver and Gertrude,' he said. 'I wonder where they are now? Swallowed up in the mists of time, or thousands of miles apart, or perhaps happily married with children, and even grandchildren, making the house glad with prattle.'

Fenton's eyes were staring from his head. For a moment he looked as if he would spring upon McLean, but then he uttered a sound like a sob, and turned his head away.

'Let's get down,' he said. 'I've got work to do. You've seen all there is here. Why should I be called upon to waste my time in this lunatic fashion? There's only the open gallery above, and it's raining cats and dogs. Want to go up?'

'Yes.'

'You would. Come on then. I'm in a hurry.'

There was nothing in the circular gallery but falling rain, and they came down again and negotiated the spiral staircase with McLean still in the rear, until they reached the bottom chamber.

'Satisfied now?' asked Fenton.

'There's still the house to do.'

'All right. Let's get it over.'

They had turned towards the door when again came the tapping which McLean had heard previously while outside the tower, but now it was much louder.

'What's that?' asked McLean.

'It's the old lightning conductor. It's come away from the wall at the top and blows against it at times.'

'But there's no wind, and the noise doesn't come from the top, but from below.'

'I tell you — '

'It's under the corn-bin,' said McLean. 'Put your hands to it and push it along.'

'I'm damned if I do. Do it yourself.'

McLean whipped the pistol from his pocket and levelled it at the infuriated man.

'Put up your hands, Oliver Galbraith,' he said. 'Put them up quick!'

Galbraith raised his hands above his head, and McLean thrust an arm through the partly open mackintosh and deftly removed a pistol from a hip pocket.

'That's better,' he said, as he pocketed the weapon. 'Now get over there, and don't move.'

Galbraith retreated, and McLean pushed with all his weight on the large bin, while still managing to keep Galbraith covered. It moved by inches, and slowly uncovered a circular hole. McLean gave a quick glance through the hole, and saw the candle-lighted cellar, with Felicity lying on the bed, and Barrington sitting on a chair raised on a table, with a chunk of wood in one hand, and a piece of metal in the other. Barrington turned his gory face upwards.

'McLean!' he gasped. 'Is it — McLean?'

'It is.'

'Oh, thank God! I've been trying to push a hole through the bottom of the corn-bin, without much success. Can you get us out of this hell-hole?'

'In a moment. I've got another matter on my hands — '

As he spoke Galbraith made a wild dash for the spiral staircase and vanished from view.

'What were you saying?' asked Barrington.

'I can deal with you now.'

'Good. Felicity first. I'll get her.'

Felicity, now aware of the changed situation, was soon standing on the chair, with her arms upstretched. McLean leaned over the hole and gripped her two hands, one hefty hoist and she was standing beside McLean, with her pallid grimy face illuminated by the ray of the torch which McLean had placed on top of the corn-bin. Barrington followed at speed, and stood gasping his heartfelt gratitude.

'This is a miracle,' he said. 'Did you guess I was with Felicity?'

'Yes.'

'But how did you find us?'

'That's a long story. What have you done to your head?'

'It's nothing serious — just a stitch pulled. But if you want to get Galbraith you'd better hurry, because he told us he was leaving this evening.'

'He's in the bag.'

'You mean — arrested?'

'Not yet. A minute or two ago he was here, but when he saw the game was up he ran up the staircase.'

'You'd better watch out. He's armed.'

'Not now. I took his pistol from him.'

'Oh, that's fine. But are you here alone?'

'Yes, unfortunately. Felicity, why don't you sit down? You look completely exhausted.'

'I'm all right — now,' replied Felicity. 'Down there I felt suffocated, but this fresh air has revived me. What are we to do now?'

'I want to send a message to headquarters, and there's a telephone at the house. But first I must get Galbraith. Are you fit enough to give me a hand, Mr. Barrington?'

'Nothing I should love better. What am I to do?'

'Come with me, and bring that length of rope with you. I want you to bind his arms to his side, and then we'll march him back to the house, and get a police car along. Will you wait here, Felicity, or go on to the house?'

'I'll wait here, and come with you,' replied Felicity.

'Good! Ready, Barrington?'

Barrington picked up the length of rope

and nodded his head. He tarried a moment to grip Felicity's hands and then went up the staircase behind McLean. The storm outside appeared to have abated and there was no sound but their footsteps on the stone steps. They saw no sign of Galbraith until they reached the top floor. This chamber was empty, but when McLean shone the torch up the stairs which gave access to the open gallery he saw Galbraith peering down.

'It's no use,' he said. 'Better come quietly.'

Galbraith's response was to hurl a large piece of rock at McLean's head, which missed by quite a narrow margin.

'Come and get me,' he screamed.

'Yes,' said McLean. 'I think that's the only way.'

Producing his automatic he began to mount the steps, with the excited Barrington two paces behind him. When they reached the balcony the sky was clear and a big moon was shining. Galbraith was not visible.

'Still as cunning as ever,' mused McLean. 'We shall have to go separate ways. You'd better take his pistol. It's in my side pocket. Make sure it's loaded.'

Barrington found the pistol and slipped out the magazine.

'All serene,' he said. 'But am I to use it?'

'Only if he attacks you. But I don't think he will.'

'He'd better not,' muttered Barrington.

It was McLean who came upon Galbraith first. He stopped and shone the torch in his eyes.

'No nonsense!' he said sternly. 'Put up your hands!'

Galbraith turned like a hare, but suddenly came face to face with Barrington, who looked even grimmer than McLean, with his horrible bandage, his levelled pistol, and the dangling rope.

'Get back!' he yelled. 'You'll never get me. I'll not hang for a lousy old swine like Grayling, who deserved to die. I'd have killed the old woman, too, but fright killed her. Go away. Do you hear? Go away!'

Suddenly he leaped on to the narrow parapet, where he stood swaying alarmingly.

'Come down,' said McLean. 'Don't be an idiot.'

Galbraith gave a demoniacal laugh, and then hurled himself into space. McLean ran to the parapet and saw the spread-eagled body strike the ground nearly a hundred feet below, and lie quite still.

'He won't need a rope now,' he said. 'You run down and take Felicity to the house. Ring up Dorchester County Police and tell them to send a car here at once, and a doctor. I'll join you later. There's a dog in the house. If he behaves badly just call him 'Bob' and I think he will be friendly.'

★ ★ ★

It was a quarter of an hour later when McLean entered the house, and found Barrington and Felicity sitting in the untidy room where he had been so recently, and with them was the big dog, behaving like the perfect host. Felicity had done something to her hair and face, and looked utterly different.

'I got on to police headquarters,' said Barrington. 'A car is on the way. Sergeant Brook is in charge of it.'

'Good.'

'What — what happened?' asked Felicity. 'Is Galbraith dead?'

'Yes. He was smashed to pieces, but remained conscious for a little while. When he realized he was close to death he became penitent, and confessed all his misdeeds.'

'You mean — he poisoned my grandfather?'

'Yes.'

'But how?' asked Barrington.

'He had been watching the house for months. He knew where the old gentleman

393

slept, and he had often seen the servant take a glass of drink into his room. Until recently there was a belladonna plant growing in the garden here, and that gave him the idea. He managed to distil poison from the roots, and this he introduced into the drinking glass that evening, while you were all downstairs in the lounge. No one saw him enter the house and no one saw him leave. He did it that night because it was the anniversary of the death of Mrs. Grayling, who, he swears, fell into the lake at sight of him two years previously.'

'He told us that,' said Felicity. 'In a fit of passion.'

'So you know the story behind all this?'

'Not very clearly. He hinted that mother had an illegitimate son, of whom he was the father, and that she had sold him like a beast at auction. What did he mean by that?'

McLean felt in his pocket and produced a crumpled, folded letter. He opened it and seemed about to read it when he changed his mind and put it back.

'No,' he said. 'I don't think I have the right to show you that letter, which was written by your mother's old nurse, before she died, just over two years ago. I knew it existed, and it contains what I expected it to contain. It was that knowledge which set Galbraith moving on his murderous quest.'

'Then — there was a son?'

'Yes.'

Felicity thought for a moment.

'I understand,' she said. 'He never knew about his son until the nurse wrote and told him, just before she died. All those years he thought he had been merely jilted, in favour of my father, and then he learned the truth. But what about the boy being sold?'

'That was a figure of speech. The nurse took him over, and looked after him until he died many years ago.'

'And she was paid to keep the secret?'

'She received a pension until her death.'

'What was his name — the boy's?'

'Oliver — the same as his father.'

'But that note which mother received mentioned Roland.'

'Galbraith thought she would recognize the association of Roland and Oliver, but presumably she didn't at first.'

'By jove, the fellow was clever,' said Barrington.

'Too clever,' said McLean. 'If he hadn't sent that note I might even now be wandering in the wilderness. As it is the case of Edward Grayling is now definitely closed, and what we happen to know about it remains strictly private.'

'Two questions more,' said Felicity. 'Was Galbraith out for a ransom?'

'Yes.'

'Did he get it?'

'No. All he got was a suitcase full of waste-paper. What's the other question?'

'Has he had an injury to his face. It looked so unnatural.'

'Yes. He deserted while his regiment was in action, and was reported blown up and killed by his brother officers, to save the good name of the regiment. I already knew that, but I didn't know until he told me that in running away he ran clean into a bursting shell, and was later picked up by the Germans, who did some wonderful plastic surgery on his face but he had had the presence of mind to hide his identity disc before he was picked up, and ultimately gave them a false name, because he feared the consequences of his cowardly act. I don't know how he eventually got to England, because he died before he could finish his story. Now I think I'll take a look round the house.'

'What about my car?' asked Barrington.

'It may be somewhere on the premises. I'll look for it.'

Left alone with Felicity, Barrington breathed a deep sigh of heartfelt relief, but Felicity was still sunk in gloom, and Barrington knew why.

'Don't brood over it, darling?' he begged.

'But it's all so terribly sad, and unjust.'

'Yes, it was. But the whole world is full of injustice, and there's so little we can do about it.'

'But what am I to say to mother? Am I to pretend that I don't know the truth? Am I to act as if it makes no difference between us?'

'Does it?'

'Yes. I can't forget that my father was deceived all through his life. That mother had that child while she was engaged to my father.'

'You have no grounds for saying that.'

'But she must have done or her parents would not have gone to such lengths to keep it a dead secret. McLean should know.'

Barrington drew her to him, and looked into her moist eyes.

'McLean probably does know, but isn't it enough, darling, that we love each other? Do you doubt your mother's love and devotion for your father while he lived?'

'No.'

'Then don't dig up any more of the past, and don't hate your mother for something which she did when she was little more than a girl, and probably under the influence of her parents. Who knows what she may have suffered through her conscience over all the years that have passed? Come — smile!'

They were interrupted by noises outside, and the sudden entrance of Sergeant Brook and another plain-clothes officer. Brook apologized and made to withdraw.

'It's all right,' said Barrington. 'The inspector is about somewhere. He came in the nick of time, too.'

'Congratulations to see you safe, sir — you, too, miss. I made a proper muck of things and got myself left at the post. I suppose you know what happened to me?'

'No.'

'I was to have got him — Galbraith. I wished myself into that job. There I was, crammed into the back of her Ladyship's car, with a pistol in my hand, ready to spring out when her Ladyship passed him the suitcase. It was all like a nice piece of cake, until I tried to push open the luggage boot. Then I found I was locked in. By the time her Ladyship had heard my banging and let me out Galbraith was well away across country, with the inspector after him.'

'You mean Galbraith locked the door on you?' asked Barrington.

'Must have done. It was unlocked when I

398

got inside. But where is he?'

'Galbraith?'

'Yes.'

'He's dead. He flung himself off the tower before he could be arrested. I expect the body is still down there. Is the doctor with you?'

'No. But he shouldn't be a minute or two. Well, I had better go and find — '

At that moment McLean came back, with a suitcase in his hands.

'Good work, Brook,' he said. 'The doctor has just arrived and has gone to the tower to view the body. Our little plan was rather like the curate's egg, good in parts, but the end is not entirely unsatisfactory. It is going to save a lot of trouble and expense. By the way, did Andrews find his motor-cycle?'

'I don't know, sir. He went to look for it while I attended Lady Gertrude. She was in no fit state to drive her car any further. I sent a man back with her. Then I telephoned headquarters, and was told to come on here. I'm sorry, sir, about that mess-up.'

'That's all right. Forget it. Now you and Webber had better go to the tower. If the doctor's finished get the body into the car. I'll join you later.'

Brook and his assistant went off.

'Your car is quite safe, Mr. Barrington,' said McLean. 'I found it in the garage next to Galbraith's. You can either go back in that or return with the doctor.'

Barrington looked at Felicity.

'Let's go in your car — now,' she said. 'I want to get away from this place.'

'I'm not surprised,' said McLean. 'I went down into the cellar just now, and found the entrance to the tunnel. Galbraith had left it open. I opened the door at the other end with a key from a bunch which I took from his pocket. It looks very much as if in the distant past the tunnel went right through to the Manor, and that the rumours that the place was used for smuggling on a large scale are well-founded. Whether Galbraith knew that that tunnel existed, or whether he came upon it by accident, we shall never know. Well, I still have a few things to do here, so I wish you a pleasant journey — and a happy future.'

A few minutes later Barrington and Felicity were seated in the little car, but at the last moment Barrington remembered his almost depleted radiator, and filled it from a can which he found close by. In the moonlight they moved across the deserted heath, looking back as they approached the steep descent to see the top of the tower, sinister against the starlit sky.

'Clever devil!' said Barrington.

'Galbraith?'

'No — McLean.'

'But he never got his man.'

'No, but I think he got what he wanted even more — justice without recrimination.'

23

It was two months later when McLean saw in the social column of a daily newspaper an announcement which caused him to utter an ejaculation of surprise and pleasure, and Sergeant Brook, who was laboriously typing, looked up from his chattering machine.

'Just an epilogue to a recent case of ours,' said McLean. 'It says here:

'Lady Gertrude Medding, after being present at the marriage of her daughter, Felicity, to Mr. Philip Barrington, left London Airport yesterday for Bermuda, where she intends to reside permanently. We understand that she has renounced her claim upon the large and beautiful estate of her father, the late Edward Grayling, in favour of her son, Sir John Medding (Bart) of Strafford Park, Dorset.'

McLEAN AT THE GOLDEN OWL
George Goodchild

Inspector McLean has resigned from Scotland Yard's CID and has opened an office in Wimpole Street. With the help of his able assistant, Tiny, he solves many crimes, including those of kidnapping, murder and poisoning.

KATE WEATHERBY
Anne Goring

Derbyshire, 1849: The Hunter family are the arrogant, powerful masters of Clough Grange. Their feuds are sparked by a generation of guilt, despair and ill-fortune. But their passions are awakened by the arrival of nineteen-year-old Kate Weatherby.

A VENETIAN RECKONING
Donna Leon

When the body of a prominent international lawyer is found in the carriage of an intercity train, Commissario Guido Brunetti begins to dig deeper into the secret lives of the once great and good.

A TASTE FOR DEATH
Peter O'Donnell

Modesty Blaise and Willie Garvin take on impossible odds in the shape of Simon Delicata, the man with a taste for death, and Swordmaster, Wenczel, in a terrifying duel. Finally, in the Sahara desert, the intrepid pair must summon every killing skill to survive.

SEVEN DAYS FROM MIDNIGHT
Rona Randall

In the Comet Theatre, London, seven people have good reason for wanting beautiful Maxine Culver out of the way. Each one has reason to fear her blackmail. But whose shadow is it that lurks in the wings, waiting to silence her once and for all?

QUEEN OF THE ELEPHANTS
Mark Shand

Mark Shand knows about the ways of elephants, but he is no match for the tiny Parbati Barua, the daughter of India's greatest expert on the Asian elephant, the late Prince of Gauripur, who taught her everything. Shand sought out Parbati to take part in a film about the plight of the wild herds today in north-east India.

THE DARKENING LEAF
Caroline Stickland

On storm-tossed Chesil Bank in 1847, the young lovers, Philobeth and Frederick, prevent wreckers mutilating the apparent corpse of a young woman. Discovering she is still alive, Frederick takes her to his grandmother's home. But the rescue is to have violent and far-reaching effects . . .

A WOMAN'S TOUCH
Emma Stirling

When Fenn went to stay on her uncle's farm in Africa, the lovely Helena Starr seemed to resent her — especially when Dr Jason Kemp agreed to Fenn helping in his bush hospital. Though it seemed Jason saw Fenn as little more than a child, her feelings for him were those of a woman.

A DEAD GIVEAWAY
Various Authors

This book offers the perfect opportunity to sample the skills of five of the finest writers of crime fiction — Clare Curzon, Gillian Linscott, Peter Lovesey, Dorothy Simpson and Margaret Yorke.

DOUBLE INDEMNITY — MURDER FOR INSURANCE
Jad Adams

This is a collection of true cases of murderers who insured their victims then killed them — or attempted to. Each tense, compelling account tells a story of cold-blooded plotting and elaborate deception.

THE PEARLS OF COROMANDEL
By Keron Bhattacharya

John Sugden, an ambitious young Oxford graduate, joins the Indian Civil Service in the early 1920s and goes to uphold the British Raj. But he falls in love with a young Hindu girl and finds his loyalties tragically divided.

WHITE HARVEST
Louis Charbonneau

Kathy McNeely, a marine biologist, sets out for Alaska to carry out important research. But when she stumbles upon an illegal ivory poaching operation that is threatening the world's walrus population, she soon realises that she will have to survive more than the harsh elements . . .

TO THE GARDEN ALONE
Eve Ebbett

Widow Frances Morley's short, happy marriage was childless, and in a succession of borders she attempts to build a substitute relationship for the husband and family she does not have. Over all hovers the shadow of the man who terrorized her childhood.

CONTRASTS
Rowan Edwards

Julia had her life beautifully planned — she was building a thriving pottery business as well as sharing her home with her friend Pippa, and having fun owning a goat. But the goat's problems brought the new local vet, Sebastian Trent, into their lives.

MY OLD MAN AND THE SEA
David and Daniel Hays

Some fathers and sons go fishing together. David and Daniel Hays decided to sail a tiny boat seventeen thousand miles to the bottom of the world and back. Together, they weave a story of travel, adventure, and difficult, sometimes terrifying, sailing.

SQUEAKY CLEAN
James Pattinson

An important attribute of a prospective candidate for the United States presidency is not to have any dirt in your background which an eager muckraker can dig up. Senator William S. Gallicauder appeared to fit the bill perfectly. But then a skeleton came rattling out of an English cupboard.

NIGHT MOVES
Alan Scholefield

It was the first case that Macrae and Silver had worked on together. Malcolm Underdown had brutally stabbed to death Edward Craig and had attempted to murder Craig's fiancée, Jane Harrison. He swore he would be back for her. Now, four years later, he has simply walked from the mental hospital. Macrae and Silver must get to him — before he gets to Jane.

GREATEST CAT STORIES
Various Authors

Each story in this collection is chosen to show the cat at its best. James Herriot relates a tale about two of his cats. Stella Whitelaw has written a very funny story about a lion. Other stories provide examples of courageous, clever and lucky cats.

THE HAND OF DEATH
Margaret Yorke

The woman had been raped and murdered. As the police pursue their relentless inquiries, decent, gentle George Fortescue, the typical man-next-door, finds himself accused. While the real killer serenely selects his third victim — and then his fourth . . .

VOW OF FIDELITY
Veronica Black

Sister Joan of the Daughters of Compassion is shocked to discover that three of her former fellow art college students have recently died violently. When another death occurs, Sister Joan realizes that she must pit her wits against a cunning and ruthless killer.

MARY'S CHILD
Irene Carr

Penniless and desperate, Chrissie struggles to support herself as the Victorian years give way to the First World War. Her childhood friends, Ted and Frank, fall hopelessly in love with her. But there is only one man Chrissie loves, and fate and one man bent on revenge are determined to prevent the match . . .